BREAK MY HEART

USA *Today* Bestselling Author

JENNIFER SUCEVIC

Break My Heart

Copyright© 2024 by Jennifer Sucevic

Published by Tangled Hearts LLC

All rights reserved. No part of this book may be reproduced in any form or by any electronic or mechanical means, including information storage and retrieval systems, without written permission from the author, except for the use of brief quotations in a book review.

This is a work of fiction. Names, characters, businesses, palaces, events, locales, and incidents are either the products of the author's imagination or used in a fictitious manner. Any resemblance to actual persons, living or dead, or actual events is purely coincidental.

Original Cover Design by Mary Ruth Baloy at MR Creations

Special Edition & Illustrated Cover by Claudia Lymari at Tease Designs

Editing by Shauna Stevenson at Ink Machine Editing

Proofreading by Kate Newman at Once Upon a Typo

Interior Formatting by Silla Webb at Masque Publishing

Join my Newsletter here!

AVA

Those four words hit me like a punch to the gut, and the ground drops from beneath my feet. My sneakers squeak against the tile floor of the corridor as I stumble to a halt. As I stare at my phone, the words blur before my eyes.

I really thought this nightmare was finally over.

It takes a handful of seconds for my brain to play mental catch up as my fingers hover over the keyboard, and I fight the urge to smash my cell against the wall. It's so tempting to ignore the message and pretend I never saw it.

How the hell did he get my number?

Again.

Every time I change my digits, he figures it out. My heart slams against my ribcage as a potent concoction of anger and frustration surges through me like wildfire.

Screw him.

That's all it takes for something to snap inside me as I stab out a response.

Nausea roils in my stomach as I hit send.

Why won't he leave me alone? It's been more than a year.

Before I can take a steady breath, my phone vibrates with another message.

UNKNOWN NUMBER:

We both know that's not true. There's quite a bit to say. In person.

No.

There's no way that will ever happen.

This time, I don't bother with a reply.

My thumb lingers for half a second before I block the number.

Not that it'll do any good.

With a frustrated huff, I pocket the phone in my jacket and shove through the door into the men's locker room.

Transferring to Western was supposed to be a fresh start. That's one of the reasons Dad took the head coaching position last summer—to give all of us a break from the mess back home.

It seems like no matter how far or fast I run, some things refuse to stay buried in the past.

The second I step inside, I'm hit by a wave of steamy moisture, thick in the air with the undeniable scent of sweat, wet gear, and damp towels.

My nose scrunches.

You'd think I'd be used to it by now, having spent my whole life around hockey teams.

But men's locker rooms?

They always reek.

I hesitate inside the door, cocking my head and listening for signs of life. The steady drip of water echoing from the showers is the only sound that can be heard.

Thank God.

Dad would totally lose it if I walked in on the guys undressing.

For as long as I can remember, there's been a strict no-hockey-players rule in place. It was never a problem because I was too busy skating to notice them.

I've been on the ice since I was four. After one of my coaches said I was a natural, my parents signed me up for private lessons. The next thing I knew, we were traveling all over the country. By the time I was twelve, we had uprooted our entire lives so I could train with a world-renowned coach. My life revolved around the rink—practice, competition—and little else.

Until last year.

I shove that depressing thought away as I swing around the corner and stumble to a halt. My eyes widen as I take in the naked guy with his back turned toward me. There's not even a towel slung around his waist to shield the view.

Somewhere in the back of my brain, I realize I should retreat or, at the very least, stop staring, but I can't pull my attention away from the sight in front of me. His back is broad and rippling with muscles, each one perfectly defined.

Before I can stop myself, my gaze dips lower. His ass is just as finely sculpted as the rest of him.

Tight.

Perfect.

Damn.

I suck in a harsh breath and almost choke. A coughing fit is the last thing I need right now. The noise is enough to alert him to my presence, and he swings around.

His green eyes lock on mine, and there's a beat of silence as the air thickens with something I can't quite place.

My heartbeat stutters.

And still, he doesn't bother to cover himself. His eyes scan me lazily, as if he catches girls sneaking into the locker room and eating up his naked body with their gazes all the time.

Who knows, maybe he does.

His gaze never wavers as he lifts the white towel to dry his damp hair. The guy is completely unfazed that he's stark naked, dripping, and on full display.

If only my reaction were just as casual.

Heat floods my cheeks, as if I'm the one who's been caught without a stitch of clothing.

My eyes do the exact opposite of what I tell them to. They should be locked on his face, but no, they take a slow and thorough tour of his body. First, the broad expanse of his chest—all hard muscle and glistening with droplets of water.

My mouth turns cottony as my attention drifts lower. I can't help but catalogue the ridges of his abs. There are eight of them, by the way. I swear, he's got abs on top of abs. It would be difficult not to appreciate every contour.

My gaze continues to meander until arriving at his—

Oh my God.

He's shaved.

Completely.

There's not a single hair in sight.

And yeah, I'm staring.

Hard.

A deep chuckle escapes from him as he breaks the silence. "Like what you see, sweetheart?"

Unsure how to respond, I remain frozen in place, my feet rooted to the floor.

Much to my mortification, my brain remains on hiatus, unable to compute anything beyond the scene playing out in front of me. I should tear my gaze away, but it's like a train wreck I can't stop staring at.

As if this situation isn't mortifying enough, he wraps his hand around the thick length and slowly strokes it. My mouth falls open as he stiffens up until his cock is pointing straight at me.

"Well," he drawls, voice thick with amusement, "what are you waiting for?"

I blink and attempt to rouse myself from the daze that's fallen over me. It takes a handful of seconds to wrap my lips around a response. "Waiting for?"

I bite back a groan of embarrassment. Under normal circumstances, I pride myself on being quick-witted, always ready with a sharp retort. But right now?

My brain has short-circuited.

There's nothing.

With his fingers still wrapped around his erection, his lips lift into a smirk. "Why don't you strip off your clothes so we can get to it."

My heart nearly stops. There's a beat of silence so loud it feels like it's echoing in the room.

Excuse me?

I force myself to say something.

Anything.

But I'm stuck, frozen in disbelief, as my mind scrambles to process what the hell is happening right now.

With a tilt of his head, he gives me another slow perusal. "My guess is that you'll look good on your knees with a mouth stuffed full of cock."

The silky words are like a bucket of icy water dumped over my head. They manage to do the impossible and wake me from my stupor.

My narrowed gaze slices to his sparkling eyes.

Even though I only started at Western in the fall, I know exactly who this player is.

Introductions aren't necessary.

Hayes Van Doren's reputation precedes him.

It's so tempting to blast this guy into next week. Instead, I force the corners of my lips into some semblance of a smile as I prod my feet into movement. As I step closer, it becomes necessary to tip my chin upward in order to hold his steady gaze.

He's tall.

Well over six feet.

I'm lucky if I top out at five foot three.

When there's no more than a handful of inches to separate us, and the heat of his body is enough to singe me alive, I reach out and knock his hand away before wrapping my fingers around his hard length and giving him a long, slow stroke.

Fire leaps to life in his green eyes, making them sparkle like emeralds.

When a shiver dances down my spine, I stomp it out and drop my voice until it turns husky. "Is this more like what you had in mind?"

It doesn't take long for his eyelids to droop and a deep groan to escape from him. "Yeah, baby. That feels so damn good."

I give his erection one final stroke before tightening my grip.

The yelp of pain he releases is sweet music to my ears.

"You're kind of hurting me, sweetheart."

With an arch of my brow, I apply more pressure. "Huh. Am I?"

He studies my expression for a long beat. "You're not my birthday present, are you?"

It's not really a question.

I purse my lips. "No, *sweetheart*. I'm not."

"Hon, is that you?"

Our gazes stay locked in silent combat as Dad's voice echoes off the orange and black cement walls.

"Yup," I say, loud enough for him to hear me from inside his office.

"Please tell me all the guys have taken off."

The corners of my lips tilt upward. "There's not a single man in sight."

His sigh is audible. "Good. I would have really hated if you'd walked in on one of them changing."

"No worries there."

Hayes winces when I give his appendage one final twist before releasing him.

Without another word, I swing toward Dad's office.

I would be lying if I didn't admit to feeling the heat of Hayes's stare boring into my back. It takes every ounce of self-control not to turn around and meet his gaze.

TenInchesofCocky

TENINCHESOF
COCKY

VAN DOREN
19
HAYES

WILDCATS

My attention stays pinned to the feisty blonde as she saunters away, half-expecting her to toss a triumphant look over her shoulder for getting the best of me.

But it never happens.

With a flick of her ponytail, she strides into Coach's office, dismissing me without a second thought.

Who the hell is that girl?

I rack my brain, trying to place her, but I'm certain I'd remember someone like her. With her golden blonde hair, piercing blue eyes, and a petite, toned frame, she's not easily forgotten.

With a wince, I glance at my crotch.

Pretty sure the vise grip she had on my junk is gonna leave a bruise.

One thing is for certain, I'm not leaving the locker room until I figure out who the mystery girl is. The low hum of conversation that drifts from Coach's office only piques my curiosity further.

I take a step toward the door before skidding to a halt.

Right... I should probably get dressed first.

With a muttered curse, I grab my boxer briefs and yank them up my thighs. This is followed by sweatpants, a T-shirt, and my Western U sweatshirt. Add the socks and shoes, and I'm good to go. I sling my duffel over my shoulder and make my way toward the office.

Since the door is cracked open, I pop my head in. With a frown, the older man's brows shoot up, and his conversation dies a quick death.

"What are you still doing here? I thought everyone had left."

The terse question he fires off only solidifies my sneaking suspicions that he's not thrilled to see me.

I glance at the girl sitting on the other side of his desk. She eyes me with a cool, unreadable expression. It's a far cry from the heated look she'd given me while staring at my hard dick.

When Coach doesn't immediately introduce us, I take matters into my own hands. "Hey there, I'm Hayes."

She barely acknowledges me. Just a halfhearted chin lift and a flat "Hi."

Awkward silence stretches between us. When she doesn't give me anything further to work with, I turn my attention back to Coach and wait for him to fill in the blanks.

With a scowl, he reluctantly mutters, "This is my daughter, Ava."

I blink.

Well, damn.

"You're Coach's daughter?" I ask, totally thrown off my game.

"Yup," she replies, not bothering to elaborate.

"Yes, she is," Coach says, in that tone that clearly means *back the fuck off and pretend you never met her.*

Now I'm even more intrigued.

My gaze shifts back to the blonde—*Ava*—and I can't help the slow smile that creeps across my face. "Nice to meet you."

One brow slinks upward. "Was it?"

I chuckle. "Definitely memorable."

When Coach clears his throat, I force myself to refocus. "Is there a reason you stopped by?"

Uh, yeah, there is. But I'm pretty sure he wouldn't appreciate hearing that I'm here to figure out who manhandled my junk less than five minutes ago. So, I pull the first plausible excuse that comes to mind out of my ass.

"I wanted to double-check the times for the clinic."

Coach relaxes, and his rigidly held shoulders lose some of their tension. "It'll run from nine in the morning until one. I'll send out an email later in the week with the drills we'll run."

I nod as my gaze slides back to Ava. "Sounds good. Looking forward to it."

"Great. Thanks again for volunteering," he adds, leveling me with a hard-edged stare.

I'm smart enough to know when I'm being dismissed. I can either walk out on my own or get tossed out on my ass, and I'd rather keep my pride intact.

Unable to help myself, I flick one more glance at the cool blonde. "I'm sure we'll see each other around."

Her lips twitch in what could possibly be a smirk. "Let's hope not."

Her icy attitude has a snort slipping free from me. Can't say I don't like it. The girl definitely has a bit of bite to her. It's a refreshing change from the groupies who hang on my every word.

"If you don't mind, close the door on your way out," Coach says, interrupting my runaway thoughts.

"Will do."

I shoot Ava one last grin before pulling the door shut and sauntering from the locker room.

AVA

ad frowns at the frosted glass before his gaze resettles on mine. "You're not acquainted with Hayes, are you?"

I shake my head. "Nope."

"Good." The relief on his face and in his voice is almost comical. "Let's keep it that way."

I shift in my chair, eager to steer the conversation in a different direction. "You wanted to see me?"

"Yeah. I was able to book the ice for six A.M.," he says, a small smile creeping onto his face. "Only the janitorial staff will be around, so you'll have the place all to yourself." He opens his desk drawer and pulls out a keycard before holding it out to me.

I take it and try not to think too hard about how good that sounds.

"Thanks." My tongue darts out to moisten my lips. "I really appreciate it."

"Just don't lose the card, or it'll be my ass," he warns, but his tone is light. "The only reason the athletic director agreed is because it's all but certain that we've made it to the playoffs."

"I won't." I tuck the card into my pocket and rise to my feet, ready to take off, but Dad pulls off his ballcap and rakes a hand through his hair, his expression shifting, as if he wants to say more but isn't quite sure how.

My stomach clenches.

Does he know about the texts?

There's no way Nathan would contact him.

Not after everything that happened.

I thought Dad would murder him with his bare hands after the scandal broke. I've never seen him so close to losing control, and I've never been so scared. Nathan should consider himself lucky to still be alive. If he has any brain cells whatsoever, he'll stay far, far away from me.

Dad's voice pulls me out of my spiraling thoughts. "Have you given any more thought to reaching out to a few of the names on the list I gave you?" Before I can shake my head, he adds, "Like maybe Nadia Petrovic? I don't have to tell you what a world-renowned coach she is. The girl who won Nationals last year trained with her."

I drop my gaze as tension coils in my muscles. "What would be the point? I'm not even sure I want to skate anymore."

The silence that follows that response is deafening.

I force myself to glance up, only to find his blue eyes filled with a mixture of confusion and sadness.

"Maybe if you just had a simple phone conversation with her or one of the others, you might change your mind." His voice is quieter now, as if he knows how close I am to bolting. "I hate to see you throw away everything you've worked so hard for because of that piece of—"

"I don't want to talk about it," I blurt, popping to my feet. I can't sit here for another moment and pretend like everything's fine when it's not.

It hasn't been for a long time.

"You've always loved to skate," he murmurs, as if trying to remind me of something I've forgotten.

"I know." My voice is tight, almost strangled.

"It was your life."

"I know," I repeat, hating just how true the statement is.

It *was* my life.

And now?

Now it feels like something that belonged to someone else.

"I hate that you're letting what happened take away the one thing you've always been so passionate about," he says, his tone low and full of sadness.

I open my mouth, but no words come out.

What can I even say?

It's not like he's wrong.

A year ago, everything blew up. My life went up in flames, and after all this time, I'm still sifting through the ashes, picking up the charred pieces.

"Dad..."

With a sigh, his shoulders sag. "I'm not going to force you to do something you don't want to, but would you at least think it over?"

"Sure." The lie slips out easily, even though we both understand that I have no intention of following through with it.

I've been telling people what they want to hear for months now.

It's just easier that way.

Easier than explaining how I can barely breathe when I think about the past. How I spent months in therapy trying to process it all, and I'm still not there.

Still not okay.

If I'd had my way, I would've walked away from skating for good.

But I just couldn't do it.

The ice is the only place that makes sense.

The only place where I can find any peace.

Irony's a bitch, isn't it?

The thing I love the most is also the thing that inflicted the most damage.

After months of fighting the impulse, I returned to the rink. I still skate, but not competitively.

It's doubtful I'll ever do that again.

Dad clears his throat, as if unsure how to keep the conversation going. "Have you been out with anyone lately?"

The question catches me off guard, but it's not a total surprise. Mom's usually the one who wades cautiously into these turbulent waters. For whatever reason, Dad seems to be picking up the slack this afternoon.

I shake my head. "Nope."

"Why not?"

"I just need time to think and figure out what I want to do with my life."

What I don't say is that dating is the last thing on my mind. That I'm too screwed-up to even think about being with someone right now. It's not something I felt comfortable explaining to my therapist. How can I tell anyone that I'm still messed-up, that I haven't been able to find anything that feels good, or that the guys I've been with couldn't give me what I needed?

What I secretly craved.

Dad would probably keel over if I admitted any of that to him.

When it looks like he might say more, I do the only thing I can and rise to my feet.

"Sorry, I really need to go. But I'll see you later?"

The smile he flashes doesn't quite banish the sadness from his eyes. "Sure. Of course." There's a pause. "I love you, Ava."

Only then does everything loosen inside me. "I love you too."

TENINCHESOF
COCKY

WILDCATS

TenInchesofCocky
VAN DOREN
19
HAYES

"Who's hungry?" Colby asks as we shove through the arena doors into the crisp evening air. "Because I'm fucking famished." He pats his belly.

"Correct me if I'm wrong, but I do believe it's Tuesday," Steele adds.

Ford grins. "Taco Tuesday it is!" He pulls out his phone. "I'll call the girls. They can meet us there."

"Guess I could put away a few tacos," Bridger adds, slinging his bag over his shoulder.

A curvy body slams into mine and I find Larsa Middleton hanging off my neck. She's got dark eyes that always seem to sparkle with mischief, and right now they're locked on mine.

"How about me? Am I invited to Taco Loco?"

I give her an apologetic smile. "Sorry, sweetheart. I won't be heading over. I've got other plans this evening."

Her lower lip juts out in a pout that probably works on most guys. "Can't you change them?"

I shake my head, not even tempted in the least. "Nope. Maybe next time."

She stretches onto the tips of her toes and nips my earlobe with sharp teeth, whispering, "That's too bad. I was hoping we could spend a little one-on-one time together. Or, if you're up to it, maybe two-on-one."

Before I can respond, movement catches the corner of my eye, and my head swivels so fast that I nearly give myself whiplash. My attention locks on the blonde striding across campus about twenty yards away. Her ponytail bounces with every determined step she takes.

Ava.

The girl I haven't been able to stop thinking about since our memorable encounter in the locker room.

As if she can feel the heat of my stare, she glances up from her phone. Her eyes narrow as soon as our gazes collide. The smile I flash is met with a scowl before she dismisses me and continues on her way.

"Hayes?"

It's only when Ava disappears around the corner of a building that I glance at Larsa and realize she's still clinging to me. "As fun as that sounds," I say, untangling her arms from around my neck, "I'm gonna have to pass."

"Boo." She swings away, eyeing Ford and Colby for a few seconds before dismissing them. Larsa knows better than to mess with either of my teammates. Carina and Britt both made sure of that. If she crosses the line again, it won't end well for her.

The grin Steele flashes her way makes his dimples pop. "You can ride on the back of my bike."

She gives it a second of consideration before setting her sights on his cousin. "No, thanks."

"Okay, the girls are in. They'll meet us at Taco Loco in ten," Ford announces, pocketing his phone.

I glance back to the last place I saw the petite blonde. The words are out of my mouth before I can reel them back in. "Did you guys know Coach has a daughter?"

Ford glances at me with mild confusion. "Yeah, there's a picture of her in his office. You never noticed?"

I frown. "Nope."

With a smirk, Bridger shakes his head. "You're totally oblivious, dude."

"Not when it matters," I shoot back.

Colby raises an eyebrow. "And when exactly would that be? On the ice and between the sheets?"

I point at him and smile. "Correctamundo."

Before the conversation can spin any further out of control, our phones buzz simultaneously with an incoming text. The air around us shifts as we all exchange uneasy glances. Ever since last semester, Bridger's been getting blasted by mass messages from the university's system. Nobody's been able to figure out who's behind it. The texts started out as a joke, but now they're way past funny.

More like brutal.

I unlock my phone and glance at the screen.

Shit.

It's bad.

The image might be blurry, but it's unmistakable.

Bridger's pants are down, and some girl's face is smashed against his groin.

Can't say she doesn't have game.

But this doesn't seem like the time to point that out.

Even Larsa's gone quiet as she stares at her phone in disbelief.

"Dude..." Steele mutters, reaching out to comfort his cousin.

But our teammate swats his hand away before snarling, "I'm so fucking sick of this bullshit."

"I know," Colby says, his usual humor nowhere to be found. "We'll figure out who's doing this."

Bridger pinches the bridge of his nose. "How? I've tried. Whoever's behind it knows what they're doing."

"Can't we talk to the cyber security department at the university? Maybe they have connections who can help," I suggest.

Bridger sighs. "My dad already reached out to them. There's nothing they can do. But I guess it's worth another shot."

When his phone rings, he silences it without even checking who it is.

"Is that your dad?" Ford asks carefully.

"Probably. I'm not really in the mood for an ass chewing right now."

Steele nods toward the parking lot. "Let's get out of here and grab some food. It'll take your mind off it for a while. Then we'll try to come up with a plan."

Bridger shakes his head. "You guys go ahead. I'm gonna stop by my dad's office before he loses it."

"Want us to come with you?" his cousin asks, a hard glint filling his gray eyes. "There's always strength in numbers."

Bridger's expression softens. "Nah, I'll be fine. Catch you guys later."

In silence, we watch as Bridger walks away. The poor guy looks like he has the weight of the world resting on his shoulders.

Colby sighs. "Who knew his old man was such a dick?"

We all mutter in agreement.

"Guess we should get moving," Ford says, heading toward the parking lot.

As we reach my beat-up truck, I realize that Larsa has vanished too. That's probably for the best. She's not exactly on great terms with the girls after the last time Carina caught her hitting on Ford.

Colby unlocks his shiny new Escalade as he and Ford climb inside. Steele beelines for his motorcycle.

"Meet you there?" Colby asks.

I shake my head. "Sorry. Like I told Larsa, I've got plans."

Ford laughs. "And here I thought you were just feeding her a bullshit excuse."

"Nope. Real plans." I wave my teammates off and duck into my ancient '96 Ford Bronco before they decide to pepper me with more questions. Those two are the nosiest bastards I know.

I fire up the engine, and the familiar rumble drowns out their voices as I pull out of the lot, driving in the opposite direction of Taco Loco. It doesn't take long for the quiet to settle around me as I enjoy the hum of the road beneath the tires. Thirty minutes later and I'm pulling into the narrow gravel driveway of the single-story house that has seen better days.

The moment I park, the front door flies open, and Theo comes barreling out like a missile. The screen door slams against the aluminum siding before reverberating on its hinges.

"Theodore!" Mom's voice carries from inside.

Theo ignores her, launching himself at me with a wide grin. The kid's only ten, but he's built like a tank, just like I was at the same age.

Ollie, my thirteen-year-old brother, lingers in the doorway, arms crossed against his chest, trying to play it cool. He's been full of attitude lately.

I scoop up Theo in a mock wrestling move. "Missed you, little bro."

"What's it been, like a week?" Ollie asks, voice dripping with teenage indifference. There's the barest glint of humor in his eyes.

I set Theo down and grin at Ollie, knowing exactly how to push his buttons.

"No—"

Before he can react, I tackle him, hoisting him up like we're about to go full-on WWE. He squirms, laughing despite himself. By the time we're done messing around, both of us are winded and our hair is mussed.

Mom stands in the doorway, watching with a smile. "Hello, sweetie."

"Hey, Ma." I straighten my clothing and shoot a grin at my brother before giving her a kiss on the cheek. With a glare, he gives me the finger. It's tempting to put him in a headlock.

Instead, I turn to my sister, Kia, who's standing by my side, grinning up at me with a gap in her smile.

"Look! I lost a tooth," she says proudly, pointing to her mouth.

I crouch down, pretending to inspect the damage. "Looks to me like you lost *two* teeth."

She beams. "The tooth fairy gave me four dollars!"

"Well, you better save it," I say, scooping her up. She's fine-boned, like our mother, and light as a feather.

Her arms tangle around my neck as she clings to me like a baby rhesus monkey.

She cups her fingers around my ear and whispers, "I hid it in Dolly's diaper so the boys don't take it."

I carefully tap the side of her head. "Smart thinking. Probably the last place they'd look."

When she flashes a dimpled grin, my heart melts. With her mess of golden curls and big blue eyes, she's way too adorable for her own good.

Dinner is simple—Hamburger Helper, one of my childhood favorites. It's comforting in all the right ways. Throughout the meal, my brothers compete for the funniest story, Kia picks at her food, and Mom just looks tired. The dark circles under her eyes never really went away after Dad died five years ago. Even though it's been a challenge, she's done her best to hold everything together for us.

After dinner, I help clean up while the kids retreat to their rooms. Once she settles at the small kitchen table with a cup of decaf, I pull a wad of cash from my pocket and set it down in front of her.

Mom stares at it for a long moment before looking up at me, emotions swirling in her hazel eyes. "You know... if we took them out of hockey, it would help with some of the expenses."

I shake my head. "Forget it. They need the structure and discipline."

She reluctantly glances at the cash again.

"They'd get into trouble without it," I add when it looks like she'll argue. "You don't need that stress."

She nods as wetness gathers in her eyes. "Oh, Hayes..." She sniffs, trying to hold it together. "I know I don't say it enough, but I'm so grateful for everything you do."

Thick emotion clogs my throat. "You don't need to thank me. We're family. We only have each other to lean on."

"Your father would be proud of the man you've become."

We sit in silence until she dries her tears. Only then do I glance at my phone, knowing I need to get back to school. I still have a pile of work to do before calling it a day. Sometimes it feels like the grind never stops.

I jerk a thumb toward their bedrooms. "I'll say goodbye to the kids and then take off."

She swipes at red-rimmed eyes before rising to her feet as I do the same.

Her fingers trail over the thick wad of bills. "That's a lot of cash." She picks it up before flicking a concerned glance my way. "I'm almost afraid to ask how you're making this much money."

I force a smile and keep my tone light. "Don't worry, it's nothing illegal."

Her teeth scrape against her lower lip before chewing it. "I really hope not. The last thing I want is for you to jeopardize your future."

I press a gentle kiss against her forehead. "You know I'd never do that. The NHL is our ticket to a better life."

Some of the tension drains from her thin shoulders. "Good."

I spend the next twenty minutes watching stupid videos online with my brothers and then read Kia her favorite book about a hound dog named Charlie before walking out of the house.

As I head back to school, I think about how different our lives will be a year from now. We'll have more money than we know what to do with. It'll be falling out of our asses. Mom won't have to worry or put in extra hours so she can make ends meet.

All the shit we've had to go through will be nothing more than an ugly, distant memory.

It's what keeps me motivated and focused on the things that matter.

My family.

Hockey.

School.

In that order.

And there isn't room for anything else.

AVA

At this hour in the morning, the rink is deserted. The hum of the Zamboni has long since faded, leaving behind a flawless, glass-like surface. Fresh ice, untouched and perfect.

Is there anything better?

I draw in a deep breath and hold it captive, savoring the chilly air that fills my lungs. For just a moment, I allow the tension in my body to melt away before exhaling. And then my blades are carving a steady rhythm as I ease into my warmup. Each glide sends a satisfying hiss through the silent arena as my breath comes out in little clouds before dissipating in the chilled air.

I move into some crossovers, feeling the familiar burn in my thighs as I pick up speed. Everything from the past year that normally eats away at me fades to the background, leaving nothingness in its place.

Once warmed up, I glide to the center of the ice and take my starting position. With my knees slightly bent and arms poised, I focus on the music in my head. It's a piece I've practiced more than a thousand times. I visualize each note, each synchronized movement, then I begin.

The first few moves are smooth and flowing, a series of elegant spirals that show off both my control and grace. I transition into a camel spin, extending my free leg behind me and holding my position steady as the centrifugal force pulls at my body. Only then do I exit the spin with a flick of my toe pick and push into a series of intricate footwork.

My focus narrows as I approach a triple lutz. I dig my toe pick into the ice and launch myself into the air, rotating quickly. My heart stutters as my blades touch down in a perfect landing.

Even after everything that happened, it's one thing that never fails to send satisfaction flooding through me.

After that, I flow into a sit spin, dropping low and holding the position, as the burn in my legs intensifies. From there, I transition into a flying camel, launching into the air and rotating into the spin mid-flight. The rush of the wind against my face is exhilarating, and confidence surges through me as I nail the landing.

The routine builds to its climax, and I push harder, faster before executing a sequence of jumps—an axel, a loop, and finally a salchow. Each one pushes me to my limits. My body is in perfect sync with the rhythm in my mind, each movement precise and deliberate.

For a second, my old coach's voice creeps into my mind.

"Bend your knees!"

"You're skating too stiff!"

I crush it before it takes hold, refocusing on the final spin, feeling the stretch, the release as I come to a graceful stop. It's only when I slow that I realize my chest is heaving. My breath comes out in small clouds before evaporating in the frigid air. Contentment floods through me. In this moment, I feel lighter, like I've finally found the missing piece of myself.

That fragile peace is shattered as slow clapping echoes through the rink.

My eyes snap open, and ice floods my veins.

For a terrifying second, I think it's *him*.

That he's found me.

My eyes lock on green ones, and a potent concoction of relief tinged with irritation rushes through me.

Hayes Van Doren loiters near the benches, a lazy grin tugging at his lips as he takes a swig of coffee.

Our last run-in flashes through my mind. The flutter at the bottom of my belly is a shock to my system.

I haven't felt anything like that since—

I slam the door on that thought and harden my stance.

There's no way I'm interested in this guy.

Not even a little.

His manwhore reputation is legendary.

He's exactly the type of guy my dad would lose his mind over if I got anywhere near. Which makes him even more dangerous. Add to that the wreckage of my past, and I'm no longer the girl who can afford a distraction.

When I remain silent, his lips lift into a crooked smile as he raises one hand in a wave before raising the container he's holding in the other to his mouth and taking a swallow.

I continue to glare, hoping my prickly demeanor will send him scurrying. It's become a defense mechanism. Even as that thought rolls through my brain, I realize it's an unlikely scenario.

This guy is much too cocksure of himself.

When he doesn't take the hint that I'm not interested in striking up a conversation or anything else he might have in mind, I skate toward him, every movement deliberate, eating up the distance between us until I stop in front of him.

That's when I realize he's not sipping on his own coffee.

He's enjoying mine.

Seriously?

My brows snap together.

Who the hell does this guy think he is?

Still breathing hard from my workout, I plant my hands on my hips and scowl.

The smartest thing I can do is shut down whatever this is before it spirals any further out of control.

A little voice inside my head wonders if it's already too late for that.

"Have you come to ask me to fall to my knees so you can..." I pause, as if trying to jog my memory, then continue, "How did you oh so charmingly put it? Stuff my mouth full of cock?"

A grin moves across his face as his eyes twinkle with humor. He doesn't look the least bit embarrassed.

"Yeah, sorry about that. Thought you were someone else."

I roll my eyes at the explanation. "That doesn't make it better."

His tongue slides over the front of his teeth as he shrugs. "No, I suppose it doesn't."

My pulse trips as silence thickens the air between us. I hold myself steady, refusing to let him see just how much he gets under my skin.

"So... you're Coach's daughter, huh?"

I lift a brow. "I'm pretty sure we established that already."

"I didn't even know he had a kid," he muses, eyes gleaming with something I can't quite place.

"Color me surprised. Is that because you're too wrapped up in your groupies to notice?" The words fly out of my mouth before I can think better of it.

His grin widens. "Ahhh, so you know who I am."

I bristle, realizing I've given him exactly what he wanted—the upper hand in this conversation.

"Stop drinking my coffee," I snap, spinning away and skating back toward the center of the ice.

"See you around, Tink." His low and amused chuckle follows me as the sound vibrates through the empty arena and settles somewhere deep in my core. I refuse to turn around, even as I feel the tug of it.

The last thing I need is to encourage him.

After a few silent minutes, curiosity wins out, and I peek over my shoulder, only to find the benches empty.

I should be relieved.

Instead, disappointment bubbles up inside me, unwanted and annoying.

I force myself to skate through my routine two more times, trying to lose myself in the movement, but it's useless.

His easy grin keeps popping into my head.

As soon as exhaustion sets in, I skate back to the benches and reach for my coffee, only to find the container empty.

Grrr.

TENINCHESOF
COCKY

WILDCATS

TenInchesofCocky
VAN DOREN
19
HAYES

ith my duffel slung over my shoulder, I push through the front door of the two-story Victorian I share with Ryder, Bridger, Maverick, Riggs, and Colby. Scratch that. Colby's off playing house, married to Britt, a singer-slash-reality star who was once in hiding but is now living her life out in the open.

There've been more plot twists and shocking reveals around here than in a freaking soap opera.

Since Colby packed up, Bridger's cousin Steele moved into the room. The house is still a rotating door of teammates, friends, and, of course, girls.

Tonight is no different.

A group of the younger guys are kicking back in the living room, cold brews in hand, eyes glued to the video game playing out on the high-def 70-inch screen. Half a dozen girls are mixed in, draped over the furniture.

"Hey, Hayes!" A hot brunette perks up as soon as she spots me walk in, raising a hand in greeting.

I give her a chin lift as I head toward the staircase.

"Come party with us!" she calls after me.

Without breaking stride, I shake my head. "Sorry, I've got some stuff to do."

She pouts, batting her lashes. "And here I was hoping to be one of those things."

A half-amused snort escapes me. "Maybe later."

Even as I throw out the possibility, I know it's not going to happen.

Not tonight.

Hell, probably not anytime soon.

It's been a week since I watched Ava skate, and I haven't been able to stop thinking about her. I'm not the kind of guy who loses sleep over a chick, but there's something about her.

Normally, it only takes a wink or compliment from me to get a girl interested. But this one?

She'd rather throat punch me than return a smile.

I probably shouldn't think that's hot, but I do.

Once I make it to my room, I shut the door and lock it before pulling off my black Western Wildcats sweatshirt and the T-shirt beneath, tossing them both onto the bed. Barely do I notice the cool air that hits my chest as I fire up my laptop and set everything up.

I've done this enough times to have it down to a science.

Once I'm connected and the home screen loads, I enable the camera, making sure only my torso is in the frame. Not my face or any recognizable marks. Nothing that could give me away. Since I don't have any piercings or tats, I don't really worry about being identified.

If there's a lady—or dude for that matter—out there who can recognize my dick, hats off to them.

I shove the chair away from the desk to give myself enough room to maneuver.

I've been doing these shows since my sophomore year. By now, I understand what my audience tunes in for.

Sometimes, I'll stretch out on the bed.

Other times, I sit at the desk.

Once or twice, I've tried to get creative with a shower scene, but that gets tricky when you live with a bunch of dudes. It tends to raise questions when you saunter out of the bathroom after a twenty-minute shower with a computer tucked under your arm.

That's the last thing I need.

I shove the buds in my ears and crank up a little mood music to lose myself in. It's a trick I picked up early on. It looks way more natural if I forget about the audience tuning in.

All I can say is, who knew jacking off online would turn out to be so damn lucrative.

Luckily for me, I enjoy rubbing one out a couple times a week.

My scholarship covers my tuition and books. My online hustle pays for my living expenses and gives me enough cash to send Mom's way at the end of the month.

It's a win-win for everyone.

It wasn't a lie when I told Mom I wasn't mixed up in anything illegal.

Although, she'd definitely tear into my ass if she discovered how I make my money. And she wouldn't accept one damn penny if she discovered the truth.

Which is exactly why I keep my online activities to myself.

No one knows about it.

Not even my closest teammates and friends.

A few months from now, *TenInchesofCocky* will retire and be a thing of the past.

I fidget with the screen until I have the perfect angle of my chest, abs, and gray sweatpants before tugging the waistband down. I squirt a little lotion on my hands and rub them together before starting the livestream. Already there are a couple hundred viewers—or voyeurs —waiting patiently in my private room.

The little red light on the camera blinks, letting me know I'm live.

I lean back in the chair and manspread.

Maybe women don't like it IRL, but they sure as hell don't mind when I'm on camera and they're getting up close and personal with the goods.

Especially when I drag the material down, freeing my dick, and proving that my screen name is one hundred percent accurate.

There's definitely no shame in my game.

My hands settle on my chest, sliding with ease thanks to the lotion. That's all it takes for me to close my eyes and lose myself in the steady thump of the music. It's something mellow that flows. I pinch my nipples before allowing my fingers to meander downward. I throw a few stretches in, so my muscles bunch and flex, before shifting on the chair.

When an image of Ava pops into my head and my dick stiffens right up, I go with it.

This is exactly what my fans clamor for.

Even though my eyes remain closed, I have zero doubts that appreciative comments are rolling across the screen.

In the beginning, I was more cognizant of them, but that takes me out of the experience. So, I stopped paying attention. The only time I tweak something is when the money dips, but I'll be honest, that hasn't happened since the beginning. My audience has only grown over the years.

I focus on the sassy figure skater as my hand drops to the waistband of my sweats before sliding over the material and grabbing the thick erection that tents the cotton.

I hiss out a breath.

The tip is already sensitive.

Who would have thought the feisty blonde could get me so hard?

My fingers drift lower, tracing the ridge of my erection until reaching my balls. I roll the sac around, massaging it before squeezing.

Damn, that feels good.

Under normal circumstances, I try to stretch out the show for about twenty minutes before the grand finale, but I don't think I'm going to make it that long.

Fuck it.

Instead of waiting, I shove down the sweats and boxers, allowing my erection to spring free. Then I pull out my balls.

They're just as much of a showstopper as my cock.

Especially since they're shaved and as smooth as a baby's bottom.

Don't believe me?

Check out the comments section.

Maybe I don't watch them scroll by, but I always read them afterward to see what people enjoyed.

With one finger, I circle the crown, gliding over the slit where moisture has beaded, before spreading it around until the bulbous head is slick with arousal. If I lift my finger, a little string of clear fluid would come with it.

Then I tighten my grip around the girth and slowly slide it up and down the shaft. Just when my balls tighten, I force myself to release the length, massaging my sac for a second time. A groan rumbles up from my chest before escaping between my lips as my head falls back and I arch, impatient to feel the slide of my hand against my dick.

It's nothing short of torture.

I'm so damn close to coming.

My teeth sink into my lower lip as I nudge myself closer to release before easing off. Then I do it all over again until I'm dancing on the precipice. When I can't stand another second, I allow an image of Ava to creep back into my thoughts.

I wasn't kidding when I said she'd look good on her knees with her mouth stuffed full of cock.

My cock.

That image is all it takes to send me flying over the edge.

With a guttural groan, my balls tighten as the first hot spurts of cum land on my lower abdomen. My orgasm seems to last forever. It's only when I've completely emptied myself that I loosen the chokehold on my dick and sink farther back on the chair.

I massage the jizz around my belly since I know the fans love it.

With a peace sign, I end the livestream.

I pluck a few tissues from the box on my desk and clean up the mess before tugging up my underwear and sweats and then heading to the shower.

I glance at the screen, zeroing in on the number of viewers.

The corners of my lips tip upward.

We're venturing into record-setting numbers, which translates into record-setting amounts of money that will hit my bank account and help pay for Mom to keep food on the table and my siblings in hockey.

There's nowhere else I could earn this kind of cash for twenty minutes of "work" a couple times a week.

Who knows, I just might miss it when I finally pull the plug at the end of the semester.

AVA

The noise is deafening as I step inside the arena. The sports venue is packed tonight with a sea of fans wearing Western Wildcats jerseys and hats. The hardcore supporters are easy to spot with their orange and black face paint. Near the plexiglass, a group of girls are holding up glitter-bedazzled poster boards in a desperate plea for attention.

The way some of these chicks lose their minds over the hockey players around here is ridiculous. It's like they forget these guys aren't out there curing cancer or solving climate change.

As I scan the crowd, I spot my new friends. Britt pops up from her seat with a wave. A smile tugs at the corners of my lips, and the knot of tension in my belly loosens as I make my way toward them. When Britt first introduced me to her crew, I wasn't sure what to expect. Girls like them—tight-knit, supportive, genuinely nice—didn't exist in my world. I was always on the ice, too busy training to make real connections. And even when I did get close to people, the relationships felt catty and filled with jealousy.

But these girls?

They've done the unexpected and welcomed me with open arms.

Britt pulls me in for a warm hug the moment I reach her. "Ava!" she chirps, her excitement contagious. "I'm so glad you were able to make it."

My muscles relax as I settle into the seat next to her. The others—Fallyn, Juliette, Carina, Stella, Viola, and Willow—are scattered around, all engaged in various conversations. It's noisy with the music blasting through the loudspeakers, hyping fans up for the game.

I try to focus on anyone other than Hayes Van Doren, but my gaze is reluctantly drawn to him. Even with the helmet covering his head and face, I can still pick him out in the crowd of players.

He's taller and broader in the shoulders than most of the others.

From across the sheet of ice, our gazes collide, and a jolt of electricity shoots through me. Instead of glancing away, he smirks.

Ugh.

His ego is so massive, he probably thinks I'm here just for him.

It takes effort to sever the connection and turn my attention back to Britt, who loops her arm through mine. Like me, she's new to this group of friends. The difference is that she's with one of the hockey players, so she fits in perfectly. All of these girls are dating—or married to—guys on the team.

The only other girl not with one of the players is Holland. She's Willow's bestie and roommate. I've only met her a handful of times. What I've noticed is that she tends to hang back and feel out the situation before loosening up. She has a razor-sharp sense of humor and seems to detest hockey players in general. The only time she shows up for games is when Willow drags her along. And she certainly never parties with them afterward.

Then again, neither do I.

It's only when Britt nudges me that I blink back to our conversation. "Where have you been hiding? I feel like I haven't seen you in forever."

Funny she would say that. Britt has no idea how close she is to the truth.

I shrug, wanting to keep the convo light. "Just busy with classes. You know how it is."

She nods. "It's a juggling act, for sure."

"How's married life treating you?" I waggle my brows. "Still enjoying it?"

Her cheeks flush as a wide smile spreads across her face. "It's pretty amazing. I couldn't be happier."

It still blows my mind that Britt and Colby secretly tied the knot in Vegas while there to celebrate the marriage of their friends, Wolf and Fallyn. From what I can tell, they're head over heels in love with each other, and he treats her like a total queen. Honestly, all the guys are that way with their significant others. My guess is that these girls have snapped up all the good ones. I've spent enough time around hockey players to know that most of them are exactly that—players who enjoy all the perks that come along with being a high-profile athlete on campus.

My attention is once again ensnared by Hayes.

As much as I try not to stare, I just can't seem to help myself.

He's way too handsome for his own good.

Mine as well.

It would be for the best if he lost interest. Although, I'm sure it won't be long before he moves on to the next warm body. I doubt he has much of an attention span.

The lights dim, and a voice booms through the arena, announcing the starting lineup. The energy in the place kicks up a notch as the Wildcats hit the ice to a chorus of cheers. Hayes is in the center of it all, probably eating up the adoration like sugary candy. This time, I do roll my eyes when a group of girls a few rows ahead scream his name, hoping to snag his attention.

He gives them exactly what they're so desperate for. With a grin, he lifts his gloved hand to wave. He's the epitome of cocky confidence.

Typical.

Finally, the coaching staff is introduced, and I whistle, cheering for my dad. He's always been my rock, and as complicated as life has become, I realize how lucky I am to have parents who love me unconditionally. They've supported me through everything—even when I made the impossible choice to walk away from professional skating.

I tamp down the grief threatening to surface, refusing to let it in.

The puck drops, and the game explodes to a start in a frenzy of motion. Hockey is fast, aggressive, and chaotic. A well-oiled machine of players crashing into each other with precision. I remind myself to stay focused on the game, but my attention continually drifts to Hayes.

He's all over the ice, involved in every play, moving with an ease and fluidity that's mesmerizing. It's hard not to notice how good he is, how he makes the toughest plays look effortless.

It doesn't take long for him to rack up three goals, securing a hat trick. His teammates surround him, slapping his back and grinning through their visors.

When he looks up, our eyes lock, and my pulse stutters.

Damn him.

I tear my gaze away, refusing to give him the satisfaction of thinking I'm impressed by his talent.

As I force myself to scan the packed stands across the ice, unease settles in my stomach. There, in the sea of fans, is a man in a black hoodie, his face obscured. My breath catches, the air freezing in my lungs.

No. It can't be.

I rise, trying to get a better look as the visiting team's fans jump to their feet when a turnover is made. Panic flares to life inside me, spreading through my veins like ice, as I search the crowd again, scanning faces, trying to convince myself it was nothing more than a trick of the light.

That Nathan isn't here.

He has no idea where I am.

"Ava?" The worry woven through Britt's voice is what pulls me back. "Are you okay? You look like you've seen a ghost."

I swallow hard and force a shaky smile, wanting to alleviate her concern. "I'm fine. Just a little lightheaded. I didn't eat much today."

Britt frowns. "Why don't we grab something from the concession stand? You don't want to pass out."

My heart continues to race as I shake my head. Even as I force the words through stiff lips, fear slithers through me, wrapping icy fingers around my heart before squeezing. It takes effort to keep the tremble from my voice. "I hate to bail, but I'm going to head out."

"Are you sure? We're not even halfway through the game."

"Yeah, I still have some work to finish up."

Her brow furrows. "You're really pale. Want me to come with you?"

The offer is tempting, but I can't drag Britt into this. More than likely, it was just my imagination playing tricks on me. "No, I'm good. I'll text you when I get home."

She gives me a hug before I say goodbye to the rest of the girls and then slip from the arena.

With my shoulders hunched, I weave through the crowd. My senses are on high alert as I scan the corridor for a familiar face—one I never thought I'd see again. The chilly night air hits me as soon as I step outside, but it does nothing to calm the gnawing fear in the pit of my belly.

Even though the parking lot is well lit, I can't shake the ominous feeling that settles inside me. The one that whispers someone is looming in the shadows, watching me.

Waiting for the perfect time to strike.

TenInchesofCocky

VAN DOREN
19

TENINCHESOF
COCKY

HAYES

WILDCATS

The bar is packed, loud, and buzzing with energy as we walk into Slap Shotz. The vibe is electric with people still riding high from our win tonight. We fought hard, making sure every play counted. The thought of not making it to the playoffs had all of us on edge. It's starting to hit me that every game could be the last one we have as a team.

A unit.

I scan the dark room, searching the sea of faces. It takes a moment to realize I'm looking for someone specific.

Someone petite and pixieish, who reminds me of a prickly little Tinkerbell.

My feet stutter to a stop.

What the hell am I doing?

I've never fixated on a girl like this before. Usually, they're all interchangeable. A pretty face and a body to warm my bed for a couple hours. That's all it's ever been. But the blonde figure skater has wormed her way into my head and refuses to be evicted.

I don't like it.

I don't like the way she knocks me off balance.

Especially when I know she'll cut me to ribbons with her sharp tongue if I step too close.

Not only that, but she's also Coach's daughter.

His *only* daughter.

The fastest way to get benched would be to screw around with Ava.

Besides, she's made it clear that she's not interested.

If I were smart, I'd let it go.

And yet... I can't stop thinking about her.

I try to shake off the strange sensations that have taken root inside me, but they refuse to be dismissed.

There are plenty of girls here tonight to lose myself in.

What I need to find is someone uncomplicated.

I glance around, the flashing lights and dark corners of the bar offering more than enough options.

All I need to do is smile, and the groupies will be lining up, vying to spend a little time with me.

Even as I tell myself that, deep down, I know it's not what I want.

I'm not looking for a tall brunette or a fiery redhead. I'm not interested in anyone else except a snarky blonde with sharp blue eyes.

And an even sharper tongue.

And that's a problem.

I release an irritated breath and spot my teammates already heading toward our usual table in the back that's reserved just for us.

"Shut the fuck up before I do it for you," Bridger snaps, his voice strung tight.

Even though Garret smirks, a mean look flashes in his eyes. "I'm just asking a question, man."

"Well, don't."

"When you can't make a clean pass, it becomes my business," Garret shoots back. "That last goal? It was totally on you."

Bridger swings toward him with his hands clenched at his sides. Only a couple of inches separate them. I've never known Bridger to have a short fuse, but the pressure inside him has been building over the last couple months. He's become a ticking time bomb. Garret's an idiot for pushing him. The last thing we need is a full-on brawl in the middle of Slap Shotz. It's one thing to get into it with your opponents and quite another to start with your own teammates.

I slip between them, shoving Garret back a few paces. "Hey, we won tonight. Let's not start shit here." Garret's eyes flash with irritation as my hand presses against his chest to keep him at a distance. "You're being a dick."

He scowls as tension crackles in the air between us. "You're always taking his side, huh, Van Doren?"

I meet his glare head-on before lifting my chin. "That's right."

Garret looks like he might say something else until Wolf steps beside me, his menacing presence enough to shut anyone down. With his tats and shaved head, Wolf's not someone you want to mess with. Garret's face pales, and he mutters something under his breath before stalking off in the opposite direction.

Wolf raises an eyebrow. "What's his deal?"

I shake my head. "Same as always. Just being an asshole."

We settle at the table, and the moment my butt hits the chair, a curvy girl drops onto my lap. She beams, flashing perfect white teeth. Her hands slip around my neck as she leans in, pressing her breasts against my chest.

"Hayes," she purrs, running her fingers through my hair. "You were amazing tonight."

I offer up a smile. "Thanks, sweetheart."

She's pretty. The kind of girl I'd usually go for without a second thought. And yet... all I can think about is how she's *not* Ava.

My brow furrows at the thoughts that have taken up residence in my brain.

"Wanna get out of here?" Her lips brush against my skin as she whispers the question.

Normally, that's all it would take, and I'd already be out the door with her on my arm.

Instead of feeling the usual rush of excitement, there's nothing.

No spark, no heat.

My mind drifts back to the other morning at the rink and the way Ava's eyes narrowed when she caught sight of me watching her. The most hilarious part was her feeble attempt at ignoring me. When that didn't work, she skated closer to verbally spar.

Does she feel the same pull I do?

It's the million-dollar question that begs for an answer.

The girl on my lap nips at my neck, her fingers curling into my hair. "So, what's it going to be? Come back to my place?"

I stare into her whiskey-colored eyes, trying to drum up a little bit of interest. But all I see is Ava. Her blonde hair, those piercing blue eyes, the way she gets under my skin without even trying.

Fuck.

With a groan, I drag my hand down my face, surprising even myself when I gently lift the girl off my lap. "Sorry, sweetheart. That game really took it out of me."

Her face scrunches. "You're leaving?"

"Yeah." I rise to my feet. "Alone."

Her lips part in surprise. "Alone?"

I nod, feeling like I've been dropped into some weird alternate reality.

This isn't me.

I don't walk away from girls like her.

But tonight?

Something's off.

And I know exactly what it is.

I force a small smile. "I'll see you around."

Without waiting for a response, I turn and walk out of the bar until the noise and chaos fade behind me. My thoughts are all tangled up in the one girl I can't seem to forget.

The one who wants nothing to do with me.

AVA

The only sound in the arena is the scrape of my blades over the ice. It's one of the few things that usually brings me comfort.

Today, though?

It sets my nerves on edge, like every muscle is stretched tight, ready to snap.

I roll my head from side to side, trying to ease the tension, but nothing helps. I'm wound up, and the more I skate, the more Nathan's voice digs into my brain.

"Lazy. Mediocre at best."

I can still hear him, criticizing my every move.

The triple salchow is one of the hardest jumps to master, but even now, I feel his judgment pressing down on me, making me second-guess every step. And it's not just the skating.

It's everything.

I landed like crap, didn't get enough sleep, and now, on top of everything else, I've convinced myself I saw Nathan at the game last night. That possibility is enough to turn my stomach.

I blow out a slow breath, trying to get my head right, and push off again. My skates slice the ice as I build speed, approaching the takeoff for a triple axel. Even though my legs are tired, I ignore it and launch into the air. The rotations feel right. The landing is solid.

It's perfect.

At least for a moment.

That moment where everything falls away, and it's just me, the ice, and the sound of my breath.

I miss that feeling.

The rush.

The power.

It's like Nathan found the smallest thread inside me, pulled it, and unraveled everything.

My confidence, my joy, my belief in myself—it all came apart in his hands.

Now I'm here, fighting to get it back.

I transition smoothly into a triple lutz-triple toe loop combination, nailing both jumps without thinking. My body knows the rhythm, the timing, better than my mind ever could.

For a few minutes, everything is simple again.

No Nathan, no scandal.

Just skating.

But it's fragile.

I glide through a Biellmann spin, my signature move. One arm reaches back to grab my blade as I spin faster, my body bending and core burning. The announcers used to rave about my spins. But Nathan's voice would cut through the praise, pointing out the smallest flaw.

"Hold it longer, Ava. That was sloppy. Do it again."

With a flick of my toe pick, I exit the spin and launch into a sequence of jumps. The final combination is a quadruple salchow, the one I always struggle with. My body surges into the air, muscles tense as I twist four times before landing cleanly. My knees bend with the impact, and for a second, I can almost imagine the roar of the crowd.

But it's all in my head. The only sound is the empty arena and my heartbeat pounding in my ears.

The peace that follows is short-lived as a chill races down my spine.

Just like that, the moment is gone.

Vanished into thin air.

I whip around, gaze scanning the seats.

It's enough to have my skin prickling with unease.

There's no sign of him, no figure lurking in the shadows, but the feeling refuses to be evicted.

It's like he's still here, somewhere, watching.

I shake my head, trying to shove the paranoia away. But ever since the text messages started, every little thing feels like a warning.

A threat.

It's exhausting, and I'm tired of looking over my shoulder.

My eyes catch movement by the benches, and I freeze.

Hayes.

He's sitting there, watching me, as if he has every right to do so.

My stomach flutters with nerves. Seeing him has become a weird kind of relief, even though I don't want it to be. Even though he's the *last* person I should be thinking about.

I take off in the opposite direction, attempting to ignore him, but it's useless. His gaze is heavy and distracting. When I can't stand another moment, I cave and skate toward him, coming to an abrupt stop a few feet away.

"What are you doing here?"

"Watching you skate," he says easily, his voice calm and brimming with confidence.

I cross my arms, narrowing my eyes. "Why?"

"Why am I watching you?" His lips quirk into a half-smile, like the answer is obvious.

I give him a sharp nod.

He leans back, eyes thoughtful. "Maybe because you're really good, and I find it... soothing."

The breath I'd been holding whooshes from my lungs, leaving me speechless.

Soothing?

My brain is usually quick to fire back with something biting, something that will make him retreat.

But this?

I don't know what to do with this.

"Do you have a problem if I like to watch?" His voice is lower now, a bit rougher, and when I meet his eyes again, there's something in them that makes my pulse jump.

Heat floods my cheeks.

I blink, trying to find my footing, but it's like he's pulled the ice out from under me. "If you're just watching me *skate*," I manage to mumble.

"I am." He grins, mischief dancing in his eyes. "Unless there's something else you had in mind." When I narrow my eyes in response, he changes the subject. "Did you used to compete?"

It's a challenge to shove the memories back down where they belong.

"Yes."

"But not anymore?"

"No."

When I don't elaborate, he asks, "How come?"

The air feels tight around me, like there's not enough oxygen to go around. "I just don't. End of story."

His gaze sharpens, and for a second, I feel like he sees more than I want him to. More than I'm comfortable with. "I don't believe that," he says quietly. "Something tells me there's more to the story. How about you tell it to me over coffee?"

I blink, thrown off by the casual invitation. "What?"

"Coffee," he repeats. "It's a drink. I'm sure you've heard of it before."

I cross my arms tightly over my chest. "Are you seriously asking me out?"

His lips curl into a smile that has alarm bells blaring in my brain. "Yeah. I guess I am."

I shake my head, trying to clear the sudden fog that has descended. The last thing I need is for it to cloud my judgment. "No. That's definitely not a good idea."

He doesn't miss a beat. "Why not?"

"You do realize who my dad is, right?" The reminder should be more than enough to make him back off.

But Hayes doesn't even flinch. "It would be hard not to."

I exhale sharply. "Look, I'm not interested."

His green eyes stay locked on mine, and I brace for the typical male reaction—annoyance, frustration, anything that might knock him off his axis. Instead, his smile widens as his eyes spark with amusement. "Just out of curiosity, are you always in the habit of lying to yourself?"

A gurgling laugh slips out of me. "Excuse me?"

"You're interested. But for whatever reason, you're too stubborn to admit it."

My jaw drops as I stare at him. How does this guy manage to throw me off-kilter at every turn? "You're really cocky, you know that?"

He hops down from the half wall with ease. "I've heard that before, Tink."

"Why do you keep calling me that?"

He cocks his head. "Because the way you skate is pretty fucking magical. Almost like you're flying. I've never seen anything like it."

The compliment does the unexpected and stuns me into silence.

He flashes a grin as his gaze remains fastened to mine until he swings away with an easy confidence that's impossible not to admire. "Give it some thought," he calls over his shoulder, "and get back to me."

Ha!

This guy is out of his mind if he actually thinks I'd consider going out with him.

Instead of telling him that, I remain silent, watching him disappear into the shadows of the arena as the sound of his laughter echoes in my ears.

TENINCHESOF
COCKY

WILDCATS

TenInchesofCocky
VAN DOREN
19
HAYES

"Are you guys excited?"

Ollie jerks his shoulders, attempting to act indifferent, but the brightness in his eyes gives him away. "Yeah, I guess."

I glance at him with a hiked brow. "You guess, huh? Well, I can always call Ma and have her pick you up if you've got better things to do with your time."

His eyes widen, panic flaring for a moment, before he quickly shakes his head. "Nah, that's all right. I'll stay and skate."

It's tempting to call him out on his bullshit, but I bite back the sharp retort. Thirteen is a rough age. Everything changes and the world feels like it's shifting beneath your feet. He's at that stage where acting like you care is uncool, but I know better. Deep down, he's still the same kid who used to look up to me like I hung the moon.

I remember what it was like, the confusion and awkwardness of trying to grow up. But that doesn't make it any less frustrating when he gives me attitude.

Theo, on the other hand, is practically bouncing off the walls, barely able to contain his exuberance. His wide grin and sparkling eyes are contagious, and I can't help but ruffle his messy blond hair. "You gonna get out there and show them how it's done, buddy?"

"Yup!" Theo beams up at me, vibrating with enthusiasm.

I glance down at Kia, her small hand safely tucked in mine. She's the youngest but just as determined as her brothers. She already loves the ice, and there was no way she'd let me bring the boys without her. Mom coaxed her to try ballet and soccer, but Kia only wants to play hockey.

Just like her big brothers.

When she looks up at me, I smile. "Ready, squirt?"

"Ready!" she chirps, voice bursting with just as much excitement as Theo's.

We head to the locker rooms to get them geared up for the clinic. I poke my head inside to make sure everyone's decent before leading Kia in to get changed. She wrinkles her nose at the distinct smell of stale sweat and gear that permeates the space.

"It's stinky in here," she says, her face scrunched with disgust.

I laugh and gently flick the tip of her nose. "Trust me, you get used to it."

I unzip her bag and pull out her gear, then she steps into her hockey pants, and I strap on her chest and elbow pads. Next come her socks, which I tape in place, and finally her skates. I tug her practice jersey over her head, then carefully secure her helmet.

"All set, squirt?"

With a nod, she hops in place with pent-up energy. Once everyone is dressed, we check in with Maverick at the registration table. He flashes a grin when he sees us, fist-bumping the kids.

"Man, you've all really grown since last year. What are you eating for breakfast, steroids?" Maverick jokes, giving Ollie a teasing look.

My brother stands a little taller, trying to look bigger than he is. He's always been on the shorter side, much to his irritation.

After we exchange a few more words, I hustle the kids onto the ice, getting them settled with their age groups.

I pat Theo on the helmet. "I'll be right over there if you need anything, okay?"

He nods as I take off. The players will rotate through different stations before scrimmaging later. I'm supposed to help Maverick, but my attention gets snagged by something—or rather *someone*—on the ice.

Ava.

Her blonde ponytail swings behind her, catching the light as she skates across the rink. Every time I've watched her on the ice, her hair has been pulled tight into a bun. Seeing the golden length flowing down her back has my mind going places it probably shouldn't. I can't help but wonder what it'd be like to wrap it around my fist and feel it in my hands while—

I change direction, my feet moving before I've even made a conscious decision. It's like there's an invisible thread pulling me to her. One that's impossible to resist.

When I catch her eye, she tilts her head and meets my gaze with a steely look of her own.

"Kind of late, aren't you?" she says, her voice dry.

I smirk, unable to resist needling her. "Anxious to see me again, Tink?"

With a snort, she crosses her arms and glances away. "I think we both know nothing could be further from the truth. And stop calling me that."

My mind comes up with and then rejects a dozen different responses.

I'm not used to playing it cool, and I sure as shit don't have to try this hard to secure someone's attention.

That realization only makes me want to break down the walls she's erected to keep me out even more than before.

"Have you given anymore thought to grabbing that coffee with me?"

"Actually," she says with an exaggerated pause, "I forgot all about it."

I press my hand to my chest. "Ouch. That stings."

She arches a brow. "Doubtful."

Even though she's doing everything possible to keep me at a distance, I refuse to walk away. There's something here, something that demands to be explored.

My guess is she feels it too.

Before I can say anything else, Coach skates over, his narrowed gaze bouncing between us.

Suspicion darkens his features. "Hayes, help Sanderson with the drills."

I blink. "I thought I was with Maverick."

Coach's stare turns a few shades colder. "McKinnon's got it under control. Assist Sanderson."

Translation: *Get the hell away from my daughter.*

"Sure thing, Coach." I give Ava one last look, but she's already skating away.

I head toward the opposite end of the rink. It's a challenge to keep my mind focused on the drills and not the blonde figure skater. Every couple of minutes, my attention gets snagged by her.

And when she drops the prickly demeanor and smiles at the kids?

It's like a punch to the gut that leaves me feeling even more off-kilter than before.

That's when I realize that whatever this is won't just fade away.

The question is, what the hell am I going to do about it?

AVA

Three hours later and I'm completely wiped. Parents are trickling in for pickup, and I didn't expect wrangling a group of hyperactive children would be more exhausting than my own two-hour practices filled with physically demanding jumps and routines.

Some of these kids have the attention span of a goldfish. They're constantly asking questions, wandering off, or worse, encouraging others to do the same.

And the ones who can't seem to focus for more than five seconds?

I keep them glued to my side.

Their parents must be saints, because there's no way I'd survive one day in their shoes.

"Coach Ava?" A small tug on my fingers pulls me from my thoughts.

I glance down into the big blue eyes of a little girl. Two teeth are missing from her smile, which only makes her cuteness factor shoot off the charts.

"What's up?" I check the white tape on her helmet that has her name scrawled in black Sharpie. "Kia?"

"I'm thirsty. Can I get a drink of water?"

"Of course."

She beams before rushing off toward the bench where the bottles are lined up like little soldiers. She's one of the few girls in the clinic, and definitely the youngest.

A couple minutes later, she's back, standing in front of me with that same wide-eyed grin. "Do you play hockey?"

The question takes me by surprise. "Nope. I'm a figure skater." A small stab of sadness twists inside my chest. That answer used to fill me with pride. Now, it's a reminder of everything I've lost.

Before I can wallow, I push the feeling aside, refocusing on the little girl. "Are you here by yourself?"

She shakes her head, pointing toward a group of boys on the other side of the rink. "My brothers are over there."

"Hockey must run in the family, huh?"

Her dimples pop as she nods. "Yup. My brother says I can play on a team next year."

"That'll be fun. So, who's picking you up? Are they here yet?"

"My brother drove us," she says.

I glance at one of the boys she pointed to and frown. "Isn't he, like, ten?"

Kia bursts into a fit of giggles. Before she can answer, Hayes skates over with two boys trailing behind him. One of them looks about twelve, the other younger, maybe eight or nine. When Hayes scoops Kia up into his arms, her face lights up.

"Did you have fun, squirt?" His tone is gentle in a way I wasn't expecting.

"Yeah! Can we come back next weekend?"

With a smile, he shakes his head. "Nope. This was a one-day thing, remember? We talked about it."

Her pout is immediate, and I can't help but soften at the exchange.

"These are your siblings?" The question slips out before I can stop it.

His gaze locks on mine, that familiar grin creeping across his face. "Yup. All three of them."

"My feet hurt," one of the boys complains, sounding every bit the pre-teen he probably is. "I think I've got blisters."

Hayes pats the top of his helmet. "I've got bandages in my bag. We'll check them in the locker room."

As they make their way off the ice, I realize the rink is mostly empty except for the Wildcats players who volunteered for the clinic.

Just as I step onto the rubber mats, a small hand slips into mine. Kia looks up at me with those big blue eyes. "Can I come with you? The boys' locker room smells bad."

The question catches me off guard, and I glance at Hayes, unsure how to respond.

He shrugs, clearly amused by the situation. "If it's okay with Coach Ava, it's fine with me."

I look down at her again. "I mean... yeah, sure."

"Yay!" she chirps before pulling me toward the girls' locker room.

A grin simmers around the corners of Hayes's mouth as we walk away. "I'll grab her bag," he calls after us.

A minute later, he hands me a pink hockey bag that's bigger than she is. It could probably fit her and one of her brothers inside. I chuckle at the thought as I lead her into the locker room.

There are only a few other girls left, all pink-cheeked and sweaty, slowly peeling off their gear. Kia chatters nonstop as I help remove her helmet, then work on unlacing her skates.

"Are you friends with my brother?" she asks, her tone curious but innocent.

I hesitate, my fingers pausing on her skates. "Umm... yes?"

She doesn't seem to notice the uncertainty in my answer, and keeps talking, completely unaware. "I miss him when he's at college. I wish he lived at our house."

"I bet that's hard. Does he visit a lot?"

"Yup! Sometimes Mama brings us to his games, and we get to yell his name really loud." She cups her hands around her mouth and shouts, "Hayes!"

When her voice echoes off the concrete walls of the locker room, I laugh. This girl is way too cute. "I bet he can hear you all the way from the ice."

"He says he can." There's a brief pause and then her voice drops. "Guess what?" She doesn't give me time to respond before blurting, "He's gonna play in the NHL next year."

I raise an eyebrow. "So I've heard."

"And when he does, we'll have lots and lots of money," she whispers, as if this is a big secret she's sharing with me. "He promised I can have a puppy."

I pause, digesting her words.

"Hayes gives Mama money so we can skate," she adds quietly, her voice growing solemn.

The innocence in her tone is heartbreaking. She says it so simply, but there's a heaviness behind her words that makes my chest tighten. This is the first time I've gotten a glimpse into the weight Hayes carries, the responsibility that must rest on his shoulders.

I clear my throat, wanting to shift the mood. "Sounds like he's a pretty great big brother."

Her face brightens again as she bounces on the bench. "He's the best!"

As we finish packing up her gear, I can't help but mentally replay everything she said. It paints a different picture of Hayes than the one I had before. Less cocky center for the Western Wildcats and more protective older brother, willing to do whatever it takes for his family.

We head out to the lobby where Hayes and his brothers are waiting. The minute they spot us, Kia runs to him, her small hand clutching his tightly.

"Who's hungry?" he asks.

"Me!" they all shout in unison.

I take a step back, raising my hand in a wave. "Well, have fun—"

"Can Coach Ava come?" Kia interrupts, her eyes wide and hopeful.

I pause, startled by the unexpected question. I glance from her to Hayes, shaking my head. "Oh, no. I don't want to intrude—"

"Please?" Kia pouts, her expression tugging at my heartstrings, making it impossible to say no. This little girl already knows how to wrap people around her finger.

Hayes smirks, clearly enjoying my discomfort. His laughter is barely contained. "You're welcome to join us, if you're up for it."

With a sigh, I check my watch. "I guess I can go."

"Yay!" Kia hops around, her energy boundless despite the hours spent on the ice.

As we head toward the exit, Hayes falls into step beside me. His siblings run ahead, eager to hit the arcade area near the concession stand.

I give him a sideways glance as my lips twitch with amusement. "You realize your sister is going to be a handful, right?"

He snorts. "What do you mean *going to be*?"

As much as I hate to admit it, for the first time since I met Hayes, I see him in a different light. Maybe he's not just an arrogant hockey player who always seems to have a smirk on his face. Maybe, just maybe, he's a guy who has a lot more going on beneath the surface.

And maybe that makes him someone worth getting to know.

TENINCHESOF
COCKY

WILDCATS

TenInchesofCocky
VAN DOREN
19
19
81
HAYES

12

The drive to Harvey's Eats and Treats is a quick fifteen minutes from the arena, but with Ava sitting next to me in the passenger seat, it feels like a longer stretch of time. She offered to take her own car, but Kia—God bless her—begged Ava to ride with us. There was no way she could say no to those big blue eyes, and I wasn't about to let her off the hook.

Without my little sister doing my dirty work, I'm sure Ava would have found an excuse to avoid my beat-up Ford Bronco. The old girl might be rusty and a little worse for wear, but I'd never replace her. Not even with the NHL salary I'm hoping to land next year. I've put too much blood, sweat, and tears into this truck, working summers in high school to afford it, then spending weekends fixing her up with my uncle. She's seen me through a lot, and there's something grounding about that.

Ava sits stiffly beside me, her fingers twisted together in her lap, eyes glued to the windshield like she's trying to will herself to be anywhere but here. Alternative rock hums through the speakers while my siblings chatter in the back seat about their morning on the ice.

After we pull into the parking lot of Harvey's, Ava pops the handle and steps out of the truck before assisting the kids. All three of them scramble from the backseat and race toward the entrance. I chuckle, watching them disappear inside as the bell above the door chimes in their wake.

"You've certainly got your hands full," Ava mutters.

I grin, locking up before we follow them inside. "You have no idea, Tink."

Harvey's is one of our favorite spots. It's got this old-school diner vibe with pinball machines, a jukebox, and a menu filled with classic burgers, fries, and the best milkshakes in town. It's not something we splurge on often, but every now and then, I like to treat my siblings to dinner out just to remind them that things won't always be this tough. That better days are ahead of us.

As we walk in, Shelley—the waitress who practically watched me grow up—spots the kids and greets them with a wide smile. "Hey! It's been a while since I've seen the Van Doren bunch! Want your usual table?"

She doesn't bother to wait for a response, already knowing the drill. The kids love the booth near the pinball machines. Her gaze catches mine, and a curious brow arches as she takes in the girl beside me. I can practically see the gears turning in her head. It's only a matter of time before she calls my mom with the latest gossip.

Once we're seated, Kia scoots close to Ava until she's practically sitting in her lap. Shelley hands out menus even though we don't need them.

"The usual?" she asks.

"Yeah, that sounds good," I say, glancing at Ava. "Do you need more time to make a decision?"

She shakes her head, a small smile playing around her lips. "I'm good. My dad and I came here last month. He loves the Salisbury steak. It reminded him of the place my mom used to work at in college."

I lean back, taking in the way her face softens as she talks about her family. This version of Ava—more relaxed, less guarded—is rare, and I find myself wanting to keep the conversation going, to tease out more from her.

"Do you have any siblings?"

With a shake of her head, she tucks a strand of blonde hair behind her ear. "No, but I've always wondered what it'd be like."

I glance toward my brothers and sister, who are busy bickering over which of them is the better hockey player. "They can be loud and rambunctious, but I wouldn't trade them for the world. It's kind of like having chaos and calm all at once."

She smiles, but it doesn't quite reach her eyes. "I bet. I'm sure your parents appreciated the help, especially with such a big age gap between you and them."

I pause for a moment, considering how to answer. This is the most we've talked about anything personal, and I don't want to say something that will send her guard shooting back up.

"Guess I got the best of both worlds. I had my parents to myself for a while, then got to be a big brother."

Before Ava can respond, Ollie breaks away from the pinball machine and rushes over. "Can we get some quarters for the games?"

"Pleeeeease," Kia adds, stretching out the word for a solid ten seconds.

Ava chuckles from beside me before covering it with a cough.

I pull a ten and two singles from my wallet before handing them over to Ollie for safekeeping. "Have Miss Shelley break it at the cash register." My gaze settles on Theo. "If I give the three of you twelve dollars, how much do each of you get?"

With a furrowed brow, he looks upward, as if the answer might be magically written on the ceiling. "Ollie and Kia get three each and I get the rest."

"Nice try. Everyone gets four bucks." I point at the three of them. "And no fighting."

Theo and Kia cheer before running off, leaving me with Ava.

If I'm lucky, I'll get a solid ten minutes alone with her before they're back, begging for more money. So I need to make the most of it.

If Ava has her way, I'll never get another chance like this again.

She stares after them with a bemused expression. With her distracted, it gives me the perfect opportunity to silently soak in the sight of her.

She shakes her head and chuckles. "They're pretty cute."

"What they are is a pain in the ass," I correct, though there's a fondness in my voice I can't hide. "They keep my mom busy, for sure."

Her lips curve as she shrugs. "I can see that. When I was about ten, I begged my parents for a sister or brother. It was always just the three of us, and there were times when it was lonely. That's when they sat me down and told me that my mom couldn't have more kids. They'd both been so sad."

It's kind of weird to think of Coach having a life outside of hockey. Maybe even a few unfulfilled hopes and dreams.

"Are you close with them?"

She nods. "Yeah, I am."

"They must be pretty protective since it's just you."

Emotion flickers in her eyes before she glances away. Just when I think she'll evade the question with a change in topic, she says, "They are." There's a pause before her voice dips. "The last year has been difficult for them."

Everything around me fades to the background as I press closer, wanting to know every detail she's willing to hand over. "How come?"

She shrugs as her teeth scrape across her lower lip. "The move and just everything that came along with it."

Even as I nod, I replay her words in my head, trying to make sense of them. I get the feeling there's more to the story than Ava is willing to tell me. What I've already discovered in the little time we've spent together is that she's guarded. If I push too hard, attempting to dig for the truth, she'll shut down, and I'll lose the tiny bit of trust I've gained this afternoon.

I glance at my phone, knowing our time together is running out. "My mom is going to meet me here to take the kids home since they live about thirty minutes away."

She picks up the straw wrapper from her drink and smooths it out before folding it accordion style. "You've mentioned your mom several times, but not your dad." Her gaze flicks upward, pinning mine in place. "Are they divorced?"

It's a fair question, one I'm used to answering, but it still stings. "He died right before Kia was born."

Ava's hand flies to her mouth as regret floods her features. "I'm so sorry. I shouldn't have brought it up."

I shake my head. "It's okay. He was a great dad. Life hasn't been easy without him, but we're managing."

She surprises me by reaching across the table, her fingers curling around mine in a gentle, comforting gesture. "Do you mind me asking how it happened?"

"Distracted driver," I say quietly. "The guy was a few years older than me, and I knew him. It was an election year, and the DA was hellbent on making an example out of him. He went to prison, but it didn't change anything. It was a tragedy all the way around."

Her eyes flicker with sympathy, and for the first time, I see a crack in her tough exterior before she glances at my siblings again as if with fresh eyes. "They're lucky to have you."

The heartfelt comment takes me by surprise. I don't talk about my dad with many people, but somehow, sharing my past with Ava feels... easy.

Right.

"Kia chattered about you nonstop in the locker room. Just in case you didn't realize it, she's your number one fan."

My lips quirk. The feeling is entirely mutual. There's nothing I wouldn't do for that girl.

And that includes burying bodies or taking someone out to the woods if they break her heart.

"It's good to know she was hyping me up."

"The entire time."

"I should probably slip her a few bucks for putting in a good word."

Our gazes cling from across the table as Kia's excited voice cuts through the air. "Mom!"

I glance up to see my mom standing near the entrance, talking with an excited Kia while Theo tugs on her sleeve, trying to get her attention. Ollie is still glued to the pinball machine.

When she finally spots me, her eyes widen slightly as they land on Ava. It doesn't take long for her to recover. She walks over, a smile already forming on her lips.

"Ava, this is my mom, Cheryl. Mom, this is Ava." I introduce them quickly, hoping Mom doesn't say anything too embarrassing.

"It's nice to meet you," my mom says, her smile warm and genuine.

"You too," the girl across from me replies politely, her earlier ease slipping away under the older woman's scrutiny.

Mom's eyes sparkle with interest as she glances between us. "Are you two friends?"

Ava's quick to say "No."

But I counter at the same time. "Yes."

Mom's brows shoot up. "I see."

I suppress a laugh as Ava's cheeks flush a deep shade of pink.

"We met recently," she clarifies.

Mom doesn't push for more info, but I can tell she's dying to. Instead, she turns back to the kids. "Well, I should get them home. Theo's got a birthday party later this afternoon."

I stand, giving my siblings a quick hug and then hugging my mom too.

"Thanks for taking them." She glances at the three of them. "Seems like they had a great time."

"They did."

With a smile, she leans in to whisper, "Text me later. I want all the details."

I roll my eyes as she herds the kids out of the restaurant. The second they're gone, the silence between Ava and me grows heavier. As much as I want to spend more time with her, I've probably pushed the envelope enough for one day.

"Ready to head out?" I ask.

With a nod, she rises to her feet and grabs her jacket. After taking care of the check, we walk back to the truck.

As we approach, I quicken my steps to open the passenger door.

Her brow arches as she smirks. "Chivalry, huh?"

I grin. "You just met my mom. Do you really think I'd survive in that house without at least learning a few manners?"

She laughs, the sound light and warm. "Fair point."

Once she's settled, I jog around to the driver's side and hop in, starting up the truck.

Without Ollie, Theo, and Kia acting as a buffer with their incessant chatter, thick tension crackles in the air between us. I rack my brain for something to say. Something that will get us back to where we were earlier at the restaurant when our conversation flowed with ease.

Instead, my mind remains frustratingly blank. Every time something pops into my head as a possible topic, I disregard it.

When have I ever had this much trouble talking with a chick?

The answer is never.

As we drive back to campus, I can't stop replaying the way her hand had settled over mine at the diner.

The way she'd softened, even if it was just for a moment.

We're halfway back to the arena when her phone buzzes. She pulls it from her pocket and glances at the screen. Fear flashes across her expression before it's quickly masked as tension seeps into her shoulders.

I don't want to pry, but it's hard to ignore the way her entire demeanor has changed. "Is everything okay?"

She swallows, slipping the phone back into her pocket. "Just someone from my past who refuses to stay there."

It's so tempting to ask for more details, but I know better than to push.

Whatever is going on, it's clearly something she's not ready to talk about.

At least, not with me.

But I can wait.

If my past has taught me anything, it's to stay focused on the long game.

Especially when it involves a certain pixie-like figure skater.

AVA

13

Relief floods my system the moment Hayes pulls up beside my silver Jetta. The parking lot, once bustling with the activity of the hockey clinic, is now quiet, with only a handful of cars left.

I'm eager to flee the close confines of the vehicle. The strange mix of emotions swirling inside me makes me desperate for a bit of distance. Before I can pop the door handle and slip away, Hayes swivels toward me.

"So, what do you think about a second date, Tink?" The intensity in his eyes belies the casualness of his tone.

My brows shoot up in surprise. "Second date? That's strange, I don't remember agreeing to the first one."

A slow grin spreads across his face. "Pretty sure I just bought you lunch. That counts as a date in my book."

I narrow my eyes, feeling that familiar pull between us. "Maybe your sister isn't the only Van Doren who needs to be watched out for."

The chuckle that escapes from him is a low and rich sound that does funny things to my insides.

"I just want the chance to get to know you better. That's all."

I glance away, knowing I should shut this down before it gets out of control.

The rational part of me screams that this is a bad idea—that nothing good can come from this growing attraction or letting him in. But there's something about the way he looks at me, like he sees more than just the snippy facade I project, that makes it difficult to say no.

"I don't think that's a good idea," I murmur, my gaze flicking back to him briefly before darting away again. "And that's not me playing hard to get. I'm not someone who plays games." I pause, unsure how to explain without giving away too much. "I just..."

I trail off as the words become lodged at the back of my throat.

I hate this.

Hate how vulnerable I feel and how tangled up in the past I am.

It was so much easier to push him away when I thought he was just another arrogant hockey player used to getting what he wanted. But now, after seeing how he cares for his family, how he's stepped up since his dad died, I'm unable to fall back on that excuse.

Instead of letting me off the hook, his fingers slip beneath my chin, gently tilting my face toward him. His touch is surprisingly gentle as his eyes search mine with a kind of patience that makes my pulse quicken.

"Just what?" His voice is soft, coaxing. "Talk to me."

I sigh, my breath shaky.

As much as I want to look away, I can't. His gaze holds mine captive, and for the first time in a while, I feel exposed—like he's peeling back the protective layers I've worked so hard to build.

"There are things that happened last year," I say carefully, "and I'm having a hard time moving past them. Whatever you're looking for, I'm not it."

He studies me quietly. It's like he's trying to piece together the parts of me I've kept hidden. What I don't like is how close he's getting and just how easily he's able to break down my defenses.

Before I can retreat, he leans in slightly, his breath warm against my skin.

"Does this have anything to do with the person who messaged you earlier?"

My stomach drops at the mention of the text I received a handful of minutes ago. The way he picked up on that so easily, how he saw through my attempts to brush it off, unsettles me.

"Yeah," I admit, my voice barely above a whisper.

The shift in Hayes is immediate. His relaxed demeanor tightens, concern flashing in his eyes. "Is it an ex?"

I hesitate.

There's so much more to it than that, but I can't bring myself to spill the details.

"Something like that," I mutter.

He watches me carefully, and for a second, I think he might press for more. Instead, he inches closer until the warmth of his breath drifts across my lips.

"Okay, let me ask you this, do you feel anything for me?"

The question catches me by surprise.

Before I can react, he continues, "Because I feel something for you. And that's not something I've experienced before, so I kind of want to figure out what this is." His voice is steady, sincere, and somehow, that makes it difficult to deflect.

I swallow hard, my heart racing in my chest. "Nothing is that easy."

A slow, lazy smile tugs at his lips. "It can be," he says, his fingers still gently holding my chin. "I promise."

Everything inside me screams to shut this down, to retreat before I get in too deep. Instead of saying no the way I should, I find myself blurting out the one word that shocks us both. "Okay."

His brows shoot up in disbelief, his eyes narrowing playfully. "Really? You're not messing with me?"

I can't help the laugh that bubbles up in my chest as the crackling tension between us dissolves. "No, I'm not messing with you."

He grins, and the warmth of his smile makes my insides flip. "Good."

The moment stretches between us, a delicate balance of uncertainty and something else I haven't let myself feel in a long time. Maybe that's what terrifies me so much. For the first time since everything with Nathan exploded, I'm allowing myself to feel again.

As much as I want to believe Hayes, to let myself be swept up in whatever this is between us, I can't shake the feeling that nothing is as simple as he makes it out to be.

And that's the part that scares me most.

AVA

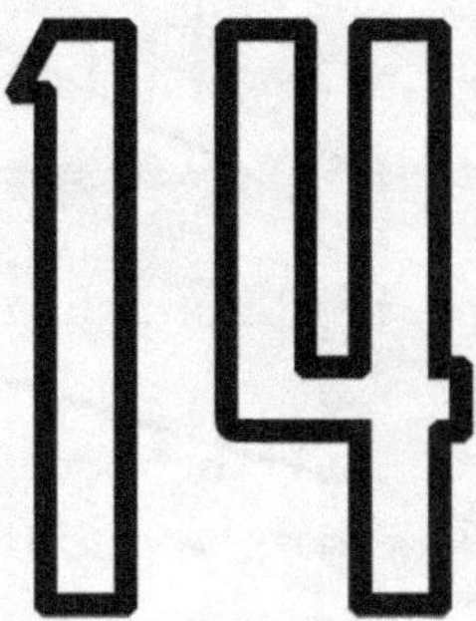

I stare at the ceiling, tracing the faint shadows that stretch across the room from the sliver of moonlight sneaking through my blinds. The clock on my nightstand ticks past midnight, and sleep feels as far away as it did an hour ago. Even though I'm physically exhausted—my body heavy and aching from practice, endless hockey drills, and wrangling kids at the clinic—my mind is wide awake, stuck on a constant loop.

I roll onto my side and try to shove thoughts of Hayes out of my head, but it's useless. His face, his laugh, the way his gaze catches mine and holds, the nickname he's given me, it all floods my brain, refusing to be silenced.

It's infuriating.

And terrifying.

Hayes wasn't supposed to be anything more than the manwhore I'd pegged him to be after our first run-in. And he certainly wasn't supposed to get under my skin, making me second-guess everything I thought I knew about him and myself.

But here we are.

I roll onto my back again, staring blankly at the ceiling, letting the memories from this afternoon wash over me.

What did he say earlier?

That he wanted to get to know me better?

To figure out what this is between us?

It's such a simple sentiment, and yet it's weighed heavily on me ever since he said it. Because the thing is, I *do* feel something for him. It would be so much easier to ignore the attraction if he were just a cocky, one-dimensional player who said all the right things but meant none of them.

I'm starting to suspect he's more than I assumed, and that's making it harder to keep my walls up.

I think back to the clinic and lunch today, watching him with his siblings. The way his little sister clung to him, how he'd made her laugh and kept her close. The way he took charge with his brothers, patient and firm but with a tenderness I hadn't expected. And then there's his mom—the way his whole face softened when she walked into the restaurant.

There was no hiding the depth of responsibility he feels for them or the pride.

It's a side of him that contradicts everything I thought I knew.

He isn't just some guy who's used to getting what he wants without putting in the work. He's carrying more than I ever imagined. Supporting his family. Balancing school and hockey with all the pressure that comes with being one of the best players on the team.

It would be so easy to push him away, to use the excuse that I'm too messed-up to be with anyone right now. That's what I've been doing, after all. Every time he gets too close, I freeze up, my instincts screaming at me to protect myself. To run before I get hurt again.

But there's something about Hayes that makes it hard to keep running.

Maybe it's the way he looks at me—not like I'm fragile, but like he *sees* me.

Like he knows I'm strong enough to handle whatever this is.

Maybe it's the way he's relentless without being pushy, always giving me just enough space to breathe but never letting me slip away completely.

I squeeze my eyes shut, trying to will away the confusion building inside me.

Most of all, I didn't expect him to burrow under my skin, to keep showing up in my thoughts when I should be focusing on other things like school, skating, and keeping myself together. He makes me feel things I haven't felt in a long time. Things I haven't let myself feel since...

The thought of Nathan slithers in like a snake, coiling around my gut and squeezing tight. My eyes snap open, and I stare at the ceiling again.

Don't think about him.

But I can't stop myself. It's like my mind is stuck in this endless loop, going back to the place I've spent the last year running from.

Every time I see Hayes, every time I hear his voice or feel his presence, that invisible wall I've built between myself and the world cracks a little more.

And that terrifies me.

I sit up in bed, running my hands through my hair, frustrated by my own emotions. This is the last thing I need. Instead of thinking about Hayes, I should focus on getting my life back together.

But then I hear his voice in my head, soft and steady, asking me that one question that's been gnawing at me since we left the restaurant.

"Do you feel anything for me?"

I hadn't answered him then, too caught off guard by his honesty to respond. But now, in the quiet of my room, I can't escape the truth.

I do.

I think about the way he stared into my eyes. The way his warm breath feathered across my lips. My lower belly flutters before the sensation settles deep in my core.

My teeth scrape across my bottom lip as my hand slips inside my panties and grazes the top of my mound. I suck in an unsteady breath before allowing my fingers to glide across my slit. It's a surprise when I find just a hint of slickness.

I squeeze my eyes tightly closed and allow thoughts of Hayes to fill my head. A shiver dances down my spine as I shift so my legs can fall open. With soft strokes, I touch my pussy. It doesn't take long before more wetness gathers. Need blooms in my core as my mind conjures up images of walking in on Hayes after his shower in the locker room. It would be impossible not to remember the hard, sinewy strength of his back that stood out in sharp relief. Even his ass had been chiseled and well-defined, and his thighs bulged with muscles.

My fingers pick up their pace as more desire floods through me.

It had almost been a disappointment when he'd turned around, his gaze colliding with mine. I could have spent hours soaking him in, visually tracing every dip and contour. In return, he'd given me a lazy once-over. Unable to help myself, my attention had fallen to the thick length of his cock.

And his shaved balls.

Sure, I'd seen that in porn before but never in real life.

It had been tempting to step closer and get a better look.

He'd stiffened up before wrapping his hand around his thickening length and leisurely stroking himself.

Everything tightens within me as those images flash through my mind like a slow-motion picture show.

This isn't the first time I've touched myself while reliving our initial meeting. As close as I've come to orgasming, I haven't been able to get there. I want—no, *need*—this time to be different.

I need to prove to myself that Nathan didn't break me.

My brow scrunches as my teeth sink into my lower lip.

I'm so close.

Dancing on the precipice.

It's right there.

It's been so long since I've felt an orgasm crash over me, dragging me to the very bottom of the ocean before allowing me to float to the surface.

It's enough to make desperation brew within. The need to sever the last chains Nathan shackled me with so I can free myself from him once and for all.

Anxiety spirals through me, and my fingers move faster as I arch my back. I focus on the slide of Hayes's hand along his thick erection. The memories of what it had felt like to wrap my fingers around his length and stroke him for myself. How hot to the touch he'd felt.

"My guess is that you'll look good on your knees with a mouth stuffed full of cock."

Those husky words ignite a firestorm within me.

But it's still not enough to push me over the edge.

It's not enough to make me come.

After a few tense moments, frustration bursts through me and my arousal vanishes like a wisp of smoke in the darkness.

I let loose an angry cry as I roll onto my side and curl up in a tight ball. Even though tears spring to my eyes, I refuse to let them fall.

Last year broke me in more ways than one.

What I don't know is if it's possible to piece myself back together again.

TENINCHESOF
COCKY

WILDCATS

TenInchesofCocky
VAN DOREN
19
HAYES

I sit perched on the edge of the couch at the Roasted Bean, my eyes glued to the door, scanning every passerby for a glimpse of familiar blonde hair. The moment Ava steps foot inside—or worse, walks past the café and ditches me altogether—I want to be ready.

It wouldn't surprise me if she changed her mind at the last minute. The girl is unpredictable, always keeping me at a firm distance, never allowing me to get too close.

I check my phone for what feels like the twentieth time.

She's five minutes late and counting.

With a shift, I fidget with my cell.

The bell above the door jingles, pulling my attention from the thoughts racing through my head. I glance up, heart stuttering, only to be met with a flirty smile from a brunette. She gives me a look that says *I'll come over if you want me to.*

I flash a polite smile and hope she moves on. If I give her the slightest bit of encouragement, she'll beeline in this direction.

That's not me being conceited.

It's just straight up facts.

Scenarios that have played out hundreds of times in the past.

Dismissing the brunette, my gaze drifts back to the door. I'm still scanning for Ava, wondering where the hell she is and why she's late. She's not the type to make things easy, and it only drives home the realization that I care.

When another five minutes slip by, disappointment gnaws at me.

It's official.

I've been ghosted.

How's that for ironic?

The first time I ask a girl out because I'm legit interested, she ditches me.

Note to self—stick with the eager bunnies.

This sucks.

I take a deep breath and force my muscles to loosen.

This was always going to be a long shot.

Ava isn't the kind of girl who's interested in someone like me. She's got walls higher than I've ever seen, and I'm not sure I'm equipped to climb them.

"Hi."

I blink back to the present and realize the girl who sauntered through the door a few minutes ago is now standing in front of me, with a friend who looks eerily similar to her. They're both sporting bags with the same Greek letters stamped across the front of them.

Sorority sisters.

Been there, done that.

Her friend beams a blinding smile my way. "We caught the last game and just wanted to stop by and say you were amazing. The hat trick was so impressive."

"You make it look so easy," the other adds.

"Thanks. Years of training can make anything look simple." My gaze flicks from them to the door when the bell dings and another customer steps inside.

Air clogs my lungs.

The physical reaction I have to this girl is the strangest sensation ever.

I can't help but want more of it.

It's only been a couple weeks, and already the feelings she rouses in me are more like an addiction.

I can just imagine how she'd react if I admitted as much to her.

She'd probably take out a restraining order.

Would I necessarily blame her for that decision?

Nope.

Is it going to stop me from pursuing her?

Probably not.

Ava meets my gaze before her own darts to the girls, and she grinds to a quick halt. One brow slinks upward. The thoughts circling around in her head flash across her face before vanishing behind a mask of indifference.

My attention never deviates from her as I pop to my feet.

When I take a step in her direction, one of the girls reaches out to detain me. "We were wondering if you wanted to grab a coffee. Maybe we could—"

Before the rest of the sentence can make it past her pink-slicked lips, I shake my head. "Sorry, I have plans, and she just walked through the door."

With matching frowns, they turn and stare at Ava.

I take their distraction as my opportunity to leave.

The last thing I want to happen is for Ava to change her mind. I might not know her well, but I can see the indecision written across her expression.

It only takes a few long-legged strides for me to eat up the distance between us. "You're late, Tink." I make a show of glancing at my phone. "By at least ten minutes."

Her gaze flicks from mine to the girls, who have their heads bent together and are whispering furiously while staring at us.

"Looks like you had company while you waited. Am I interrupting a fan club moment?"

Not bothering to glance in their direction, I shake my head. "Not at all."

Unable to keep my hands to myself for another second, my fingers wrap around her elbow as my other hand settles at the small of her back, propelling her toward a couch in the back, away from the girls.

Once she's settled, I nod toward the counter. "I'll grab us a couple of coffees. Anything specific you'd like?"

With a tilt of her head, the corners of her lips quirk. "Surprise me."

I arch a brow. "Hmmm. Why does this feel like a test?"

"Not sure."

When mischief sparks in her eyes, I narrow mine for a second or two before swinging toward the counter. Once there, I ponder the array of drink options written in colorful chalk until one catches my eye, and I order two of them.

The entire time I wait, my attention strays to Ava. I'm half afraid she'll disappear. Most girls are thrilled if I give them a little bit of attention.

This one couldn't be more different.

"That was a hell of a game the other night. I couldn't be there in person, but I watched the highlights on ESPN."

I glance at the barista. "Thanks."

He rests his elbows on the counter, as if settling in for a long chat. "Yeah, I used to skate back in the day."

"You don't say."

With a nod, he puffs out his chest. "I wasn't half bad."

My gaze slides to Ava.

Well, hell.

The brunette sorority sisters have descended, flanking her like vultures.

My attention stays pinned to them as I clear my throat. "Are the drinks ready?"

He straightens to his full height. "Cara? Put a rush on the Van Doren order!"

Less than thirty seconds later, a girl bustles around the corner with two cups. Her cheeks are pink and her hands tremble as she sets them on the counter. "Here you go! Sorry about the wait!"

"No worries. Thanks."

As I step away from the register, she raises her voice. "Bye, Hayes Van Doren!"

Without turning, I lift one of the drinks. "Have a good one."

As I make my way to Ava, I notice the girls have settled on either side of her, sandwiching her in. By the look on her face, she's not thrilled about the situation.

Her gaze fastens to mine as I approach.

The sorority sisters straighten as their eager expressions lock on me like heat-seeking missiles.

One of them flashes a sly smile. "We were just getting to know your friend."

It would be impossible not to notice the way Ava's jaw tightens.

"Yeah! Now we're all besties," the other adds, trying to slip her hand around Ava's smaller one. With a frown, Ava tugs it free.

"Thanks for keeping her company while I was getting our coffees."

"No problem!"

"Now, if you two wouldn't mind..." My voice trails off, not wanting to be rude.

"I'd love a coffee!" the girl on the left chirps.

"Me too!" the other agrees.

"Sure." Their smiles widen before I nod toward the counter. "Mark would be happy to assist you with that."

They blink a few times before understanding dawns across their faces.

"Oh."

That's all it takes for awkward silence to descend.

"Um... I guess we should leave you two alone, then?" Her brows draw together, as if that's not what I could possibly want.

My smile widens as comprehension finally dawns on them. "That would be great. Thanks for understanding."

They take their sweet time vacating the couch, as if they fully expect me to have a change of heart.

Yeah, that's not going to happen.

I want this girl all to myself.

The sorority sisters hesitate for a long beat before finally rising to their feet, their exit slow and reluctant. "It was nice meeting you," one of them says to Ava, her tone sweet but insincere.

Ava watches them go, then turns back to me with a shake of her head. "Do you have a fan club that stalks your every move?"

I grin, trying to lighten the mood. "Only when you're around."

Once they're across the shop, I huff out a relieved breath before settling next to Ava and passing over the drink.

"Finally," I mutter. "Alone at last."

Confusion flashes across her delicate features. "Certain that's what you really want?"

"One hundred percent. I'm interested in getting to know you. Kind of hard to do that with other people hanging around."

She stares at the girls for a second or two before bringing the container to her nose and taking a delicate sniff. With her gaze pinned to mine, she takes a sip. As soon as the hot liquid hits her tongue, her eyes widen before fluttering shut as she savors the rich medley of flavors. Pleased with my selection, my muscles loosen as I relax against the cushions.

Even though I can tell she likes it, I want to hear her admit that I picked out a winner.

"So, what's the verdict?"

She takes another drink. "Not bad." Lifting the cup, she stares at it. "Which one is this?"

"The McNichols Special."

There's a beat of silence before she shakes her head. "Of course it is."

"You might not have realized it since you're new to Western, but Colby McNichols is pretty popular around here."

She snorts. "Oh, it would be difficult not to notice."

A prick of something foreign blooms in the pit of my belly. It takes a handful of seconds to realize what it is.

Jealousy.

It's not a sensation I've experienced before.

I don't like it.

Even more disconcerting is that it's impossible to shake off.

What doesn't make sense is that I've shared girls before and didn't care one way or the other who they liked more.

So why is this strange emotion rearing its ugly head now?

With someone who'd prefer not to spend any time with me at all?

My brow furrows as I stare at Ava. The words shoot out of my mouth before I can stop them. "Do you have a thing for Colby?"

Her face scrunches. "Hardly. For one, I don't date hockey players. And two, even if I did, he's married to my friend."

My rigidly held muscles loosen with that acknowledgment as I take a sip of my own drink and attempt to get this runaway conversation back on track again. "Don't date hockey players, huh?"

"Nope." With a shake of her head, she pops the P at the end of the word.

"Is that a firm stance or is there room to maneuver?"

"It's impenetrable."

I settle on my seat, all the while watching her carefully. "You know, I get the feeling you don't want to be here."

Her gaze flicks to mine as uncertainty flashes in her eyes. "It's not that," she says slowly, as if choosing her words carefully. "I'm just... not used to this."

"To what?"

"To you." With a shrug, she glances away. "You're not what I expected."

"Good surprise or bad one?" I ask, my voice softening.

She hesitates, her gaze meeting mine for a moment before darting away. "I'm still trying to figure that out."

I lean forward, straining closer. "I can wait while you do."

As Ava stares at me, I can almost see the walls she's built start to crack. She's unsure, still guarded, but there's something else there, something that makes me believe I'm getting through to her, even if it's only a little.

"You're very persistent," she mutters, taking another sip of her coffee.

I grin. "You have no idea."

With a laugh, she shakes her head, as if she can't quite figure me out. "I'm not sure what you're after."

I keep my gaze locked on hers and my tone serious. "I'm after *you*, Ava."

She blinks in surprise, and I can see her inner conflict. As much as she wants to believe me, something holds her back. Something I can't put my finger on yet.

"Nothing about me is easy," she warns.

"I know," I say, leaning back. "But I think you're worth the effort."

Instead of responding, she clears her throat and changes the subject. "Did your siblings have fun at the clinic?"

"They did. The boys have been participating in them since I started freshman year. This will be their last one." A punch of sadness hits me. As much as I want to move on with my life, I've enjoyed living so close and spending time with them. That won't be the case next year. Plus, Ollie will be in high school. His schedule will be packed with academics and hockey. I'll probably blink, and Kia will be going off to college herself.

"I'm sure they'll miss it."

"I think we all will."

As excited as I am to make my move to the pros, so we have more financial security, I won't be able to spend as much time with them as I have these past couple years. It's an unfortunate trade off.

"Hi, Hayes."

I glance at Larsa Middleton, who has sidled up to us while I was focused on Ava. I'm still getting used to the idea that everything around me ceases to exist when we're together.

"Hey, Larsa. Stopping in for a coffee?"

Her gaze flicks to Ava before she dismisses her without any acknowledgment. "If you're not busy, I was thinking we could hang out at my place for a while. My professor just canceled class for the afternoon." She flashes a knowing smile. "I'm sure we could figure out something to occupy ourselves with."

I nod toward Ava. "Sorry, I'm a little busy at the moment."

Larsa's brows slant together. "Oh?"

"Yeah, Ava and I are having coffee."

She drops down on the chair situated across from us. When she crosses one long leg over the other, the short corduroy skirt she's wearing slides higher up her thigh. "I can wait."

"Sorry, Larsa. We're hanging out."

Her face scrunches. "Together?"

"Yeah, that's right."

The petite figure skater shakes her head. "We're not together."

I slip my hand around hers and give her fingers a squeeze. "We're definitely together."

Larsa takes a closer look at the girl sitting next to me. "Wait a minute. Aren't you Coach Philips's daughter?"

"Yup, I am."

Speculation brews in Larsa's eyes. "Interesting. Is she tutoring you or something?"

"No, she's not." With my hand locked around Ava's, I rise to my feet, bringing her up with me. "If you'll excuse us, we were just about to head out."

"What about my coffee?" Ava asks.

"Leave it behind," I mutter. "We'll get you another one later. Let's just get the hell out of here."

We're halfway to the door when a tall, lanky guy steps in front of us. "Hayes! That was an awesome hat trick you scored against the Titans."

"Thanks."

When he launches into my stats, I give Ava a bit of side-eye. I don't need to know her well to realize she's seconds away from leaving me behind in her dust. I have one chance to change her impression of me, and we're only fifteen minutes into this date, and I'm already blowing it.

"I appreciate your support, but I'm kind of in the middle of something."

He glances at Ava, as if seeing her for the first time.

What the hell is wrong with people around here?

"Oh."

I clap him on the shoulder. "Thanks for your understanding."

"Sure thing, Van Doren!"

With that, I hustle her ass out the door. It's only when it closes behind us with a resounding thud and the small group doesn't follow us out, that I breathe a sigh of relief. Under normal circumstances, I don't mind shooting the shit and talking hockey with the fans, but that's the last thing I want to do when I'm with this girl.

Before she can come up with a reason to bolt, I blurt, "Can I take you somewhere, Tink?"

AVA

16

Absolutely not.

That's exactly what I *should* have said.

It's what any smart girl would've said, especially one who's still piecing herself back together.

"I guess."

The response slipped out of my mouth before I could stop it, and now, here I am, walking beside Hayes Van Doren, hand in hand, completely unsure how I got myself into this.

What is it about this guy that makes me deviate from every instinct I've built over the past year? Hayes is everything I should avoid—a major player on campus, someone who probably views relationships like a game with easy rules and no attachments.

That's never been my type.

Then again, what *is* my type?

It's not like I have much experience to go on.

Nathan didn't leave much room for learning that on my own.

I shove that thought down before it can tank my mood.

Hayes's grip on my hand tightens as he flashes a boyish grin, the kind that should set off alarm bells in my brain. Instead, my stomach does that stupid swooping thing like I'm on a roller coaster about to plunge over the steepest drop.

I glance around as we walk across campus, noticing how people stare. Some wave and call out his name, others throw lingering looks his way. And he just takes it in stride, as if none of it fazes him.

"It's like you're a celebrity," I mutter, more to myself than to him.

"You think so?" He shrugs. "I don't really notice it anymore."

That remark catches me off guard. I was expecting him to bask in the attention, to maybe even thrive on it.

But he's indifferent.

"How can you not notice?" I ask, honestly curious. "People act like they're waiting for their chance to get your autograph."

He slows his pace a bit, like he's mulling that over. "It's been like this since high school. Our old college coach recruited me early on, and once that happened, the attention just kind of followed." He gives me a sidelong look. "But it's never been about that for me. After Dad passed away, I knew hockey was my way to take care of my family. That's what I focus on. The rest? It's just noise."

That's not the answer I was expecting.

My defenses, the ones I've carefully held in place since Nathan, reluctantly shift. Even if it's slightly.

"They're lucky to have you," I say softly.

His gaze turns serious as his voice dips. "Nah. I'm the lucky one. They mean everything to me."

And just like that, the walls I've built around myself crack even further.

Before I can react, we stop in front of the ice arena, and I blink in surprise. "Are we here to skate?"

He flashes that grin again, the one that makes it hard to stay detached. "Nope."

My face scrunches in confusion. "We're not?"

Instead of answering, he pulls me toward the building, leading me inside like he owns the place. Which, given how people treat him around here, maybe he does. It takes me a moment to realize that we've been holding hands since leaving the Roasted Bean.

No wonder people were staring.

Inside, the scent of the rink hits me—cold, crisp, and familiar. It's comforting in a way I can't quite explain, even though I'm no longer competing. The ice has always been a refuge, and I guess, in some way, it still is.

Hayes walks beside me as we head deeper into the arena, exchanging casual greetings with the employees like they're old friends.

"Hey, Tony!" Hayes calls to one of the custodians, who waves back from the concession stand. "How's the family?"

"Doing well! I'm taking the wife on vacation next week," the older man replies with a grin.

"I'm jealous. I could really use one of those," Hayes responds easily, still leading me forward.

I give him a sideways glance, baffled by how he manages to knock me off balance at every turn. "Are you on a first-name basis with everyone around here?"

"Most of them. Tony's wife bakes banana bread and usually sends a few loaves my way. Best damn stuff I've ever had. They run an animal shelter, and every year, the Wildcats do a fundraiser for them, and then we spend a weekend in the spring helping with cleanup and repairs. I love the clinics for kids, but the ones for animals hold a special place in my heart."

Everything he just admitted swirls through my head before reluctantly settling deep inside me.

I grind to a halt and stare at him. "I'm sorry. Who exactly *are* you?"

He stops too, turning to face me, his expression half amused, half serious. "What do you mean?"

"Ever since I started here, all I've heard is that you're this huge player who lives for parties. That's it. But now, you're telling me you help out at animal shelters and know the life story of everyone at the rink."

He lifts a brow, his grin turning a bit more wicked. "Well, it's true. I do like to party. But there's more to me than that. I just don't feel the need to talk about it with every person I meet."

I blink, trying to wrap my head around this new version of Hayes. It's impossible not to state the obvious. "But you're telling *me*."

"Maybe that's because I want you to know who I really am."

His earnest explanation sends a shiver racing down my spine. I don't know if it's the chill in the air, but standing here with him suddenly feels like teetering on the precipice of something I have no idea if I'm ready for.

When he reaches the doors to the rink, he pulls the handle open and extends his arm in invitation. "Are you coming or what?"

His voice yanks me back to the present as I hustle toward him. When I'm once again within striking distance, he snags my fingers, and instead of leading me toward the locker rooms, he heads to the stands, pulling me up the concrete stairs to the very top row. Uncertain what we're doing, I settle beside him and survey the quiet arena below.

"Looks different from up here, doesn't it?"

I shift on the hard plastic and stare at the pristine sheet of ice below.

He's right. It does look different from this vantage point.

As if it's miles and miles away.

Maybe even a different life.

Or someone else's life.

"Yeah," I whisper, taking in the view. "It does."

We sit in silence for a few moments as the cold air seeps through my jacket and into my bones. I shove my hands deeper into my pockets, trying to keep warm.

What doesn't make sense is that the quiet between us feels... nice.

Like there's no pressure to fill it with words.

There aren't many people I feel comfortable with.

How weird is it that Hayes is turning out to be one of them?

I glance at him and notice the way his muscles have loosened. "Do you come to the nosebleed section often?"

"Actually, I do. It's a good place to think. There's always a shitload of people at our house, and it can get pretty noisy. There's nowhere I can go on campus and just get away. Even in town. So, I'll come here and sit in the cheap seats and just breathe in the icy air. It never fails to clear my head." There's a pause. "Do you have a place like that?"

I turn the question over in my mind. It never occurs to me to hold back. "I feel like that when I'm on the ice, running through an old routine." My voice is barely more than a whisper. "Everything bothering me just melts away."

Hayes leans back slightly as he continues to watch me. "You're really good, Tink. Better than that. So why aren't you competing anymore?"

The question sits between us, heavy and suffocating. My chest tightens, and for a second, I'm tempted to shut him down. I've been perfecting that move for months, the art of deflecting, of keeping things light and easy so no one probes too deep.

Instead of allowing instinct to take over, I let out a gradual breath, the air escaping my lungs like a slow puncture. The words hover on my tongue, but they're hard to release. Even after all this time, it's still difficult to talk about.

He must sense the weight of my silence, because his grip tightens around my hand, offering something that feels dangerously close to comfort. "You don't have to tell me," he says softly. "I just... You're so damn talented. Watching you makes me forget about everything else going on in my life, and I can finally breathe."

The unexpected admission hits me hard. His words wrap around me, warm and solid, making it difficult to speak.

When I finally find my voice, my words come out quiet and scratchy. "Thank you."

"You've probably heard it before," he says with a shrug, like it's no big deal.

My throat tightens as I shake my head. "Not like that."

For a moment, we just sit. The weight of unspoken words presses down on me as I stare at the untouched sheet of ice.

The girl who used to glide across it with dreams in her eyes and hope filling her heart feels so far away now, buried beneath the heaviness of the past.

It's almost a surprise when I hear myself say, "Something happened last year..." My chest constricts as I trail off.

His steady gaze never wavers, and for the first time, I'm grateful for the darkness of the arena. It's safer somehow. Like the shadows give me permission to let the past out, even though every part of me wants to shove it back down and keep it buried.

I never intended to tell anyone, least of all Hayes. But there's something about him that makes it hard to lie or hide. Maybe it's the way he listens without judgment, his fingers wrapped around mine, grounding me in the moment.

"Nathan Covington was my coach," I begin, my voice shaky but determined. "He found me at a local competition and told my parents that I had something special. He said I was a natural and that he'd take me all the way if they let him. My parents were thrilled. Within months, we uprooted our whole lives and moved to Utah."

Even though Hayes remains silent, I feel the tension building in him. His fingers are still wrapped around mine, but his grip tightens just enough for me to notice. I glance at him and find his expression unreadable but his eyes sharp, focused.

"I skated all day, every day. I had private tutors for academics, ballet classes, strength training, and cardio—you name it, I did it. It didn't take long before I was winning competitions and moving up the ranks. Ever since I was a little girl, my goal had been to qualify for the Olympics. With Nathan focusing all his time and energy on me, there was no way it wouldn't happen." There's a long pause as I gather my thoughts, the memories painful and raw. "But then... things changed."

Hayes sucks in a sharp breath but doesn't interrupt.

"It didn't take long for Nathan to become my everything. He was my coach, my mentor, the person I trusted most in the world. We trained together, traveled together, and ate together. He'd help with homework. And I suppose I had a crush on him. When I turned eighteen and our relationship crossed a line, it never occurred to me to question it. I thought it was just the natural progression of things. I thought it was love."

Hayes exhales harshly, his jaw clenched tight. "Ava..."

I force out the rest, because if I stop, I won't be able to do it. "I didn't realize Nathan saw me as something he could mold and control. At that age, I was impressionable and desperate for his approval. I trusted him. I believed every word he said, every compliment, every promise.

"What hurt was that he weaponized my feelings against me. He was a master at mind games and manipulation. He was capable of cutting me down with a few sharp words. A look. That's all it took for me to spiral. All I wanted to do was please him. It became more important than anything else. By the end, I was a mess. Nervous, high-strung, depressed. It was almost a blessing when people found out about our relationship. Except that it was like a bomb went off, destroying everything I'd spent my life building. I was a scandal. The girl who had an affair with her coach.

"It didn't matter that I wasn't even twenty or that Nathan was in his forties, someone I'd looked up to and worshipped for years. It didn't matter that he'd been grooming me long before our relationship became physical. The world saw me as complicit. As *willing.*" I shake my head as a wave of confusion crashes over me, and I squeeze my eyes tightly shut, wanting to block out the memories. The guilt. "I don't know, maybe I was."

His knuckles are white where his fingers are clenched around mine. "No, you weren't. You were just a kid. Impressionable. Innocent. He took advantage of you. Of your feelings."

I shrug as misery continues to eat at me.

"Your parents didn't know? They didn't suspect anything?"

With a shake of my head, I bite my lip. "No. By that time, he was like family. More often than not, he spent the holidays with us. They trusted him."

His gaze burns into me, but he doesn't speak. It's like he's waiting, giving me the space I need to finish.

"That wasn't even the worst part of it all. After our relationship was exposed, I found out that I wasn't the only girl he'd done this to. He'd had relationships with other skaters—girls like me, girls who were younger, who were vulnerable and eager to please. I'd thought he loved me. I hadn't realized I was just another name on a list, another body in a long line of broken girls he'd left behind."

The shame of it still clings to me, suffocating and heavy. No matter how far I've tried to run, it's always there, like a shadow that won't disappear. It's the reason why I've kept everyone at arm's length since then. Why I haven't let anyone get too close.

Because trusting someone, letting them in, is dangerous.

Hayes's reaction is immediate. His grip tightens as his eyes darken with unspent fury. "Fuck, Ava. I'm so sorry you went through all that."

The raw emotion in his voice takes me by surprise, and for the first time, I feel tears burn at the back of my eyes. It takes effort to blink them away and swallow hard, wanting to keep it all contained. "It came out after one of the other girls saw us and reported it. There was an investigation, and everything fell apart. My parents were devastated. And I... I felt so stupid. Gullible. Used."

I look away, embarrassed now that I've laid it all out in front of him. The ugly truth, the baggage I've carried with me for so long. "That's why I stopped competing. After that, I just couldn't do it. I couldn't hold my head up. I hated that everyone knew what happened and were judging me. The snide comments and whispers."

For a long moment, Hayes remains silent. His hand rises to cup my cheek as his thumb brushes away a tear I didn't realize had fallen. "None of that was your fault. Do you hear me? He took advantage of you. Of your age and his position of power."

Even though I nod, the words don't sink in.

How could they?

I went along with it all. I was happy to hide our relationship from everyone, including my parents. I lied for him.

It still sickens me.

"Wait a minute... Is he the one trying to contact you?" Hayes asks, his voice tight with barely restrained anger.

"Yeah. He sends messages from different numbers. I've blocked them all, even changed my number a few times, but he always finds a way."

"Jesus Christ." Hayes's jaw flexes, his anger palpable. "Does Coach know?"

"No," I say quickly. "And I don't want him to. He'd lose it. That's why we moved here—to get away from all of it, to start over. I don't want to drag my family back into that nightmare again."

His expression softens as he pulls me into his arms, holding me tight against his chest. For a second, I freeze, the instinct to pull away, to protect myself, kicking into high gear. But then I force myself to relax and let him hold me, allowing myself to feel the comfort of his strength.

For the first time in what feels like forever, I don't feel so alone, so isolated.

I pull back slightly, just enough to meet his gaze. Our faces are so close, his breath warm against my skin. My heartbeat picks up tempo, and for a moment, I think he'll brush his lips across mine. It's a shock to realize that for the first time in more than a year, I *want* someone to kiss me.

But just as quickly, he pulls away, his expression unreadable. "It's getting late. We should probably get moving."

The disappointment that crashes over me is unnerving, but I remain silent. Instead, I follow him out of the arena, my heart pounding a steady tattoo as confusion floods me.

Despite everything, I wanted Hayes to kiss me.

Even more surprising than that, I might just want him to stick around.

TenInchesofCocky

TENINCHESOF
COCKY

WILDCATS

VAN DOREN
19
HAYES

17

With a quick peek at my phone, I take the stairs to the second floor two at a time. As I round the corner to my bedroom, Bridger steps into the hallway. The purple smudges under his eyes and the tightness around his mouth tell me everything I need to know.

"Hey, man," I say, slowing down. "You doing all right?"

I almost wince.

Stupid question.

Of course he's not.

It seems like every day a new message is popping up and his father is up his ass about it.

His jaw tightens as he drags a hand through his already mussed hair. "Yeah. I'm fine."

"Any closer to figuring out who's behind this shit?" I ask, crossing my arms against my chest.

His gray gaze flicks to mine. Frustration is written across the tight lines of his face. "No. But when I do, I swear, I'm going to bury them."

With a frown, I shake my head. "I don't get it. Who could hate you enough to do this?"

Bridger's one of the easiest guys on the team to get along with. He's smart, athletic, and popular, but he's not a dick about it. The idea that someone's out there with a grudge big enough to go after him like this... it doesn't add up.

He exhales sharply, the tension in his shoulders never easing. "I don't know. But I'm so fucking tired of it. I'm going through hell while they hide behind a screen like a coward."

"Yeah, it's messed-up." I clench my fists. "If there's anything I can do, just let me know."

His lips twitch, but it's a far cry from a smile. "Thanks. I appreciate it."

With a nod, I twist the handle to my door. "Seriously, if you need anything..."

"Yeah, I know." He gives me a grim smile. "A few of us were gonna go out and grab some food. You want in?"

"Wish I could, but I've got a paper due at midnight."

"Good luck with that," he mutters, already walking toward the stairs. "I'll catch you later."

I watch him disappear before slipping into my room. After closing the door behind me, I twist the lock and lean against it for a second as Ava's face flashes in my mind. I haven't been able to stop thinking about the way she dropped her guard and opened up at the rink. The pain that flooded her voice as she told me about her old coach. The way she was groomed and manipulated by someone she trusted.

It's so fucked-up.

It takes effort to refocus my attention on the business at hand. I've got two minutes to clear my mind. I strip off my clothes in record time, leaving them in a heap on the floor. When I'm wearing nothing but my boxer briefs, I grab my laptop and drag the desk chair over to the bed, positioning it before flipping it open. The camera light blinks on, and I adjust the angle until it's a perfect shot of me stretched out on the mattress.

Earbuds in, music filling the silence, I close my eyes and force myself to get into the right headspace. It's been a routine for a while now, something I've perfected over the years.

It's easy money.

Usually.

But tonight, I can't shake the heaviness sitting in my chest.

I see Ava's face again. Her eyes, wide and uncertain, the raw pain in her voice when she told me how it all went down with Nathan.

How he'd crossed every line and shattered her trust.

It makes me fucking sick to my stomach.

I'd like nothing more than to find that asshole and make him pay for what he did to her.

For the damage he caused, the way he made her feel small and used.

Even when the first few comments pop up on the screen, people already tuning in, all I can think about is how much I hate the idea of her still having to deal with him.

Still receiving those texts.

I flex my abs and shift on the bed, needing to get my head back in the game, but it's useless. The more I try to push Ava out of my mind, the more I feel this growing need to protect her.

To be there for her in a way no one else has been.

And that's the scariest part of all.

Since those thoughts aren't conducive to what needs to happen, I force them from my head for a second time and allow my hand to stroke over my chest. It's so damn tempting to rush through this, but I refuse to do that.

That's not what these people are paying for.

And since I need the money, I force myself to slow my roll and draw out every touch and stroke of my hand.

At the end of the day, it's not about me.

It's about them.

The people paying good money to see me get off.

With lazy movements, my fingers circle around one nipple and then the other until both stiffen. I've given serious consideration to piercing them. I bet the fans would go fucking crazy over that, but I've just never found the time to get it done. And now that there's only a few months left until graduation, there doesn't seem to be much point. As soon as I sign my NHL contract, my little X-rated performances will be a thing of the past.

As the music thumps a steady beat, everything inside me loosens, and I allow both hands to wander, caressing every inch of exposed flesh. They continue their descent before one slides along the thick length of my erection pressing against the cotton of my underwear.

The moment I squeeze the tip, thoughts of Ava shove their way back into my brain. What it felt like to wrap her up in my arms and offer comfort. Her warm weight nestled against me. How close we came to kissing before guilt slammed into me, and I yanked myself back from the precipice.

It had been so damn tempting to brush my lips across hers.

The need rushing through my veins had been like nothing I'd ever experienced before.

I cup my balls and massage them. A guttural groan escapes from me as I shift, my cock growing even harder.

When I can't stand another second of the torture, my hand slips beneath the elastic band of the boxers, and I shove them down until my dick can spring free of the confines. My teeth sink into my lower lip as I fist the hot length, tightening my hold until it turns borderline painful.

Even though I'm conflicted about Ava and how to proceed with her, I can't stop thoughts of her lithe body from rolling through my head. I want to stretch her out naked and lick every silky inch of her skin. I want to run my tongue over her pussy until she's writhing beneath me and screaming out her orgasm. That image alone is almost enough to make me lose control.

Which never happens.

I'm always the one calling the shots.

A tortured groan makes its way past my lips as I bow my spine, and hot spurts of cum jet from my cock, landing on my lower abdomen.

My breathing turns harsh as I strangle the life out of my dick until every last drop has been wrung from it, and I'm softening in my palm. Only then do my muscles loosen as I relax against the mattress.

I stretch my arms above my head as endorphins flood my system, making me drowsy and satisfied. Music pours through my earbuds as I rub the jizz around my belly.

I give it a few moments before rolling to the side, throwing up the peace sign, and ending the video. Five hundred comments and a whole hell of a lot of emojis greet me from the screen, but I'm not in the mood to go through them.

After slamming the laptop closed, I grab a few tissues and wipe up the cum before tossing them in the trash can near the nightstand and pulling the elastic band back over my cock. Once the earbuds have been removed, I sit on the edge of the bed as the sassy figure skater shoves her way back into my brain for the umpteenth time today.

I have no idea what to do about her.

If I'm honest with myself, she's become something of an obsession.

No matter how hard I try, I can't stop thinking about her.

She's not what I expected.

And that's the problem.

After everything she confided this afternoon, I'm unsure how to move forward.

Or even if I should.

What can't be denied is that she's been to hell and back.

The last thing I want to do is inflict more damage.

The funny thing is, she doesn't come across as someone who's fragile, but deep down, I think that's exactly what she is.

I drag a hand through my hair.

I really need to think about this.

She's not a girl I can fuck around with and then flee the scene of the crime.

There's also the fact that she's Coach's daughter.

If I have any brains whatsoever, I'll cut my losses and avoid her for the foreseeable future.

Graduation is right around the corner, and then I'll sign my contract and play in the pros. My family will be taken care of. At the end of the day, that's the most important thing.

My family.

But...

I'm afraid it might be too late to bail.

My life has always been complicated.

How the fuck did it get even more so?

As those thoughts circle through my brain, my belly grumbles. Only then do I remember that it's been hours since I grabbed something to eat. With that, I rise to my feet before throwing on a shirt and sweatpants. I make a pitstop in the bathroom to wash my hands and then head down to the first floor.

I step inside the dark kitchen and stumble to a halt when I find Willow, Maverick McKinnon's newly minted girlfriend. Our gazes catch as she tucks a stray lock of blonde hair behind her ear.

We've known each other since elementary school. Her twin brother River and I played hockey on a lot of the same teams while growing up.

My lips settle in a smirk as memories of the first time I caught her sneaking out of our house at the butt crack of dawn after spending the night with Maverick. Given his contentious relationship with her brother, it had been a shock.

Especially since Mav hadn't known the identity of his one-night stand.

I'm not gonna lie, watching their relationship play out with all the secrets and subterfuge had been hilarious.

A small smile simmers around the edges of her lips as she rolls her eyes. It's like she can read the thoughts in my head.

I've always liked Willow. She was diagnosed with childhood leukemia in high school. She's been in remission for a couple years now, and it's nice to see her thriving. I'm glad she and Maverick worked out. He's a good dude, and he seems to genuinely care about her.

River, on the other hand?

He's not as thrilled about his twin's new love interest.

From what I've seen, they're both trying to get along for Willow's sake.

I beeline to the fridge and peek inside. Disappointment bubbles up inside me when I don't find much in the way of sustenance. With my fingers tapping against the door, I throw out the question. "How's it going?"

"Pretty good. And you?"

"Same."

From the corner of my eye, I watch as she grabs a piece of fruit from the counter before taking a few steps toward the living room.

"Willow?" Her name shoots out of my mouth before I can think better of it.

She glances at me with raised brows from the other side of the threshold. "Yeah?"

Now that she's staring at me with curiosity brimming in her wide blue eyes, I'm unsure what to say.

All right, that's a lie. It's all there on the tip of my tongue. I just need to grow a pair of balls and force out the words.

I stare past her into the living room and see Maverick is sprawled out on the couch with a controller in his hand as he stares at the big screen TV mounted on the far wall.

I clear my throat and drop my voice. The last thing I need is any of these nosy bastards eavesdropping on our convo. "Do you, um, have a moment?"

Surprise flashes across her face as she steps back inside the kitchen. "Sure. What's up?"

Well, hell.

I have no idea how to bring this up without sounding like a total puss.

When I remain silent, she hikes a brow.

Fuck.

Why does this feel so hard?

I drag my hand through my hair. "So, I kind of like someone."

She blinks, as if that was the last thing she was expecting me to say. "You do?"

"Yeah."

A smile curves her lips. "What's the problem with that?"

I huff out a breath before sidling closer. "I don't know. The situation is complicated."

"Is it more complicated than sneaking around behind your twin's back because you've been seeing the one guy he can't stand?"

I snort out a laugh as some of the tension filling my shoulders drains away. "Probably not. It's more like she's been through a lot in the past year or so, and I'm afraid of inflicting further damage."

Her expression softens. "If you're thinking along those lines, then you're probably already being careful with her. Anyone would appreciate that."

I let her words settle inside me.

"Yeah, I guess." With a nod, I break eye contact. "I'm just not sure if it's better to walk away now before anything gets too serious between us."

"How does she feel about the situation?"

"I don't know."

"Maybe you should talk to her about it first before you make any decisions." There's a moment of silence before she adds, "After I went into remission, one of the hardest parts was how my friends and family acted like I was made of spun glass. I hated it so much. All I wanted was to be treated like everyone else, not like I was weak or constantly on the verge of relapse. I don't know anything about this girl, but I can almost guarantee she doesn't want you to view her through the lens of her past, like she's breakable."

I release a pent-up breath from my lungs. "It's different with her."

"I get that. But don't you think it might help to have an open and honest conversation with her before you make any decisions? Especially if you have feelings for her."

"Thanks for the advice." Everything she just said somersaults through my head. "I'll give it some thought."

She flashes an easy smile. "Want to give me a clue as to who the lucky girl is?"

I shake my head. "Nah. Like you said, I should probably talk to her first and get everything figured out."

"All right. Sounds like a plan. Good luck."

"Thanks."

I'll probably need it.

AVA

18

I glance down at my phone, my stomach twisting into knots at the latest message. Another one from a new number. No matter what I do, he continues to find ways to get to me.

The words blur on the screen, sharp with hostility.

The demanding tone in the message is unmistakable, and the implication makes me sick. His texts used to be sporadic, popping up here and there. Now, they come daily, each one more aggressive than the last.

Angrier.

Like I owe him something.

Unsure what to do, I squeeze my eyes tightly shut until my cell chimes with another one.

It's like I'm being bombarded.

Beaten down.

As I stare at the new message, I realize my hands are trembling.

My belly pinches at the thought of bringing this up to my parents. But what other choice is there?

I can just imagine Dad's reaction.

He's going to lose it.

And Mom will get upset all over again and blame herself for allowing us to get so close. For not seeing what was happening beneath her nose. I hate the guilt she carries regarding the situation.

They'll threaten to pick up and move again, and I don't want that to happen.

Not now.

Dad loves his new coaching position, and I've finally made some good friends. Real ones. I don't want to lose that and start all over again.

I shove my phone into my jacket pocket, hoping it's possible to block out the creeping sense of dread. But the feeling of being hunted continues to linger.

"Ava!"

I blink out of those thoughts before lifting my hand in a wave. For a split second, the tension in my chest loosens.

"Hey, Britt!" It takes effort to force a smile to my face.

She loops her arm through mine as we walk toward the Union, weaving through the dinner crowd. Britt has become my best friend, the one person I can actually be myself around. She gets it—being thrown into the public eye at a young age, her rise to fame, and now her need for something real. Britt left LA to escape the spotlight, and even though I wasn't a celebrity or household name like her, I under-stand that craving for a fresh start, for normalcy.

She scrutinizes my face for a long moment. "Is everything okay?"

I glance at her and then away. "Yeah, just tired."

It's not a total lie, but it's nowhere near the full truth. A prick of guilt hits me. I hate lying to her, but I'm not ready to reveal what's been going on.

"Well, you've been juggling classes, skating, and everything else. But don't forget to take care of yourself too."

I nod, appreciating her concern, even though I know it's more than that.

After ordering sandwiches, we scan the space, looking for the rest of the group we're meeting. As soon as Carina pops up and waves, we navigate through the crowd until we reach a long stretch of table where we settle in.

"I'm so glad you could make it!" Juliette says before digging into her salad. She found out last week that she was accepted into med school. That girl is always at the library studying her ass off.

Well, when she's not spending time with her hunky boyfriend, Ryder McAdams.

Fallyn's sparkly engagement ring catches the light and nearly blinds me. It's a gorgeous ring. Wolf did an amazing job picking it out.

Her attention gets snagged by it for a second or two. "Sometimes I still can't believe I'm married." She flashes a smile at Britt. "You too."

Britt glances at the blingy rock on her own finger. "It's gone by so quickly."

The conversations that buzz around me are all normal—comforting in a way—but I can't help feeling out of place.

"What about you?" Britt asks, nudging me playfully.

I almost choke on my water as an image of Hayes flashes in my brain along with the way he made me feel and how I stupidly opened up to him at the arena. That vulnerability I showed him now feels like a mistake. I haven't heard from him since, and it stings more than I care to admit.

"Are there any prospects on the horizon?" Viola asks. She and Fallyn are cousins and live together off campus.

I shake my head, forcing a casual smile. "Nope, I'm just focused on school."

I never should have entrusted Hayes Van Doren with my secrets.

What if he tells his friends, and it spreads like wildfire across campus? That thought is enough to have nausea stirring in the pit of my belly.

"It wouldn't be a hockey player even if you did," Stella adds.

Juliette nods. "Your dad would probably lose it."

I can't help but grimace.

That's not a scenario I want to imagine playing out.

"He definitely wouldn't be thrilled about it." Even though my parents want me to move on from the past and get involved with a nice boy and have a normal relationship, there's no way they'd want me to date one of his players.

As tempting as it is to share all that with my new friends, I keep the truth locked up tight where it can't see the light of day. When it comes down to it, I'm afraid of the judgment I'll find in their eyes.

If only it were possible to blot out the last three years and pretend it never happened. I'd give anything to be the naïve girl I'd once been.

When my phone buzzes in my pocket again, the muscles in my belly contract until it becomes painful. My appetite vanishes as I shove my sandwich to the side.

If this keeps up, I'll lose another five pounds. Mom commented on my weight loss the other day and asked if everything was all right. The concern in her dark eyes was obvious, and it brought me right back to the past.

To the secrets I'd kept from them.

The loneliness that had eaten away at me.

The sense of being trapped.

For a second or two, I considered coming clean but decided against it.

This situation is different than the one before.

It's nothing more than texting.

If I refuse to engage, he'll eventually get bored and go away.

Right?

That's the hope I'm currently clinging to.

"Hey, babe."

I blink back to the present and find Colby McNichols locking lips with Britt. There's a besotted expression on her face that matches his when they break apart.

"Jeez," Bridger grumbles. "Always with the PDA."

Colby grins, throwing an arm around his wife. "You jealous, bro? Want a hug? I've got enough love to go around."

"Nah, I'm good." Bridger chuckles while shaking his head as the group dissolves into laughter.

Colby gives me a chin lift in greeting when our gazes collide, and I scoot over so he can settle next to Britt.

"Thanks, Philips. Appreciate it."

"No problem."

Most of the guys from the team are friendly toward me but nothing more. It makes me wonder if Dad fired off warning shots at the beginning of the season.

"Is it all right if we crash your dinner?" Ryder asks before squeezing in next to Juliette. I have to admit they're perfect for one another.

A few more of their teammates stop by with trays loaded with food.

Our group continues to swell as Ford, Wolf, Madden, Riggs, and Steele crowd around the table, pulling chairs up, and the babble of voices escalates. I can't help but look at each face. Over the past semester, they've all become my friends.

I try to relax and enjoy the moment, but then I feel it again. A prickling sensation that makes me wonder if I'm being watched. As soon as I glance up, our gazes collide.

Hayes.

My breath catches. After a few days of absence, I'm hungry for the sight of him. Even though he's standing with a few teammates, his attention is focused on me. I can't read his expression, and part of me doesn't want to. It's been days since we talked, and not hearing from him after everything I confessed hurts.

I can't do this.

Not with everything else going on in my life.

Decision made, I push back from the table. "I need to get going."

Britt frowns. "What? I thought we were going to hang out after this."

Heat floods my cheeks as people turn and stare. "Sorry, I've got some stuff to take care of. I'll text you later, and we can figure out another time to get together. Promise."

"You better."

I force a small smile and grab my bag before weaving through the crowded building. My heart slams in my chest with the need to distance myself from Hayes.

From the awkwardness and the rejection.

As soon as I push through the doors and step into the crisp evening air, a mixture of relief and sadness pumps through me.

"Ava, wait."

I freeze as my pulse thrums in my ears. There's no point pretending I didn't hear him. With a sigh, I turn and find Hayes standing in front of me, his expression soft but unreadable.

"What do you want?" My voice comes out sounding sharper than intended. But I can't help it. I'm hurt, and the last thing I want to do is show it.

"Can we talk?"

I cross my arms, as if it's possible to guard myself from further pain. "What's there to talk about? We hung out twice. That's all it was."

His jaw tightens, and for a second, I think he's going to back off. Instead, he steps closer, his gaze locked on mine. "And here I'd thought it was more than that. Was I wrong?"

My mouth goes dry as my tongue darts out to moisten my lips. Refusing to answer his question, I fire off one of my own. "Why are you doing this?"

His brows furrow. "Doing what?"

I shift, impatient to get moving and away from him. Allowing him to get close was a mistake, and I've learned my lesson. I was an idiot for thinking he was anything more than a player.

"Acting like there's something between us."

"Because there is, and I want to spend more time together and see where it goes." When he steps closer, bridging the distance between us, it becomes necessary to tilt my chin upward. "Is that something we can do?"

Air escapes from my lungs like a tire with a slow leak.

It's a terrible idea.

Nothing good will come from spending more time with Hayes.

"I don't know," I mumble.

"What don't you know?"

I force my gaze from his, hoping it's enough to break the spell he's woven around me. I don't know how he does it. Every time we're together, all rational thought flies out the window.

A few people walking by stare in our direction with interest. It's just another reminder that this is Hayes Van Doren I'm dealing with.

"Why we're bothering to do this," I mutter as my cheeks heat.

He hikes a brow. "You don't?"

With my lips pressed together, I shake my head. I don't think I've ever felt more confused or conflicted in my life. But there's something else buried beneath those emotions. Something I'd rather not inspect too closely. I'm afraid of what I'll find if I do.

It's a surprise when his fingers slip beneath my chin, and he turns it until I have no other choice but to meet the steadiness of his gaze.

"I like you, Tink. Maybe I haven't done a good job of showing it, but I do."

"Is that the reason you've been avoiding me?" The question shoots out of my mouth before I can reel it back in. The last thing I want is for him to think I care.

It's painful to admit that I just might.

There's a moment of silence, as if he's mulling over the question.

"That's not what I was doing," he says, his tone turning serious. "I just... I needed time to think."

"About what?" I demand, my frustration bubbling to the surface. "About what I told you? Did that scare you off?"

His eyes soften. "No. It didn't scare me. But it did make me think. I don't want to hurt you. Not after everything you've been through."

There's something in the way he says it that makes me pause. It's like he's genuinely afraid of screwing this up and causing me pain.

For some reason, that hits me harder than anything else, and my anger drains away. "So, what now?"

He exhales slowly, like he's been carrying the weight of the world on his shoulders. "I want to move forward. But I want to be careful. I want to do this right."

I stare at him, my heart racing. "You want to keep seeing me?"

The smile he flashes makes my stomach flip. "Yeah, I do. If you'll let me."

It's crazy.

The last thing I should do is let myself fall for this guy. But standing here, looking at him, I realize it's a risk I'm willing to take.

"Okay."

A grin spreads across his face as he reaches for my hand and threads his fingers through mine. "Are you free for the rest of the night? I want you to come with me."

"Yeah. Are you going to tell me where we're going?"

"It's a surprise," he says, leading me down the path, his thumb brushing against my hand. "Do you trust me?"

I hesitate for a moment and search his face. It's almost a shock when I admit what's in my heart.

"Yeah, I do."

TenInchesofCocky

TENINCHESOF
COCKY

WILDCATS

VAN DOREN
19
HAYES

19

The air in the ice arena feels familiar, almost like coming home, as Ava and I weave through the crowded lobby. I grew up in this place, spent hours on the ice, goofing around with teammates, and later, coaching my little brother's team to help Mom with the bills. This arena is in my blood, and yet tonight, it feels different. It's not just about hockey or family, it's about the girl walking beside me.

I steal a glance at Ava.

The knot of anxiety that's been sitting in my chest for days starts to loosen.

I want to bring her into my world and share the things with her that matter to me. I'm hoping it'll help break down some of the walls she's built around herself, the ones I understand so much better after what she confided.

Ollie's team is already warming up on the ice. When I catch his eye, he lifts his chin in a gesture that makes him seem older than he is. I nod back, feeling that familiar burst of pride every time I see him out there. He's grown into a hell of a player.

Before I can take another step, small arms wrap around my legs, and I look down to find Kia grinning up at me.

"Hey, squirt," I say, hauling her into my arms. She squeals before trying to wriggle away when I blow a raspberry against her neck.

Ava watches, a smile tugging at her lips.

I nod toward the blonde at my side. "Remember Coach Ava from the clinic?"

Kia's face lights up in recognition, but she quickly ducks her head against my neck, giving Ava a shy wave.

I almost laugh.

Kia, shy?

Yeah, right.

The kid doesn't have a shy bone in her body.

"It's nice to see you again," Ava says. "Have you been practicing some of those hockey moves since I last saw you?"

Kia straightens in my arms, all bright eyes and bouncy curls. "I had a lesson with Coach Jay on Saturday! It was fun."

Ava smiles at her. "I'm glad. Having fun is the most important thing."

Kia nods before turning back to me. "Can we get popcorn and a pretzel?"

I narrow my eyes. "Did you eat dinner?"

She gives me a mischievous smile. "We had grilled cheese."

"You sure about that? 'Cause I don't want Mom yelling at me for feeding you junk food again."

Her grin widens, and I get the feeling she's playing me, but I can't say no to her. "All right, fine," I grumble, setting her down. "If Mom says otherwise, you're in big trouble."

She grabs my hand and pulls me toward the concession stand as Ava trails behind us. We load up on popcorn, pretzels, and drinks before settling on the bench next to my mom. She greets Ava with a smile, but I can tell she's surprised to see her again. Mom knows I don't bring girls to family events. She's definitely going to have questions.

As the game gets under way, I can feel my attention split between Ollie on the ice and Ava beside me. Kia has climbed onto Ava's lap, and Theo is practically glued to her other side, asking a million questions. It's moments like this—seeing her here with Kia, with my family—that make me realize how much I want her to be part of my life.

Ollie's skating out there like a pro. He's definitely got moves. I've watched him grow from a wobbly kid, clutching the boards, to a player who commands attention when he's on the ice. Every time he gets near the puck, anticipation builds. Then he makes a break for it, weaving through the defense, his eyes locked on the goal.

The arena erupts when he scores, the sound deafening in the small rink. Ollie pumps his fist in the air, and for a second, our gazes meet across the ice. All I see is my little brother, beaming with joy as his teammates swarm him in celebration. In that moment, I'm proud of the player he's become.

If Ollie continues to grow and improve the way he has these past three years, there's no way that Division I schools won't be vying for him to play for their programs. It makes all the hustling I've done while in college totally worth it.

How could I regret any of it when I've been able to give my siblings everything they need?

Dad would be proud that we've managed to hold everything together in his absence. It wasn't easy, but we've done it.

A thick lump of emotion rises in my throat. When my gaze gets snagged by Mom's, her lips lift into a soft smile that doesn't quite reach her eyes, and I get the feeling she's thinking about him as well.

After Ollie's team pulls off a win, all the fans flock to the lobby. They talk about the highlights and grab snacks while waiting for the players to get released from the locker room. I glance over at Ava, who's still chatting with my mom. It would be hard not to notice that Kia's hand is wrapped in hers, as if they've known each other forever.

Fifteen minutes later, Ollie finally emerges, grinning from ear to ear.

We bump fists. "Good game, little bro. You were on fire out there."

He shrugs, trying to play it cool, but I can see how much he's buzzing from the win. "Thanks."

I ruffle his sweat-soaked hair. "Keep playing like that, and you'll have college coaches knocking down your door."

His eyes light up, but he jerks his shoulders again, trying to downplay it. "Yeah, that might be cool."

"It would be more than cool, dude. It'd be amazing."

Mom comes over, gathering Kia and Theo. She looks at Ava with a warm smile. "Thank you for joining us tonight. I know it meant a lot to Ollie."

Ava smiles back. "I had fun. I'd love to do it again sometime."

Mom glances between the two of us, and I know she's filing this moment away for later interrogation. "We'd love to have you."

As we say our goodbyes, I slip a little extra cash into Mom's pocket, and she squeezes my arm, her eyes shining with appreciation. "I love you, Hayes."

"Love you too."

I hug Theo and give Kia a kiss on the cheek before we part ways.

The drive back to campus is quiet, the kind of comfortable silence I don't usually experience with girls. The radio hums softly in the background as I glance at Ava. The way she interacted with my mom and siblings tonight... it did something to me.

Something I didn't expect.

"I like your family," she says after a while, breaking the silence. "Your mom is really nice."

I nod, keeping my eyes fastened to the road. "Yeah, she's the best. It's been tough since Dad died, but we're hanging in there. I try to help out as much as I can."

Ava reaches over, her fingers gently resting on mine. It's a small gesture, but it makes something tighten in my chest.

"You're a great big brother. It's obvious how much they all look up to you."

I swallow hard. It would be impossible not to feel the weight of her words. "I'm just doing what I can. After Dad... it's like we didn't have anyone else to lean on but each other."

There's a pause before she shifts in her seat, her voice soft. "I noticed you gave your mom money before we left. I didn't realize you have a job."

My fingers tighten on the steering wheel as I keep my tone casual. "Yeah, I do some freelance stuff online. It helps pay the bills."

My muscles remain tense as I wait for her to bombard me with questions. None of my teammates work. There aren't enough hours during the day when you're a Division I athlete. Hockey is like a full-time job with school. There's a lot of guys who refuse to get into relationships because it's just another time commitment that pulls them away from their sport.

When a handful of seconds ticks by and she doesn't say a word, I glance at her with a cocked brow. "Not going to ask about the specifics?"

Our gazes lock for just a heartbeat or two before I force mine to the dark ribbon of road stretched out beyond the windshield.

"Nope. I really hate when people stick their nose into my business. So I'm not going to be a hypocrite and do it to you."

Her honesty hits me, and before I can stop myself, I blurt, "I hope you realize I'm still going to be all up in your business because I want to know every damn thing about you."

She gives me a small smile, but there's something in her expression that makes me think she's still holding back. After what she's been through, I can't blame her. It's going to take time for her to open up completely.

But I'm willing to wait.

As we drive, her hand stays wrapped in mine. The simple contact feels more intimate than anything I've experienced in a long time.

Maybe ever.

"My sister really likes you," I say, breaking the silence again.

"I like her too," Ava replies softly. "I like all of them."

I glance at her, my heart thudding in my chest. "How about me, Tink? Do you like me as well?"

The question comes out before I can stop it, but I don't regret it.

I need to know where I stand with this girl.

AVA

My heart races, each beat reverberating in my chest as Hayes's question lingers in the air between us.

Do I like him?

It's not a question I was expecting, but now that it's out there, there's no way to avoid it.

I take a breath, trying to sort through the whirlwind of emotions swirling inside me. Hayes isn't what I thought he was. He's deeper, more genuine, and that scares me as much as it excites me. I can't deny the attraction, the pull toward him that feels impossible to resist.

"Yeah, I do," I finally admit. It makes me feel vulnerable to say it, but at the same time, it's liberating.

A slow grin spreads across his face as he glances at me, his fingers wrapping around mine before squeezing.

"Good," he says, his voice low and soothing. "You might not have realized it, because I've been keeping this under wraps for a while, but I like you too. A lot."

His words send a rush of warmth through me.

I didn't expect him to be this honest or direct.

Even though a part of me is screaming to guard my heart, another part—the one that's tired of being afraid—is desperate to trust him and wants to see where this goes.

I bite my lip, hesitating as the familiar walls I've built around myself crumble further. "I don't know what I can give you. My head is still messed-up from everything that happened."

His gaze softens in understanding. "I'll take whatever you're willing to give, and we'll go as slow as you need to."

I shake my head in confusion. "I don't get it. Why are you doing this? You could have anyone. There are so many girls who would be easier than me."

For a moment, he says nothing.

The silence stretches, making my nerves tighten.

When he finally speaks, his voice is steady and sure. "Did you ever consider that I'm not looking for easy?"

A few minutes later, we're pulling into the parking lot of my building. Before I can say another word, he's out of the truck, rounding the front, then opening the passenger door. He extends a hand, and despite the inner voice telling me to push him away, I take it. His fingers are warm around mine.

"You don't have to walk me to my door," I say softly as we head toward the entrance of the building.

"I know," he replies, flashing me a lopsided smile. "But I want to."

When we reach the lobby, we step inside the elevator, and just as the doors begin to close, four girls pour inside, filling the small space. A brunette with wavy hair locks eyes with Hayes and then beams at him.

"Hey, Hayes," she says, her voice dripping with familiarity. "It's been a while."

The jealousy that flares to life in my chest is sharp and unexpected. From the corner of my eye, I watch as Hayes acknowledges her with a casual chin lift. "Hey, Olivia."

My heart sinks at how easily her name rolls off his tongue. Before I can dwell on it, his arm snakes around my waist, and he pulls me flush against his side. The heat of his body seeps into mine. It's enough to dissolve the jealousy simmering inside me.

Olivia's smile falters, the confidence in her gaze wavering as she glances at me for the first time.

When the elevator dings and the girls file out without another word, Hayes doesn't bother saying goodbye. He's too focused on me, his hand resting possessively on my waist as we step into the hallway.

"What's your apartment number?" he asks, his voice cutting through the silence.

"406," I mumble, feeling slightly off-balance from the entire interaction.

Why does he have this effect on me?

He tangles everything up in my head until it's impossible to think straight. Especially when he's this close.

Once we reach my door, I swing around to face him. My heart hammers almost painfully in my chest at the intensity that fills his gaze. When his hand rises to cradle my cheek, I find myself leaning into his touch.

How is it possible for our closeness to feel so natural and right?

It's terrifying.

"Would you believe me if I told you that you're the first girl I've ever wanted to get to know?" he murmurs, his thumb gently brushing against my skin. "I don't care about easy. I don't care how slow we need to go or what you think you can give me. I just want to be with you while we figure it out. Together."

His words hit me straight in the chest, sending a flutter through my stomach.

He's so sincere, so honest, and it leaves me feeling raw.

Exposed.

His quiet sentiment has a million butterflies winging their way to life within the confines of my belly.

And yet...

There's no way to keep the skepticism from my voice. "Are you sure about that? I've heard all the gossip that circulates around campus."

"I won't lie to you." His gaze is unwavering. "There's truth in those rumors. I spent the last few years screwing around because it helped me escape everything else going on in my life. But those girls? They were distractions. None of them meant anything to me. The difference is that you do."

My teeth sink into my lower lip.

More than anything, I want to believe him.

I want to trust him.

"How can you be so sure?" My throat closes up as I force out the rest. "I don't want to get hurt. After everything that's happened, I'm afraid to put myself out there."

He strums my cheek with his thumb. "That's why we'll take this at a glacial pace."

"Glacial?"

"Super slow."

Even though this is no laughing matter, a snort escapes from me. "I know what glacial means. Won't you get bored?"

His lips tug into a smile as his brow arches slightly. "Bored? With you? Never. You keep me on my toes, and I like that."

I huff out a soft laugh, the tension between us easing just a bit. He's saying all the right things, and I hate how much I want to believe him.

"What about my dad?" I ask, voicing the concern that's been nagging at me.

"Well, I'm going to be honest with you. I'm not really interested in dating him."

I roll my eyes. "I would hope not. What I meant is that I think we should keep this between us. He won't be happy that I've become involved with one of his hockey players."

He releases a long, slow breath. "I get that, but I really don't like lying to people. Especially ones I respect. And I respect Coach."

It's tempting to shake my head.

Could this guy be more perfect?

"I just want to make sure this is actually going to go somewhere before we tell my parents."

"Okay, I get that. For the time being, we'll keep everything on the downlow."

"Thank you." Relief floods through me.

His heated gaze dips to my lips, and warmth rushes to all the places that have spent the last year cold and dormant. Hayes is gradually waking my body back to life again.

My tongue darts out to moisten my lips. "Any chance we're going to seal this with a kiss?"

He smirks, his voice dropping to a husky whisper. "Is that what you want?"

My heart thuds painfully in my chest as I nod.

"Then, yes, Ava. I'm going to kiss you."

There's no rush in the way he lowers his mouth. It's slow, deliberate, like we have all the time in the world. When his lips finally brush against mine, they're softer than I imagined. The kiss is gentle at first, a tease, his tongue lightly brushing against my bottom lip. Heat sparks in my core, spreading like wildfire through my veins.

His hands tighten on my waist, pulling me closer, and I melt into him as everything around us fades away.

There's only him.

His scent, his touch, and the way his lips make me feel like I'm floating.

It's a kiss that makes me forget every reason why I should be afraid.

Just as I sink deeper into the moment, he pulls back, his breath mingling with mine.

"You taste good. I'm definitely going to want more of your sweetness."

I blink, dazed and breathless, as I struggle to form a coherent thought.

"Keys," he says, holding out his palm.

It takes a second to realize what he means. "Oh," I murmur, fumbling in my purse until my fingers lock around the cool metal.

After I drop them in his hand, he unlocks the door and pushes it open. His beachy scent wraps around me, cocooning me in familiarity. It's so tempting to invite him in, but I hesitate.

That feels like a big step.

Maybe too big for where we are at the moment.

As if sensing my inner conflict, he retreats. "I'll see you tomorrow."

"Tomorrow?" I echo, still trying to play mental catch up with everything that's happened this evening.

He flashes his signature lopsided smile. The one that makes my heart flutter. "Yeah. Tomorrow. We've got more to figure out."

"Okay," I whisper, feeling lighter than I have in a long time.

With that, he turns and heads to the elevator. As I stand rooted in place, my fingers drift across my lips. I can still feel the soft pressure of his mouth sliding over mine, and it sends a shiver dancing down my spine.

He swings around and walks backward, his gaze pinned to mine. "You can think about that kiss inside the apartment. Make sure you lock the door behind you."

Heat floods my cheeks at being caught in a daze.

A grin flashes across his lips, as if he knows exactly what thoughts are running rampant through my head.

For the first time in a while, hope fills my heart.

Whatever this is between us feels like the start of something real.

Something that has the potential to last.

TENINCHESOF
COCKY

WILDCATS

TenInchesofCocky
VAN DOREN
19
HAYES

I balance the steaming cups in one hand as I rap the knuckles of the other against Ava's door. My heart's already pounding, nerves tingling as I wait. After about fifteen seconds, I knock again.

It's possible that I already missed her.

Just as I raise my hand to knock one last time, the door swings open, and I find Ava blinking at me from the other side of the threshold. Surprise flickers in her eyes. She's wearing tiny sleep shorts and a tank top, her blonde hair tumbling down her shoulders in loose, messy waves.

My mouth dries.

She looks incredible.

"What are you doing here?" Her voice is thick with sleep.

I shrug, trying to act casual even though my pulse is racing like I just finished a sprint. "I know you usually practice at six, so I thought I'd drive you to the arena."

Her gaze dips to the travel containers. "Is one of those for me?"

"Yeah." I hand over a cup, watching as she lifts it to her lips.

Fuck. The way her mouth curves around the lid sends a wave of heat straight through me. I shift my weight, trying to focus on something other than how much I want this girl.

I promised we'd take things slow.

"Thanks." Her eyes linger on mine before she takes another sip.

For a second, I think about how good it would feel to kiss her again, but I shove that thought aside.

Slow, Hayes.

Glacial.

I clear my throat. "Why don't you change, and then we can head out? I wouldn't want you to miss your ice time."

She glances down at her outfit, as if only now remembering she's still in her pajamas. "Give me five minutes," she murmurs, turning toward her bedroom with her coffee in hand.

As she disappears, I force myself to stay rooted in the living room and take in her private space. It's neat, minimalist. There's a small couch, a table, and a few pictures on the shelf. I pick one up and study it closer. It's a black-and-white photo of her mid-spin, three or four feet above the ice, with her arms tightly pressed against her chest.

She looks powerful.

It's a stark contrast to the vulnerability that lurks in her eyes.

"I'm ready."

I turn, startled from my thoughts.

She's transformed in minutes. Black leggings, a fitted pink sweater that clings to her curves, and her blonde hair pulled up into a tight bun. The change is almost jarring, like a mask she wears to keep everyone at a distance. All I want to do is strip it away, layer by layer, until she lets me in completely.

She tilts her head. "You good?"

I clear my throat and force a smile. "Yeah. Let's go, Tink."

I hold out my hand, hoping she'll take it.

Her gaze drops to my fingers, and hesitation flickers in her expression. After what she's been through, I don't blame her for being cautious.

It feels like an eternity before she finally slips her hand into mine. It's a small gesture that has something in my chest loosening.

I pick up her duffel bag, slinging it over my shoulder as we head downstairs to my truck. The arena is only a five-minute drive from her apartment building, and the morning is still pitch black as we pull into the empty parking lot.

As we reach the arena, Ava walks ahead, her movements sure as she unlocks the door to the rink and pushes it open. We make our way through the building until arriving at another set of glass doors. Once inside, the air hits me—the cold, familiar smell of ice.

When she drops down onto a bench, I jerk my thumb toward the men's locker room. "I'll grab my skates and be back in a minute."

She nods, already slipping off her shoes and pulling her white skates from her bag. I cut across the space to the locker room before shoving inside. The lights automatically turn on, illuminating the echoing area.

When I return, Ava's already gliding across the ice with that same effortless grace I caught a glimpse of in the photo. I can't help but stop and soak in the sight of her. She's poetry in motion—spinning, twisting, floating across the ice like she's weightless.

I've only caught glimpses of her like this when I watched her from a distance. This isn't the guarded, careful girl who looks at me with uncertainty. This is the real Ava. The one who comes alive on the ice.

It pisses me off all over again that her former coach stole something so precious from her. That he tried to ruin this part of her life.

She deserves to have the future she worked so hard for.

I skate a few laps around the perimeter while she practices jumps and spins in the center. My eyes stay locked on her, mesmerized by the way she moves. The determination etched into her face is sexy as hell, and it makes me want to pull her off the ice and show her exactly how I feel.

She transitions into a spin, pulling her leg up until the blade of her skate is over her head. The skill and flexibility it takes to execute that trick is mind-blowing.

I move closer, drawn to her like a moth to a flame.

When she finally comes to a stop, I find myself unable to hold back. As soon as my fingers nab hers, I tug her toward me with measured movements, wanting to give her enough time to put a stop to the intimacy. My arms wrap around her, pulling her against me. For a second or two, her muscles stiffen. Just when I consider setting her free and stepping back to give her space, she relaxes, her body melting into mine.

"You're too talented not to compete," I murmur, my voice low. "You realize that, right?"

Sadness floods her eyes as she looks away. "There's no longer a place for me in that world."

I lift her chin, forcing her to meet my gaze. "I don't believe that. And deep down, neither do you."

Before she has a chance to respond, I brush my lips across hers. It's a gentle kiss, slow and teasing, but it's enough to set every nerve ending on fire. Her palms settle on my chest before sliding upward until her arms tangle around my neck.

A groan rumbles up from deep within my body as she presses against me.

This is what I've been waiting for.

This connection.

The feeling of being so close to her that nothing else matters.

My hands tighten around her waist as our tongues brush, and I sink deeper into the kiss.

Somewhere in the distance a door opens, and a voice rings out. "Ava?"

We splinter apart, our eyes wide.

Coach.

I grab her hand and tug her toward the bench. We barely make it to the edge of the ice when she stumbles, crashing into me. I twist at the last second and take the brunt of the fall as we hit the rubber flooring. She lands on top of me with a soft grunt. Our bodies are flush as my arms tighten around her.

"Ava?" Coach's voice echoes closer, sending a jolt of adrenaline through me.

We're a mess of limbs, tangled up together, and I'm pretty sure the massive hard-on I'm sporting isn't helping matters. Even with her dad seconds away from finding us, all I can think about is the way her lips felt against mine.

Heat floods her eyes, turning them a deep cerulean hue. The situation turns dire when she wriggles against my groin, creating friction.

Instead of giving in to the pleasure flooding my system, my fingers tighten around her slender hips. "You need to stop, or we're going to get caught. I don't think either of us want that."

Humor flares to life in her eyes, mingling with the arousal.

Have I ever seen them spark with such laughter?

When she continues to squirm, her breath catches and her pupils dilate, the black swallowing up the blue. It makes her look even sexier than before.

"That feels so good," she whispers, her voice turning smokey.

"Way too damn good," I groan in agreement. "Keep that up and I'll come in my sweats."

Her teeth scrape across her lower lip. "I'd like to see that happen."

Her hips continue to gyrate as the flush in her cheeks grows and a dazed quality enters her eyes. Each movement forces me closer to the precipice.

I wasn't kidding when I said I'd come in my pants. My cock is impossibly hard, and my balls are tightening, drawing up against my body. It wouldn't take much to shove me over the edge.

How embarrassing would that be?

I release a steady breath, attempting to get a hold of myself. I have no idea how this situation spiraled so far out of control.

She releases a soft whimper as she continues to shift against me.

The tortured sound is like a punch to the gut.

Fuck.

My hands tighten around her again, trying to stop what now feels inevitable.

When her eyelids feather closed, my grip intensifies.

"Look at me, Ava." Her name comes out sounding more like a growl.

She cracks her eyes open just enough to meet my gaze.

It's only when I have her complete attention that I mutter, "As much as I want to make you come right here and now, I don't want it to be like this." I pause for a beat. "The first time I give you an orgasm,

I want to take my time with you and draw out your pleasure. You deserve nothing less than that."

Her teeth scrape over the plump flesh of her lower lip. "I'm so close."

Now it's my turn to squeeze my eyes tightly closed against the way her blue depths plead with mine. Part of me wants to give her exactly what she's begging for.

But... after what she's been through, I want her thinking clearly and making good decisions for herself. The man who took advantage of her innocence and abused his position of power didn't give her that choice.

I refuse to be anything like him.

It would fucking devastate me if she regretted anything we did together.

"I know, baby. But you told me that you needed to take this slow, and that's exactly what I'm trying to do." I search her gaze as it begins to clear. "No regrets."

Some of her arousal fades as she releases an unsteady breath. "No regrets," she repeats.

When a door slams in the distance, the sound echoing in the cavernous space, I realize we're once again alone, but it won't last much longer. Pretty soon the place will start to fill up.

"Ready to get out of here?"

With a nod, she brushes her lips across mine. Just as my resolve snaps, she pulls away and rolls to the side before rising to her skates and stepping onto the ice. I release a slow breath, willing my boner to deflate, before doing the same.

Already I know that I'll be rocking a pair of blue balls for the rest of the morning.

AVA

22

My hands twist together in my lap as we drive back to my apartment. I can't stop thinking about how good it felt to be stretched out on top of Hayes. Everything about him is hard and sculpted. Especially the thickness of his erection. It had been perfectly nestled against the V between my legs. Even thinking about the way I'd ground against him has arousal pooling in my core like warmed honey. Unable to help myself, I squirm on the seat before clenching my thighs to stymie the need that rushes through me, turning me on all over again.

It's been such a long time since I felt this kind of all-encompassing desire.

Nathan isn't the only man I slept with. There were a few others after him. Guys who did nothing to turn me on or give me what I needed. One of them actually made me feel bad about what I like in the bedroom.

That thought is like a punch to the gut.

Will Hayes react the same way?

It's a scary thought.

One that I shove away, not wanting to dwell on it.

I chance another peek at Hayes from beneath the thick fringe of my lashes, unable to believe I'm sitting beside him in his truck. That a relationship, if that's what this actually is, has sprung up between us out of nowhere.

If you'd told me a few months ago, even a few weeks ago, that I'd want Hayes Van Doren to kiss me, I would have laughed my ass off and told you to lay off the drugs.

And yet, I can't deny the truth of what's unfolding.

I force the air wedged in my lungs from my body.

I have no idea if a relationship can even work between us.

We're so different.

And then there's my father to consider.

I wince thinking about what would have happened if he'd caught us in such a compromising situation. The man would have definitely stroked out.

When I continue staring at Hayes, lost in the turmoil of my thoughts, he flicks a concerned look my way.

"Tell me what you're thinking."

The deep scrape of his voice reverberates throughout my body, echoing in every cell of my being, and it brings me right back to what it felt like to be pressed against him.

I clear my throat and force myself to admit the truth. "I'm wondering what would have happened if we'd kept going."

Fire ignites in his green eyes as his voice turns husky. "I would have made a real fucking mess in my boxers."

With a nod, my heart rate picks up tempo. His honesty forces me to reveal my own. "It was the same for me. It's been a long time since I've been so turned on. I almost forgot what it feels like."

The atmosphere in the truck turns charged as my admission hangs heavy in the air. A few seconds later, he turns into the parking lot of my building and pulls into a space before cutting the engine. It would be impossible not to notice the way his hands shake.

I'm not the only one who's been affected by what happened.

It's almost a shock when I blurt, "I want to feel more of that."

He shifts until our gazes collide. The longer he studies my face, the more heat scalds my cheeks as uncertainty slams into me full force.

Did I make a mistake in allowing myself to be vulnerable with this guy?

Just as I consider bolting from the vehicle, he asks, "More of what? Tell me what you need, Tink."

It's so tempting to shy away from this embarrassing conversation. Instead, I force myself to be honest. At least a little bit. "I want you to kiss and touch me like you did at the rink. I want to see if I can..." My voice trails off as I swallow down another burst of nerves.

"Come? You want to see if I can make you come?"

"Yes."

He reaches out to stroke my lower lip with the pad of his thumb. "Has that been a problem for you?"

Humiliation crawls up my neck as I glance away.

"We're not going to do anything else if you can't hold my gaze while having this conversation."

My cheeks feel like they're on fire as I force myself to turn back to him. I've never admitted this to anyone. Not even my therapist.

"Yes, it's been a problem since my world imploded."

I stare into his eyes as he continues to caress my face. His gentle touch is enough to settle everything that rampages dangerously inside me.

"I want to give you what you need. Trust me, I do. But I also want you to be sure about what you're asking for."

A pent-up breath rushes from me as relief courses through my veins.

"I don't need to think anything over. That's what I want." There's a beat of silence before I confess, "I'm tired of feeling damaged."

His brow pinches, and his lips flatten in a tight line. I blink, surprised to find anger brewing in his green depths.

"The last thing you are is damaged. Not by a long shot. And you know what I'm going to do?"

I shake my head.

"Prove it to you."

Hope cautiously rises within me.

More than anything, I want to believe him.

But how can I when the person I trusted most in this world broke his word?

It's only with the passing of time that I understand how Nathan manipulated me, wielding the love and respect I felt for him against me.

It took months of intense therapy before I came to that devastating conclusion.

The idea of opening myself up enough to trust someone else again isn't an easy one.

With shaking fingers, I pop open the door, wanting him to follow through on his promise. I live alone and have the entire apartment to myself. We can take care of business. Maybe a few times and then... who knows?

Or... he'll take a peek inside my head and change his mind about this budding relationship.

Anything's possible. I want to temper my expectations.

As I slide from the seat, I throw a glance at Hayes, who hasn't moved a muscle.

"Are you coming up?"

His attention stays pinned to me as he shakes his head. "Can't. I have class in twenty."

Well, damn.

All the anticipation, excitement, and the little bit of fear swirling around inside me nose dives before erupting into flames.

I blink, thrown off by his response. "You do?"

The disappointment that floods my system is palpable.

"Yeah, and I can't afford to miss."

I chew my lower lip and throw out the offer before I can think better of it. "Tonight, then?"

Warmth enters his eyes as his lips quirk at the corners. "Count on it, Tink."

I release a shaky breath with a nod. "Okay. Guess I'll see you then."

As soon as I slam the door closed, he backs out of the space and takes off from the parking lot.

I stare at the back end of the beat-up truck and wonder what I've gotten myself into.

But the excitement he was able to rouse within me...
A shiver slides through me before settling deep in my core.
And that right there is the reason I need to explore this.

TenInchesofCocky
VAN DOREN
19
HAYES

TENINCHESOF
COCKY

WILDCATS

23

I drop my stick into the holder by the door and head straight to my locker with one thought dominating my mind.

Ava Philips.

Ever since she walked in on me naked a few weeks ago, she's been living rent free in my brain. It started out as curiosity, and now it's turned into something I can't shake no matter how hard I try.

"All right, team, gather around!" Coach Philips's voice booms across the locker room, snapping me back to reality.

I turn, joining the guys as we form a loose circle around him. Despite everything between me and Ava, my respect for her dad is unwavering. The man's a legend. He played most of his career in Chicago, and now he's coaching us to the playoffs.

But damn, seeing him brings a tidal wave of guilt, knowing I'm thinking about his daughter in ways he wouldn't like.

"We've worked hard all season to get here," Coach starts, his voice commanding our attention. "But now it's time to dig deeper. The playoffs are a different beast. Every shift, every second counts. You've all proven you can hang with the best. Now it's time to prove you *are* the best." He pauses, eyes scanning the room, and I can feel his words settle over us like a weight. "Remember why you're here. For the love of the game, for your teammates, for the fans. You wear this jersey with pride. When you hit the ice, leave everything out there. No regrets."

A roar rises from the team, our adrenaline already kicking in.

"Wildcats on three!" Ryder calls out. "One, two, three—Wildcats!"

The chant reverberates throughout the room. Even as we break away, it doesn't take long for my thoughts to drift back to Ava. She's been in my head all day, and I need to see her. Need to feel that connection again, like I did this morning.

I unlace my skates, carefully setting them in my locker, while the other guys toss their gear aside without a second thought. Most of my teammates have no idea what it's like to hustle for hand-me-down equipment. I don't take the university's gear for granted.

By the time I strip down and hit the showers, I'm already thinking about heading over to Ava's place.

Colby knocks my shoulder on my way out. "Hey, Van Doren, you down to grab food with the guys?"

I shake my head. "Not tonight, man. I've already got plans, but thanks."

Colby, the nosy bastard that he is, arches a brow, all too interested. "Plans, huh? Who's the chick?"

"No one you know." I keep my answer vague. The last thing I need is for the guys to catch wind of this. It's not that I don't trust them, but word spreads fast in the locker room.

For Ava's sake, I'd rather keep it under wraps a little longer. I can't help but glance at Coach's closed office door.

My teammate's expression turns gleeful. It's like the guy can sniff out a lie within seconds of it leaving my lips.

"Oh, really? Why don't you give me a name, and we'll see just how true that assessment is?"

Yeah, that's not going to happen.

Can you imagine if any of these guys found out I was hanging out with Coach's daughter?

Maybe "hanging out" isn't quite the right term for it.

But I still won't be sharing that with Colby.

As soon as I shove my feet into my shoes and grab my bag, I stride from the locker room.

"Hey, where are you going? You didn't answer the question! Inquiring minds want to know who you're spending time with!"

I give Colby the finger before disappearing through the door with a sigh of relief.

Those fuckers I call my friends can be relentless.

Ten minutes later, I'm standing at her door, knocking. I've never been so impatient to see a girl. My pulse speeds up with each second that ticks by.

What if she's changed her mind?

What if she decided this—*us*—is too much?

Before my brain can spin further out of control, the door swings open. Ava stands across the threshold in black leggings and a cropped pale-blue sweater that shows just enough skin to drive me crazy. Her hair is still up in a bun. My fingers itch to take the tie out and watch the golden mass spill down her back.

Every time I see her, I'm bowled over by her beauty.

No. Not just her beauty. Everything about her.

"You look amazing."

"Thanks," she murmurs. "Want to come in?"

It doesn't take long for the tension we always seem to generate to crackle in the air like an impending storm. She leads me to the couch, and we settle a few inches apart. Her hands twist together in her lap as she glances at me and then away.

The only need pumping through me is the one that demands I put her at ease.

I reach out and cover both her hands with my larger one. "You know we don't have to do anything, right? I meant what I said the other night. We'll take this at whatever pace you need. I'm not in a rush."

She releases a breath, and her shoulders sag, as if a heavy weight has been lifted from them. "I don't understand you at all."

"What do you mean?"

"I don't know," she mumbles. "I didn't expect you to be so nice. Or thoughtful. Or understanding."

"Well, I guess with the right person, I can be all of those things."

When her gaze lifts to mine, her eyes are filled with doubt and something else that pulls at me. "Are you saying I'm the right person?"

Unable to resist, I slide her onto my lap until her thighs straddle mine. My hands rest on the gentle swells of her hips before pulling her a little closer so I can feel the heat of her body nestled against me. Her breath hitches, and her lips part slightly as our gazes cling.

At every turn, I'm falling deeper for this girl.

"I think you might be," I admit, the words feeling more real than anything I've said in a long time.

Her hands slide upward to my neck before her fingers thread through my hair. "Can I tell you something?"

I nod as my heartbeat picks up tempo. "Anything."

I want to know every little thought that pops into her brain.

"I haven't been able to stop thinking about how you kissed me this morning."

Her words send a jolt of heat straight through me. "I've been thinking about it too. More than I should."

I've had plenty of girls whisper the filthiest things imaginable in my ear, but none of them have turned me on the way Ava does while admitting something so innocent.

It makes me realize just how different everything is with her.

How much she matters.

For the first time in my life, I want to take care and make sure the person I'm with doesn't get hurt.

I want to do whatever is necessary to protect her.

Even though we didn't know each other before, I wish it were possible to go back in time and keep her safe.

I'll do the next best thing and put her needs above my own.

She leans in and brushes her lips against mine in the faintest, sweetest kiss. It's as if I'm sinking further into something I didn't realize I was already too deeply entrenched in to escape from.

My hands tighten on her hips, pulling her closer as our kiss intensifies. Her lips are soft, her breath warm as she moves against me, and for a moment, everything else falls away.

Her past.

Her doubts.

My own guilt about Coach.

None of it matters at this moment.

When she shifts, brushing against my erection, I bite back a groan.

There's no doubt about it. This girl will be my complete undoing.

And you know what?

I've never wanted anything more.

Just like earlier this morning at the ice rink, heat flashes in her eyes, turning them darker. My cock stiffens as she repeats the movement.

"I like the way it feels when I slide against you," she whispers, mouth hovering over mine.

"You're killing me, Tink."

Her lips lift into a smile.

That's the moment I realize I'll do whatever it takes to keep that expression on her face.

There's never been a girl who's made me want to think long term, but that's exactly what happens when we're together. The scary part is, I might be the only one doing it.

I remind myself to slow my roll.

We have time to figure out what this is.

"Sometimes I think about walking in on you in the locker room."

"Tell me what you're doing when you think about me."

She draws her lower lip between her teeth. Just when I think she'll refuse to answer, she says, "Touching myself." Her brows pinch as frustration flickers in her eyes. "But it's never enough to get me there." She glances away. "Ever since Nathan... I just can't seem to..." Her voice trails off as heat gathers in her cheeks.

"Get off?" I palm her backside, squeezing and massaging her ass. "That's nothing to be embarrassed about."

"I know." Sadness weaves its way through her tone. "It just sucks. I hate it."

I search her face, wondering if there's more she isn't telling me. "Are there other issues?"

When her gaze darts away, I slide my fingers beneath her chin and gently turn her face until there's no other choice but for her to look at me.

"Tell me. Whatever it is, we can work through it together. I promise."

She releases a shaky breath. "This is so humiliating."

"It shouldn't be. How can I help if I don't know what you're struggling with?"

After a few silent moments, her shoulders wilt. "I think what I like might be a little fucked-up."

"That's doubtful." My fingers stroke the silky-soft skin of her jaw. "Give me an example."

Her teeth scrape across her lower lip before she whispers, "I like when there's kind of a thrill to it."

A thrill?

I blurt out the first thing that comes to mind. "Like having sex in public?"

She nods.

Her admittance has my cock hardening even more than before. "Okay. Nothing strange about that. Plenty of people do."

This time, her words come a little easier. "I like being spanked."

"Who doesn't?" Even though I'm not bored in the least, I force a yawn. "Anything else?"

Her brows rise. "Anal. I've always wanted to try it."

Well, fuck.

"Sometimes I like to use toys."

It's entirely possible I just came in my boxers.

I shake my head in genuine confusion. "There are a lot of people who enjoy those things. Why would you think any of it makes you fucked-up?"

Color flags her cheeks. "Because Nathan would tell me what a dirty little whore I was for liking everything he did to me. He made sure I knew no one would ever be able to get me off the way he did." She presses her lips together before admitting, "I think he might be right."

Air leaks from my lungs in painful little bursts.

If I didn't already hate the bastard for what he put her through, her soft confession would do the trick. I'd like to wring his neck for planting these ideas in her head. He introduced her to sex and then made her feel bad about it.

It's so twisted.

It takes every ounce of self-control not to swear a blue streak.

Instead, I cup her cheeks and force her to meet my steady gaze. I need her to see the earnestness in my eyes. "There's nothing messed-up about you, baby. And there's certainly nothing wrong with the way you enjoy having sex when it's between two consenting adults. He's the one who was messed-up in the head. Not you." I draw her face close enough to brush my lips across her forehead. "Never you."

A shuddering breath falls from her lips. "Thank you."

"For what, baby? I haven't done anything but tell you the truth."

"You've done a lot more than that. You're the first person to tell me there isn't anything wrong with what turns me on. That it doesn't make me some kind of deviant."

"The last thing you are is a deviant." I hold her cheeks in my palms. "Do you hear me?"

"Yeah." Her eyes search mine. "I've told you all the things that turn me on. What about you? What gets you off?"

I flex my hips. "I think you can feel that everything you just mentioned gets me hard."

For the first time since this conversation began, a small smile lifts the corners of her lips as she rubs herself along my erection.

"Do you ever masturbate? Or is that a stupid question because you can pretty much have sex whenever you want?"

"It's not a stupid question. And yes, I jerk off."

Her eyelids grow heavy as she continues grinding against me. "When was the last time you took matters into your own hands?"

"This morning after class."

"Did you think about me?" Her voice dips, becoming low and husky.

"You're the only one I thought about. The only one I've been thinking about since we met."

A devilish glint enters her eyes. "Good."

When she shifts again, a tortured groan escapes from me. Whether she's deliberately trying to or not, this girl shreds every bit of my self-control.

"You know what I like most about masturbation?" I say more conversationally than I'm feeling.

She shakes her head.

"That there's no need to worry about someone else getting off. It's all about what you like and how you feel. You get to be as selfish as you want with your pleasure."

Her smile fades. "I wish it were that easy."

"It is. Maybe you just need someone to guide you through it."

Her eyes widen. "You would do that?"

"Only if you wanted me to."

"Wouldn't it be weird?"

"Of course not." Before I have the chance to think about the offer, it's out of my mouth. "We could do it together."

She stills. "Really?"

"Yeah. We don't have to make a big deal about it." When she remains silent, I blurt, "Maybe I shouldn't have brought it up. The last thing I want to do is make you uncomfortable."

"No. I don't want to forget about it. I want to do it." She sucks in a deep breath before expelling it from her lungs. "And I want you to help me. But I want you to do it too. Okay?"

"Yeah, babe. It's okay. I just want you to be sure before this goes any further. That's all."

"I am." She untangles her arms from around my neck before her hands float to the hem of her sweater. In one swift motion, she yanks it up her body and over her head before dropping it to the carpet.

Even though it's tempting to glance at her nearly-naked chest, I keep my gaze focused on her face. I'm trying so hard not to look down that I don't realize she's reached around her ribcage and unsnapped her bra until the silky straps slide down her shoulders and arms. She plucks the material away before it joins the crumpled sweater on the floor.

My gaze dips.

Oh fuck.

I force my attention back to her face.

One of her hands drifts to my cheek before stroking the line of my jaw. "Aren't you going to look?"

"Do you want me to?"

Any moment, my tightly strung control will snap like an over stretched rubber band.

At this point, it wouldn't take much.

"Yes, I do."

I inhale a sharp breath and almost choke on it.

Only then do I allow my gaze to fall again. Holy mother of God, she's got the most glorious breasts. They're small and perky. The perfect handful. Before I realize it, I'm reaching out and cupping each one in my palms. My thumbs stroke over her nipples until they stiffen.

She whimpers as she arches into my touch.

I flick a glance upward to meet her eyes. "Are you one hundred percent positive about this?"

"I am, Hayes. I'm sure."

"Okay then, hang on."

Before she can ask any further questions, I drop my hands from her breasts and slide them back around to grip her ass before rising to my feet. With a gasp, her arms twine around my neck as her legs lock around my waist. Her mouth is so close that the warmth of her breath feathers across my lips.

It's a dizzying sensation.

One I want more of.

I swing toward the short hallway. Before I can move a muscle, there's a knock on the apartment door.

Our heads swivel toward the tiny entryway.

Her brow furrows. "Ignore it."

As soon as I take a step, there's another, more insistent knock.

"Expecting company?"

"Not that I know of."

"Want to answer it?"

"Not really."

When there's a third knock, Ava swears under her breath. "Fine, I'll answer it."

My lips tremble with a smile at the frustration pouring off her in heavy waves. If I'd wanted to rekindle the spark from earlier this morning, that mission has been accomplished with flying colors.

Our gazes stay locked as she slowly slides down the length of my body before her toes touch the floor. My cock is painfully hard as she swings around and picks up her bra and sweater, slipping both on in record speed. Only then does she pad to the entryway.

"Let me see who it is."

I step into the hallway, so I'm out of sight, before readjusting my erection.

With a huff, she yanks open the door.

"Hey! What took you so long? I was just about to have Colby break down the door to make sure you were all right."

Recognition slams into me.

Britt.

"Oh. Ummm... sorry. I was in the bedroom and didn't hear it." There's a pause. "What are you doing here?"

"We're heading to Blue Vibe to dance the night away. You have to come with!"

And apparently Willow.

So not only are Colby and Britt here, but Willow and Mav too.

Well, shit.

That throws a definite wrench in the works.

"Oh... that sounds fun, but tonight's not good for me," Ava hedges, trying to turn down the invite without rousing too much suspicion from her friends.

"What are you talking about? Of course it is. This is exactly why I didn't bother calling first. I knew you'd try to bail." Before Ava can say anything more, Britt continues. "A guy from my psych class is going to be there, and I want to introduce you. His name is Jack, and I think you two would really hit it off."

Um, excuse me?

Over my dead body is that happening.

Before I can think better of it, I step out of the shadows and stalk to the door. Maybe Ava wanted to keep this on the downlow because of her father, but her friends need to understand that she doesn't need help finding a man.

She's already got one.

"Plus—" Britt's voice comes to an abrupt halt as soon as she catches sight of me.

Once I'm directly behind Ava, my hands settle possessively on her shoulders. "That won't be necessary," I tell her, just so we're clear on the situation.

Britt's eyes widen. "Well, this is one plot twist I didn't see coming."

A slow grin spreads across Maverick's face as Colby mutters, "No one I knew, my ass."

Willow beams as she puts two and two together. "Perfect. Now both of you can join us."

AVA

I'm tucked beneath Hayes's muscular arm as we step through the back door of the club. The bouncer takes one look at the guys and waves us in. Blue Vibe is like an assault on the senses. The techno beat pulses off the black walls as strobe lights cut through the darkness. The interior can only be described as sumptuous. There's a long stretch of glass bar at the far end of the room with booths and tables scattered around the perimeter. The dance floor is located on the opposite side of the space. Even on a Wednesday night, the place is jam-packed. There's a surprising range of people inside, from students in college to adults in their mid-to-late twenties. A DJ sits perched high above the crowd in a booth, mixing music.

This isn't the first time I've been here, but it's different walking in with Hayes. Usually, I feel more like a fifth wheel. I keep catching glances from my friends. I haven't said a word to them about Hayes. As soon as they got me alone in my room, I was bombarded with questions. Ones I didn't have answers for.

My attention is drawn back to Hayes when his warm breath ghosts over my ear, and a shiver dances down my spine.

"Have I mentioned how amazing you look?"

My fingers flutter over the short black dress that barely skims my thighs. Britt found it in the back of my closet when she was rifling around for something I could wear. Apparently, a sweater and leggings weren't going to cut it. She threatened to make a pit stop at her apartment to grab something for me.

Before I can respond, he adds, "Or how much I love when you wear your hair down?"

The thick mass has been left long and loose around my shoulders. I'm used to wearing it up so it's out of the way when I skate. Most days, I forget to style it differently.

"Thank you."

"Are you cool with your friends knowing we're together?"

"Is that what we are?" Air gets trapped in my lungs as I blurt out the question. "Together?"

"I certainly hope so."

The tension filling my muscles dissipates as happiness bubbles up inside me. I couldn't tamp it down even if I tried. I have no idea how everything will play out in the future, but for tonight, I'm going to go with it and just enjoy myself.

"Who wants a shot?" Colby asks.

Willow shakes her head. "Nothing for me."

She recently confided that she was diagnosed with childhood leukemia in high school. So she does what she can to keep her immune system as healthy as possible without missing out on the things she wants to do.

Maverick also shakes his head.

Until this year, alcohol was only something I indulged in when celebrating my birthday or winning a competition. When you're in training, there's no place for it.

But tonight, I'm going to make an exception.

"I'll have one," I say.

Hayes jerks his head in a nod. "One for me as well."

Colby returns with four shots, two in each hand, before passing them out. We all clink our glasses before belting back the smooth liquor. The cinnamon flavor burns as it slides down the back of my throat.

Colby raises a brow. "One more?"

"Probably not—" Hayes begins.

"Yes," I cut in.

"You sure that's a good idea, Tink? My guess is that you're a lightweight when it comes to shots."

"Oh my God, did you just call her Tink?"

I break eye contact with him to glance at Willow.

A wide grin lights up her face. "That's so cute."

Slow smiles spread across Maverick's and Colby's faces.

"Yeah, super cute," Maverick adds with a laugh.

Hayes groans from beside me. "Shut the hell up, McKinnon."

Colby chuckles as he returns to the bar for a second round.

Already I feel the effects of the alcohol warming me from the inside out. Some of the constant worry that's been gnawing at me ever since the messages from Nathan began popping up with more frequency melts away, and there's something freeing about that.

When Colby returns with another round, we all take them.

"Guess there's no chance we'll end up married for a second time, is there?" Britt jokes.

Colby winks at her. "Interested in hopping a flight to Vegas and having a do over?"

Her shoulders shake with laughter. "It'll certainly be one hell of a story to share with our kids one day."

"I wouldn't have it any other way, Firecracker," he says before they clink their glasses.

Colby McNichols was one of the biggest players on campus.

Until Britt came along.

Now he couldn't be more domesticated.

They both seem happy.

Content.

It's nice to see, and it gives me hope for the future.

My gaze unconsciously settles on Hayes, and a zip of electricity sizzles through my veins when I find him watching me.

We tap the tiny glasses together before throwing back the shots. Our gazes stay locked the entire time. Much like the first one, the liquor sends a fiery trail down the back of my throat before settling at the bottom of my belly.

Just as Hayes plucks the glass from me, Britt locks her fingers around my wrist and drags me to the dance floor, Willow leading the way. It doesn't take long before I lose sight of Hayes.

The three of us shove our way through the crush of bodies before carving out a small space. With the alcohol rushing through my system, I forget about everything else and lose myself in the heavy beat of the music. My eyelids feather closed as I tip my face upward, enjoying the sensation of letting go and allowing my mind to wander.

How long has it been since I was able to cut loose and feel free?

My mind tumbles back over the years.

Maybe never.

It's a jarring realization.

Ever since I was twelve years old, and started working with Nathan, skating has been my entire world. There was never time for fun or fooling around. There were always competitions to train for.

I glance at the two girls I'm with. I'm so grateful for their friendship. Without it, I probably wouldn't be experiencing any of this, and that would be a real shame.

Plus, now there's Hayes.

I have no idea if we'll actually fit into each other's lives, but for the first time ever, I can have fun trying to figure it out.

I let those thoughts go as one song bleeds into the next. Laughter falls from my lips as Britt grabs my hand and twirls me around before doing the same with Willow. Smiles light up our faces as we shake our asses. It feels good to do nothing more than live in the moment as the mass of writhing bodies presses in on us from all sides.

The club is a sprawling space, but there are so many people on the dance floor, it's impossible to tell whose limbs belong to who. The music echoes off the walls before gradually seeping into my bones as alcohol rushes through my veins, making me feel alive and free.

If only this feeling could last forever.

My eyelids fly open when strong hands wrap around my hips and drag me against a steely body. I don't have to twist around to know who's snuck up on me. Already I've come to recognize the beachy scent of Hayes's cologne as it invades my senses, reminding me of sunshine and lazy summer days.

I just want to inhale a big breath of him and keep it trapped in my lungs forever.

His arms tighten around me as my spine presses against his front. Everything about this guy is hard and sculpted. There's nothing soft about him. He's a wall of muscle.

I never thought I'd find myself attracted to a guy like him, but that's exactly what I am.

Even though it's scary and I'm unsure of myself, I love it.

Love these new feelings that rush through me when he's near.

All I have to do is think about the hot hockey player, and my belly swoops.

And when he lays his hands on me?

I forget about the past and all the pain tied to it.

"You're so damn sexy, know that?"

I shake my head. I've never felt sexy before, and it boggles my mind that Hayes Van Doren thinks that about me.

"With all these guys checking you out, I knew I'd better stake my claim before anyone worked up the courage to shoot their shot. No way I could let that happen, Tink."

I twist my head enough to meet his gaze. Even in the darkness of the club, possessiveness shines brightly from his eyes.

My pulse thrums an unsteady beat as his face looms closer until his lips can brush across mine. We stay locked together as the music pulses around us. With his arms wrapped protectively around me, I feel safe and insulated. His grip tightens as he pulls me close enough to feel the hard length of his erection pressing against my lower back.

When his tongue sweeps across the seam of my lips, I open, allowing him entrance. Everything that happened earlier this evening tumbles through my head. As much fun as I'm having at Blue Vibe, part of me wishes my friends hadn't dropped by and invited us out.

Thoughts of how he touched and kissed me earlier have heat exploding in my core before throbbing a harsh beat in perfect rhythm to the music. His hands glide along my ribcage before settling beneath the swells of my breasts. When I whimper, an answering groan works its way up from deep within his chest.

Arousal dampens my panties as his mouth roves over mine until our tongues can tangle. Hayes nips at my lower lip, tugging it between sharp teeth before releasing it.

My eyelids crack open just enough to meet his heated gaze. The need I find swirling there sets my pulse racing. I can only imagine the same intensity is echoed within my own.

This man makes me feel alive in a way I've never experienced before, and the rush of sensation through my veins has already become addictive.

"Fuck, baby."

I whimper when he takes a step in retreat and cool air slides across my bare flesh.

Before I can say anything, he slips my hand into his larger one and then we're on the move, cutting a path through the thick crowd. Hayes is so tall and broad—a force to be reckoned with—that people scurry out of his way rather than get run over.

Even if you didn't know he was a hockey player bound for the NHL, his size and demeanor would be intimidating.

We take the stairs to the second floor, where the VIP lounge and a glass bar are located along with a circular balcony that overlooks the dance floor. The lighting up here is muted, making the vibe sexier. It's difficult to see what's taking place in the shadows.

I gravitate to the railing and stare down at the mass of writhing bodies below that's illuminated by the flashing strobe lights.

Hayes slides directly behind me, his bigger body overshadowing my own.

"Wrap your fingers around the railing." His heated breath against my sweat-slicked skin causes a shiver to dance down my spine as I follow the directive.

"Good girl."

My panties dampen at the praise as my teeth sink into my lower lip. He hasn't even touched me yet, and already my body is vibrating with excitement.

His hands settle on my shoulders before massaging the muscles until they're malleable. Only then do his fingers drift along my bare arms, goose bumps erupting in their wake.

His fingertips sweep across my wrists before his larger hands wrap around mine. When he presses closer, I feel the insistent length of his erection nudging my backside.

A groan escapes me as I tilt my hips, greedy for the slightest contact.

"Do you feel how hard you make me?"

It would be impossible not to. His cock is so long and thick.

"Yes." There's little point in lying. Not when I've revealed all my secrets to him. The ones I keep buried deep down inside.

He retraces his path along my arms before grazing my sides with a featherlight touch. His knuckles drag against the curve of my breasts and then ribcage, igniting a firestorm of need within me. After his hands settle on my hips, he pulls me close enough to feel the grind of his thick length. There's no escaping it. And I wouldn't want to. My eyes roll back in my head with each languid movement.

One hand glides down my hip before settling on the V between my thighs. Only then does he stroke my center through the thin layers of clothing that separate us. I can't help but flex, pressing into his hand.

"Do you like having your pussy played with?"

"Yes. It feels so good."

"Oh, Tink. This is just the beginning. I'm going to give this little pussy all the love she deserves."

I believe him. Beneath his touch, my body comes alive, and a moan works its way past my lips.

That's all the encouragement he needs to continue the delicious torment. His fingers spread wide as he squeezes before flexing and repeating the caress.

His other hand drifts upward until his palm can cover one breast, and his lips devour my neck, licking and sucking. Nipping at the flesh. All the sensations he's roused whip around inside me, creating an inferno of need.

What I experienced at Nathan's hands was nothing like this, and I can't help but glory in every single difference. My former coach tried to tell me no one would ever turn me on the way he did, and for a long time, I was terrified he was right, but Hayes is proving him wrong.

And I'm so grateful for that.

He kneads me with both hands until my knees weaken, and I'm in danger of sliding to the floor. It doesn't take long before my body is tightly strung and dancing on the precipice.

"I want you to tell me exactly what my touch does to you."

I can't help but squirm against his hold, craving more of the riotous sensations that scratch and claw dangerously beneath the surface. Almost as if he's awoken something inside me, and it's now fighting to break loose.

If I'm completely honest, I've always secretly felt that way.

Wanting more.

Needing it.

But unsure how to ask for it.

Or find someone I could trust enough to give it to me.

As much as I hate Nathan for what he did, he created a longing inside me that refuses to be suppressed or denied. A craving that is now a part of me. Only now am I trying to make peace with that knowledge.

Desire crashes through me as his fingers stroke my lower lips through the thin fabric of my panties and dress.

He pinches my nipple. "I'm waiting."

"It turns me on and makes me feel achy," I say on a gasp.

His mouth drifts across the outer shell of my ear as his voice dips, turning husky. "Where does it make you feel achy?"

Unable to help myself, I shift against him, looking for more contact. "My pussy and my breasts."

When he tweaks me for a second time, I groan. It's like a straight shot to my core, and my panties flood with more heat.

"I bet you're soaked, aren't you?"

"Yes."

"Should I take your word for it or find out for myself?"

My breath catches at the back of my throat as excitement crashes over me.

After a beat of silence, he prods, "Well?"

"Find out for yourself."

"Are you sure? Anyone could look over and see the way I'm playing with you."

As tempting as it is to keep my eyes shut and sink into his touch, I force them open before glancing around and then at the mass of bodies below.

I hate how much the thrill of someone watching us turns me on.

"Yes."

A growl vibrates deep within his chest as one hand slips beneath the material of my dress before gliding up my bare thigh to the place that's desperate for the stroke of his hand.

Right when I think his fingers will slip beneath the fabric of my panties, they drift along the cotton, tracing the seam of my lips.

"You're right. Completely soaked."

I whimper as he shoves the fabric to the side, and one finger slides inside me. My body sags against his as he withdraws and circles the entrance before thrusting for a second time.

Each pump of his finger forces me closer to the precipice.

Closer to tumbling over the edge and into oblivion.

I want the orgasm so much; I can practically taste it.

I turn my face toward him. "Please."

"Mmm, that is such a pretty word falling from those pouty lips. It'll play on repeat in my dreams tonight."

Just as my muscles tighten and it feels like I'll shatter into a million broken pieces, his finger slips free of my body, and a garbled protest escapes my lips.

His dark chuckle tickles my ear. "Just like this morning at the rink, I'm not about to give you an orgasm for the first time in the middle of Blue Vibe. Although, I won't promise not to do it next time."

The thought of there being a next time has my belly spasming.

His mouth hovers near my ear as he brings the finger that had been buried deep inside me to my lips before sweeping it across the plump flesh, as if painting them with lipstick.

He taps his finger against my mouth. "Open up so you can taste how creamy I make you."

It never occurs to me not to follow the directive. As soon as my lips part, the digit slides inside. The taste of my arousal explodes on my tongue along with the slight saltiness of his skin. It's an addictive combination.

"Good, isn't it?"

"Mmmm."

"Now I need a taste."

The velvety softness of his tongue licks at my mouth before his lips crash onto mine.

Just as I grow dizzy from lack of oxygen, he pulls away enough to ask, "How am I ever going to get enough of you?"

His mouth hovers over mine before nipping at it. It's only when his fingers squeeze my breast do I realize that his palm is still covering me.

When I'm with Hayes, everything that normally bothers me falls away until it's just the two of us.

Until anything seems possible.

As I sink back into his touch, unease prickles at the base of my skull, and I get the strangest feeling we're being watched. As much as I want to ignore the creeping sensation, I can't. My gaze travels around the space before narrowing. Movement from the shadows catches my attention, and my heart slams against my chest before pounding into overdrive as I sift through the darkness only to find nothing.

It leaves me to wonder if anyone was there in the first place or if it was a figment of my imagination all along.

A shiver skates down my spine, and the mood shatters. As much as I want to make myself believe it was nothing, I can't.

I'm a little freaked out.

"What's wrong, Tink?"

It's tempting to confide my fears about Nathan, but I have no idea if I'm overreacting. I took two shots and am on sensory overload. It's not difficult in a place like this.

His hand falls away from my breast as I twist in his arms. "Would you mind if we get out of here? I'm ready to head home."

One side of his mouth hitches. "That works because I'm more than ready to take you there."

TenInchesofCocky
VAN DOREN
19
WILDCATS
HAYES
WILDCATS

TENINCHESOF
COCKY

It doesn't take long before I'm pulling into the parking lot of Ava's building and cutting the engine. I glance at her, only to find her steady gaze already pinned to me. Even in the darkness, it feels like I could drown in her fathomless blue depths. She studies me, making me feel like she's seeing way more than I'm comfortable with. More than what I project to the outside world. Even my teammates, who I consider more like brothers, don't know the finer details of my life.

"Are you going to come up?"

I hesitate, turning the question over in my head.

I've never been the good guy.

But for her, that's exactly who I want to be.

"Is that what you want?"

Her gaze drops to my mouth as she angles her body toward mine before pressing closer. The moment our lips brush, electricity hums through every cell of my being. It makes me feel more alive than anything else ever has.

Including hockey.

Nothing has ever been able to give me the same rush.

"Does that answer the question?"

I can't resist the smirk that lifts my lips. "I think it does."

With that, we exit my beat-up truck. As much as I'm dying to lay my hands on her, I remind myself to let her set the pace.

Those thoughts swirl through my head as we meet at the front of the vehicle before walking to the entrance of the building. Unable to stand the distance that separates us, I slip my arm around her waist and tug her close. I love the feel of her slender form pressed against me. The way we fit together perfectly.

It's a jarring thought.

I don't understand how this girl has come to mean so much to me in such a short period of time. It doesn't make sense.

We step inside the elevator. As soon as the doors close, her arms tangle around my neck, and she draws my mouth to hers. There's the stroke of tongues and the scrape of teeth. It's like going from zero to sixty in two seconds flat. Need spirals through me, setting fire to everything in its path until I'm consumed by it.

By *her*.

She presses me against the wall as the car rises through the building.

When I can't stand another second, I spin her around until I'm able to cage in her smaller body. As soon as my hand shoots out to slam the emergency stop button on the panel, the elevator jerks to a halt.

My mouth coasts over hers before sliding to her jawline and nipping the point of her chin. And then I'm moving along the delicate column of her throat. I lick the pulse that flutters beneath the fragile skin. My hands rise to cup her breasts, squeezing the rounded softness before pinching her nipples through the fabric of her dress. It doesn't take long before they stiffen right up. Unable to resist, I lean down and bite one and then the other until a moan escapes from her, and she's shifting against me. Her fingers tunnel through my hair, as if to lock me in place.

It's totally unnecessary.

There's nowhere else I'd rather be than here with her, giving her as much pleasure as she's willing to take.

I drop to my knees and stare up into her face.

Fuck, but she's so beautiful with her hair mussed and cheeks flushed.

She looks wild and free.

I love it.

Love that I've been able to tease out this side of her.

I play with her breasts, all the while staring into her eyes. There's something sexy about being on my knees in front of her. Our gazes hold as my fingers fall to the hem of her short dress before gathering up the material and lifting it until her light-blue panties come into view. The cotton is damp with arousal. I bury my nose against the V between her thighs and inhale until her scent floods me.

Fuck.

She smells so damn good.

I'm desperate for a taste of her.

"Don't stop," she whispers. Her voice is low and husky, vibrating with need.

"Wasn't planning on it." I nip at her mound before drawing away. "Hold your dress up for me, baby girl."

She doesn't need to be told twice. Her fingers grip the silky material.

"Higher."

Her breath catches as she lifts it to her belly button.

"Perfect." My thumbs slip beneath the elastic waistband of her panties before slowly drawing the cotton down her slender hips and thighs, revealing a shaved pussy in the process.

But that's not the reason why my breath gets lodged at the back of my throat.

My attention is riveted on the tiny glint of silver just visible between her pretty pink lips.

I drag my gaze upward to meet hers. "You have a piercing?"

Her teeth scrape across her lower lip. "Yeah."

A mixture of emotions crashes through me. "When did you do this?"

"A few months ago. I was hoping it would help."

"Has it?"

She shrugs.

"Have you been with anyone since you got it?"

"No."

Even though it wouldn't matter, I'm glad I get to be the first one to touch her, to play with it.

My gaze drops back to the piercing.

While I've contemplated one of my own, I've never been with a girl who had one. It's just as sexy as I imagined it would be.

"Step out of the panties."

She releases the fabric of her dress as she lifts one leg.

I give her mound a little tap. "Don't let the material fall, baby. Nothing shields this pussy from my view. Understand?"

She lets out a whimper.

I tap her clit again. "That's not an answer."

"Yes."

"Good girl."

I flick my gaze upward again. "Once I kiss this sweet little cunt, it belongs to me. Got it?"

She nods before tilting her hips. "I understand."

Once her underwear has been removed, I tuck the scrap of material into my pocket for safekeeping. Then I raise one leg over my shoulder so she's opened nice and wide, and I'm able to get a better view of the silver circle that pierces the hood of her clit.

"So fucking gorgeous," I mutter.

Unable to hold back, my tongue darts out to give her pussy a long lap. The taste of her honey explodes on my tastebuds, and it's almost enough to make me dizzy.

One lick, and I'm addicted.

A moan escapes from her as she opens her legs wider.

My tongue dances around the piercing before gently sucking it into my mouth and tugging.

I keep my attention pinned to her face, not wanting to miss a single flicker of emotion.

"That feels so good."

I release the piercing before licking her flesh and dipping my tongue inside the heat of her body. She's so damn wet, and I'm greedy for her taste.

Just when her muscles tighten and her hips pick up tempo, I pull away, sitting back on my heels.

Her eyelids fly open. "Why did you stop?"

"Because there's not enough time to take care of you properly." I tilt my head. "The alarm is going off, and it won't be long before someone comes to check it. I'd rather they not find us with my face buried between your legs."

Her eyes widen, as if she just realized the sharp bell is still trilling.

With one final kiss against her soaked flesh, I rise to my feet. My gaze settles on the V between her thighs. As much as I love staring at her...

"Cover up that sweet little pussy. I'm the only one who gets to see it."

She releases the material, and the hem of the dress settles around her thighs. "I was so close."

I brush my mouth across hers. "Don't worry, Tink. I'm going to give you all the orgasms you want."

Hope sparks in her eyes. "Promise?"

My lips drift over hers for a second time. "Absolutely."

When she opens for me, my tongue slips inside to tangle with hers. Without breaking contact, I slap my palm against the button, and the elevator jerks into motion.

I pull away just enough to whisper, "Do you taste yourself on me?"

"Yes."

"Just so you know, I'm going to want more of that. Every chance I get, I'm going to lick your pussy until you're crying, sobbing for relief."

As soon as the elevator doors open on the fourth floor, I sweep her into my arms and carry her down the hallway until we arrive at her apartment door. Her fingers tremble as she reaches into her purse to take out her keys. After a few fumbles with the lock, I snag the ring from her hand and insert the key before twisting the handle.

I carry her inside and close the door behind me.

"Are you still good with this?"

"Does it seem like I'm not?"

"No, but I just want to make sure. I promised you slow. This isn't exactly it."

"This pace seems perfect for us, don't you think?"

That's the crazy thing. "I do."

"And I appreciate you checking in and making sure I'm good." Our gazes cling. "Even though we haven't known each other long, I feel safe with you. You're the first person I've been with who's listened and really heard me. I feel like I can be honest, and you won't judge me."

"I would never do that." She drops her purse on the table as I carry her to the bedroom. "I know what it's like to be judged, and I'd never want to make anyone feel like that. Especially someone I care about."

Surprise flashes across her features as she searches my expression for the truth. "You care about me?"

"Yeah, I do. Like you said, it hasn't been all that long, but I can't deny what I feel. And I don't want to play games. Not with you."

Her eyes soften as her hand rises to cup my cheek. "It's the same for me. Whatever this is between us, I want it to be straight-forward. After all the head games in my past, that's what I need most."

"I get where you're coming from. And that's exactly what you'll get from me."

It's only when we reach her bedroom that I set her down gently on her feet. Her body slides against mine, igniting all those sparks of arousal that had flared to life earlier at the club and then in the elevator before our conversation turned serious.

"I want you to stay here tonight," she whispers, her warm breath feathering against my lips. "I want you to finish what you started."

One side of my mouth rises in a smirk before I press my lips against hers. "I think that can be arranged."

"I would be disappointed if it couldn't."

"I'd probably go home and beat off. A few times."

Her lips tremble with a smile. "Now that, I would like to see."

It's tempting to tell her about my side hustle, but I decide to save that for another time.

Tonight is about Ava.

Giving her all the pleasure she can take.

I need her to understand that she's not broken. Or some kind of deviant. She can enjoy what she craves without judgment.

I press one last kiss against her lips before murmuring, "Turn around."

Instead of questioning the directive, she spins in a semi-circle until the long line of her spine faces me.

"Hold up your hair, baby girl."

She gathers up the long strands of blonde hair in her hands as I tug the zipper down until the black material gapes open, revealing the creamy expanse of her back.

I didn't realize she wasn't wearing a bra.

With a glance over her shoulder, she meets my gaze before allowing her hair to spill from her fingers down her back in a golden waterfall. Then she shrugs out of the dress. The material slips down her slender body before puddling around her feet until she's in nothing but heels.

Fuck.

This girl is gorgeous.

I could soak in the sight of her for hours.

And maybe someday, I will. But not tonight.

My gaze slides down the length of her before settling on her ass. It's perfectly heart shaped. She's tight and muscular from hours spent on the ice.

The sight of her has my cock stiffening up even more, until it's borderline painful.

"You're so fucking beautiful."

I close the distance between us before dropping to my knees. My palms settle on each ass cheek, squeezing the firm flesh and massaging it with my hands. Her ass is like a juicy peach, and I just want to take a bite of it.

Actually, that's exactly what I'll do.

My teeth sink into the muscle before sucking at the skin. I want to mark this girl as my own.

Possessiveness rushes through me. I want every dude on this campus to understand that Ava Philips belongs to me.

It's not an emotion that's ever coursed through me before.

I've never liked anyone enough to claim them.

But that's exactly how I feel about her.

Whether she realizes it or not, she's mine now, and I'll do whatever it takes to keep her safe and happy. To fulfill her needs. Including the secret ones she's too ashamed to admit out loud.

I'll give her as much pleasure as she can withstand.

And then I'll ply her with more until she's drunk with it.

I haven't even been inside this girl and already I feel this territorial. I can't imagine what it'll be like when the heat of her body is wrapped around my dick like a glove.

"You're way too perfect," I murmur. "You know what you're going to do now?"

"No."

"Lie on the bed and spread your legs nice and wide so I can see every pink inch. Then I'm going to make a fucking meal of you because the taste I had in the elevator wasn't nearly enough to satiate me."

Her breath catches.

When she doesn't move, I smack her ass. "Now."

With a yelp, she jumps and kicks off her heels before scrambling to do my bidding.

I stifle a groan as she climbs onto the bed and her little rosebud winks at me. The fact that she admitted to wanting to try anal is enough to make me come all over myself. There's something different about being buried in a woman's tight ass rather than her pussy. Something so submissive and intimate about it. As much as I'd love to indulge in that tonight, it's not going to happen.

Maybe things are progressing faster than anticipated, but I'm not going to rush her. Ava is the one who sets the pace, and when she's ready for that kind of intimacy, she'll let me know.

Once she's reclined against the pillows, her gaze fastens to mine as her thighs fall open until they're touching the mattress, and I'm reminded of just how flexible she is.

"Damn, baby."

As hungry as I am to get my hands and mouth on her, I just want to take a moment and soak in the sight of her stretched out on the bed naked, waiting for me with her legs spread wide. My gaze drops to her pussy. It's already swollen and glistening from our earlier foreplay.

My mouth waters for a taste.

The silver that glints from between her lips is one of the sexiest things I've ever seen in my life. No matter how long I live, it's a mental snapshot I'll never forget.

"When you masturbate, do you play with your titties?"

Her tongue darts out to moisten her lips as she gives her head a quick shake.

"Why not?" I know how good it feels when I stroke my hands over my own chest. I imagine it would feel the same for her.

"I don't know. I guess I never thought about it."

I swallow up the space between us before settling on the edge of the bed near her outstretched legs. It takes every ounce of self-control not to reach out and stroke my hands over her center or bury my face between her legs and lap up the honey that glistens on her flesh.

"Maybe that's part of the problem. You need to touch yourself and get into the mood. What are you? A seventeen-year-old dude going straight for the goods?"

She snorts out a laugh. "I guess so."

"I want you to touch your breasts."

Her hands rise to cup the soft swells.

"Now squeeze them. Massage them."

Her expression relaxes, and I can tell she's enjoying it. As much as I want to be the one touching her, it's more important that she's able to do it for herself.

She should be able to pleasure her own body any damn time she wants or needs. She shouldn't have to wait for someone else to do it.

Or worse, ask someone only to have them judge her or not be able to get the job done properly.

"Feel good?"

"Yes." Her eyelids feather closed. As much as I want her looking at me, I want her to get lost in her pleasure even more.

"Pinch your nipples."

She tweaks the little buds between her thumb and forefinger.

"Now tug them."

The whimper that slips free from her is like a straight shot to my dick. I'm throbbing. It's tempting to take out my cock and stroke my hard length.

Instead, I keep my attention focused on her. "Tell me how your pussy feels."

"Achy."

"Good. I'm willing to bet it needs to be played with."

With a groan, she shifts. One hand trails down her ribcage and belly before arriving at her spread legs.

Again, it takes effort to hold myself back.

"Do you play with the piercing when you touch yourself?"

"Yes, but it only gets me so far." For the first time since we started, her brow furrows. "I can never quite get there."

"It's all right," I soothe, not wanting her to stress. "Let's test that theory. Keep massaging your breasts. Pinch your nipples. I bet they would look beautiful pierced."

"I thought about it."

That image has a groan rumbling up from deep in my chest.

"I want you to rub soft circles around your clit." My gaze stays focused on the wetness that gathers on her lips as she plays with herself. Her back arches ever so slightly off the mattress. "Does that feel good?"

"It does."

"Then keep doing it. Tug the piercing. Not too hard. Just enough to send waves of pleasure through you." I give her time to play. "I want you to caress your lips. Back and forth. Yes, that's it. Just like that."

Fuck.

If I'm not careful, I'm going to come.

I've never been so turned on in my life.

And that's saying something.

All it does is make me realize how special this girl is.

And how much I want to make her mine.

She might not realize it, but I'm already formulating plans in my head. Plans that would probably freak the fuck out of her if she knew. But that's all right... it can be my little secret.

I'm willing to bide my time.

For now.

I get lost in the movement of her fingers and all the cream she's rubbing around.

"That feels good, doesn't it?" My voice comes out sounding as if it's been roughed up by sandpaper. "Maybe I should check for myself." My hand wraps around hers before I lean forward and bring the digits to my lips, sucking them into my mouth to savor.

"Delicious." My tongue darts out to lick her fingers, not wanting to miss a single drop of her honey. "Do you think you can get there on your own or do you want help?"

Her brow furrows. "I need help."

"Okay. Pretty sure you know I'm happy to assist."

I twist and settle between her spread thighs before burying my face against the heat of her center and dragging my tongue from the bottom of her slit to her clit before flicking the silver piece of jewelry with tiny balls on each end. With a groan, her fingers tangle in my hair to hold me in place.

"Mmm, your pussy is drenched. You're the one who did that, baby. You just need a little more practice, and you'll be getting yourself off in no time."

"I hope so."

"You will be. Promise."

I lick every inch of her. When her muscles tighten, I know she's close. I keep my gaze locked on her face, wanting to see the moment she falls to pieces. When I draw the little ring into my mouth and suck it gently, she lifts her hips to press closer.

"Oh, Hayes..."

"Just let it happen, baby. You're safe with me."

My soft words are all it takes for her to shatter beneath my mouth.

She screams out her orgasm. It's the best damn sound in the world, and means more than any other girl who's ever cried out my name. I continue licking and sucking her shuddering flesh until her muscles loosen, and she sinks into the mattress, a boneless heap.

It's only when she's completely sated that I press my lips against her pussy one last time and then crawl up her body, stretching out on top of her before brushing my mouth against hers.

She searches my eyes. "Thank you. It's been a long time since I've orgasmed, and that felt amazing."

"No need to thank me. I loved helping you get there."

A satisfied smile curves her lips, and I love that even more. It's the first of its kind that I've seen from her, and in that moment, I know I'll do whatever it takes in the future to put that look on her face.

"What about you?"

"What about me?"

"I'd be more than happy to return the favor."

As tempting as it is, I shake my head. "Tonight was all about you, Tink. I'm going to take a raincheck."

Her brows rise. "Really?'

"Yeah." I glance at the clock. "In fact, I should probably get moving. I'm sure you need to get up early and be out the door for practice tomorrow morning. I don't want you to miss your ice time."

"What I really want is for you to stay."

"Are you sure?"

Her arms tighten around my neck. "Positive."

"Okay. I'll stay."

"Good."

When I don't move, she says, "Wouldn't you be more comfortable if you took off your clothes?"

"It has more to do with what you're comfortable with."

The corners of her lips quirk. "You just watched me masturbate—"

"And loved every minute of it."

She chuckles. "And then you were all up in my business."

"Have I mentioned how much I love being in your business and that I hope to do it again soon?"

"I liked it as well. That being said, I think you can take off your clothes."

I press another kiss against her lips before rolling from the bed and coming to my feet. "Okay. You've convinced me."

My gaze dips to her core, and I groan. "I'm gonna need you to cover that pretty little pussy, or I'll be all up in your business for a second time tonight."

"Don't you mean third?"

"Well, they do say the third time's a charm."

"I look forward to testing out that theory."

My hands settle at the hem of my gray Henley before dragging it up my body and over my head until I'm just as bare chested as she is. Now it's her gaze that dips. My muscles tense as I stand in place, allowing her to look her fill. The heat in her eyes nearly singes me alive.

"What about the jeans?"

I can't resist teasing her. "I was thinking of keeping them on."

"Off."

I jerk a brow. "Kind of bossy, aren't you?"

A smile tugs at the corners of her lips. "Maybe a little."

With a snort, my fingers drop to the button before flicking it open and dragging down the zipper. In one swift movement, I shove the denim down my thighs. Her attention drifts lower. It would be impossible to hide the boner that strains against the cotton of my underwear.

I love the feel of her eyes eating me up.

"You're really beautiful," she whispers.

"You stole my line. I was just thinking the same thing."

She slips between the sheets before tossing them back, an invitation for me to join her. Once I settle beside her, I pull her naked body against mine and wrap her up tight in my arms. That's when something deep inside me clicks into place.

A comfortable silence falls over us, and it doesn't take long before her breathing turns deep and even. I press my lips against her hair and draw in the subtle scent of the floral shampoo that clings to her.

For the first time in my life, complete contentment washes over me.

The feeling is just as addictive as she is.

And I don't want it to ever end.

AVA

I t's the bright sunlight filtering through the gauzy curtains of my bedroom window that pulls me from the best sleep I've had in a long time. As my eyelids flutter open, I'm slammed with two realizations.

The first is that I'm naked.

The second is that I'm not alone.

A warm body is pressed against me.

Not to mention, that body is hard.

Definitely hard.

Since waking up beside another person isn't a normal occurrence for me, I rack my brain to try to figure out what happened. It doesn't take long to remember making out with Hayes before being interrupted by Britt, Colby, Willow, and Maverick. We ended up at Blue Vibe, dancing the night away. Hayes pulling me up to the second floor and touching me flickers through my head like a slow-motion picture show.

The man has magic hands.

A shiver slides through me as a burst of heat dampens my core.

I crack open my eyelids and cautiously peek beneath the sheets.

While I'm naked, Hayes is still wearing a pair of black boxer briefs that hug his sculpted hips and ass. The man looks more like he was carved from marble than made of flesh and bone. He's so finely chiseled.

I know exactly the kind of time, commitment, and discipline

musculature like that takes. His physique wasn't achieved by spending an hour a day in the gym. More like hours on the ice and a few more spent in the weight room. And then cardio added to the regimen to increase stamina.

We didn't even make it up to the apartment before I'd been on him. As soon as the elevator doors closed, I was pressing him against the wall before he flipped us around. The way he'd knelt in front of me and taken my panties off while I'd held up my dress sends another burst of heat sizzling through my veins.

Just when I thought I'd find my release, he popped back to his feet and carried me to my apartment before stripping off my dress and watching me touch myself. Another thick shiver makes its way through me.

There's no way I should feel so comfortable with him.

But that doesn't erase the fact that I do.

I've confided my secrets to this man.

More than that, I trust him to keep them safe.

For the first time since my life imploded, I'm at peace with myself.

And that has everything to do with Hayes.

After he gave me the most delicious orgasm, we fell asleep wrapped up in each other's arms.

My gaze slides from his six pack abdominals to the broad expanse of his chest. Even when he's relaxed, everything is well defined. There's not an ounce of fat on him.

It's so tempting to reach out and run the tips of my fingers over every sinewy muscle.

"Whatever you're considering, you should do it."

I squeak as my gaze slices to his. His green eyes twinkle with both mischief and heat. It's a lethal combination. One that makes my pulse race.

He stretches his arms above his head, and all those mouthwatering muscles tighten and lengthen.

I wasn't lying last night when I called him beautiful.

He is.

Ridiculously so.

He folds his arms behind his head before stacking his hands beneath it. When his attention drops to my chest, I'm reminded of my naked state. As tempting as it is to cover myself, I resist the urge. The desire that darkens his eyes turns them a deep emerald hue.

There's something about the way this man stares at me that ignites a firestorm of need deep in my belly.

It's addictive.

Instead of overthinking matters, I pull myself up to a seated position and settle on top of him before straddling his thick thighs. His gaze stays pinned to mine as his hands remain behind his head. The only reactions I'm given are the tightening of his jaw and the tension that fills his muscles.

I still can't get over how much pleasure he showered me with last night, taking none for himself. It makes me want to give him just as much in return.

His boxers are tented in the front and already there's a damp spot on the cotton. I reach down and rub my finger over the wetness.

"You look good naked on top of me."

I flick my gaze to his. His eyelids are lowered to half-mast as he watches me.

Impatience to see every inch of him rushes through me, and I slip my fingers into the cotton before dragging it down so his erection can spring free. His cock is hot to the touch, and clear fluid beads from the slit as I stroke him.

My gaze clings to his as I lean forward and kiss the tip of his erection before nuzzling it. He's hard as steel and yet silky soft. I run the tip of my tongue from the bulbous head, down the length of his shaft, to the root before drifting lower to circle one ball and then the other. They're shaved clean and are smooth against my tongue.

When I suck one into my mouth, another groan explodes from him as he gently brushes the hair away from my eyes before tunneling his fingers through the thick strands.

"That feels amazing."

His breathing picks up tempo as I play with him. Arousal curls in the pit of my belly like a whisp of smoke, intensifying the ache in my core.

I release one ball with a soft pop before licking the other and giving it the same attention. Once my tongue dances over every inch of his sac, I kiss my way back up his cock and draw the tip between my lips. His fingers tighten around the sides of my head as his eyelids droop.

Each time I slide along the hard length, I take him deeper, until he nudges the back of my throat. Another groan rumbles up from within his chest as I keep up a steady rhythm.

"Fuuuuck."

With a tilt of his pelvis, he thrusts forward. When my mouth turns voracious, his muscles tense before he attempts to shove me away. Instead of allowing that to happen, I stare up at him as I continue sucking his dick.

"If you're not careful, you'll make me come," he mutters, jaw clenched. His voice is so tightly strung, it sounds as if it'll shatter into a million jagged pieces.

When his balls draw up against his body, I realize he's seconds away from finding his release. That's all it takes for me to double down on my efforts.

"Ava," he growls as the first drops of cum splash against the back of my throat, and I greedily swallow them down. His fingers sink into my scalp, holding me close as he orgasms. It's only after he softens that I set him free.

He reaches down, hooking his arms around my upper body, and hauls me upward until I'm fully stretched out on top of his body. The moment his mouth fastens to mine, I open so his tongue can delve inside to tangle with my own.

A few seconds later, I'm breathless.

He draws away just enough to stare into my eyes. "There's nothing sexier than the taste of me on your lips."

"I could say the same."

With a grin, he says, "Know what I could go for right about now?"

"Breakfast?"

"Well, I'm definitely hungry. But that's not exactly what I had in mind."

"Oh?"

I gasp when he rolls us over so he's on top. A wicked glint fills his green eyes. It's enough to make my belly swoop. He presses a kiss against my lips before working his way down my naked body. When he reaches my breasts, he draws one hard tip into his mouth until I'm squirming beneath him. My fingers tangle in his hair as he releases my nipple before sucking on the other. Need explodes through me as my core throbs a steady, insistent beat.

He descends, licking and sucking my flesh until arriving at the V between my legs. I can't help but spread them wider, giving him full access.

It's amazing how free and uninhibited I feel with Hayes. Like we've been together for months.

He wraps his hands around my inner thighs, spreading them even farther apart as he stares at me. I can practically feel the heat of his gaze sliding over my core as wetness gathers between my legs.

"Have I mentioned how fucking beautiful you are?"

"Maybe once or twice."

He flicks his gaze upward to meet my eyes. "Such a smart mouth."

"You certainly didn't have a problem with my smart mouth when it was wrapped around your cock."

He smirks before sinking his teeth into the delicate flesh of my inner thigh.

A moan breaks loose from me as I wriggle beneath his grip. His hands tighten, holding me firmly in place.

"I loved the way you sucked my dick almost as much as I enjoy eating your pussy."

He tongues the little piece of jewelry decorating my clit, circling it before drawing it into his mouth.

Barely has he touched me, and it feels like I'll go off like a rocket. Just when my muscles tighten, he pulls away.

"Ready for that breakfast?"

My eyes widen as I screech, "Are you being serious?"

"Nope. Not at all." He smirks before burying his face against my drenched flesh. A few lashes of his tongue and a tug of the piercing send me tumbling over the edge as I scream out my orgasm.

It's only when I huff out a contented breath that he presses a kiss against me.

"Now I'm ready to feed you."

AVA

27

The second our professor dismisses us for the evening, students scatter from the lecture hall like rats from a sinking ship. I close my laptop and shove it into my backpack, trying not to get caught up in the rush. As I sling the bag over my shoulder, a sense of relief washes over me, but it's quickly replaced by unease. It's always like this lately. My mind is never fully at peace.

I push through the glass doors of the building and step into the chilly night air. Even though the days are warming up, the evenings still have a bite to them, and I burrow deeper into the collar of my jacket as I make my way down the path toward my apartment. It's only a short walk—just a quarter mile from campus—but every step tonight feels heavier than the last.

As I pass by the humanities building, the sound of quick footsteps behind me makes my heart leap into my throat. My mind jumps to the worst-case scenario before I can stop it. My pulse races as I swing around, half-expecting to find the man who refuses to stay buried in my past.

But it's not him.

It's just a guy from class jogging to catch up with the girl in front of me. He drops his arm around her shoulders, and they continue walking, laughing and chatting like they don't have a care in the world. My stomach is a tangle of knots as I force out a slow breath. I'm constantly on edge, waiting for the worst to happen.

It's exhausting.

I hate how jumpy I've become, how every little thing has me thinking about Nathan, about the messages he keeps sending. I thought severing our connection and moving across the country would be enough. Every time my phone vibrates, I wonder if it's him again. If he's still there, lurking in the background of my life, refusing to let me move on.

I'm so fucking tired of Nathan controlling my every waking thought when he's more than likely half a dozen states away, teaching learn-to-skate classes in a small town where no one knows who he is or what he did.

The couple ahead of me turns to the left as I move in the opposite direction.

My shoulders droop with the realization that it might be time to return to therapy. Clearly, I haven't worked through everything like I'd hoped.

I keep my pace steady, though the prickling sensation of being watched lingers, making the hairs on the back of my neck stand on end. The blue safety lights lining the path do little to offer comfort. They're more like spotlights, illuminating my presence as I hurry past.

When a twig snaps to my left, fear crashes over me. My heart kicks into overdrive as I whip around and scan the darkness for signs of movement.

Could someone be hiding there?

My mouth turns bone dry.

The thought of Nathan, or anyone, following me, makes my chest tighten until I can't breathe.

Can't think straight.

It's all too much.

I don't want to continue feeling paranoid. Like I'm always looking over my shoulder, waiting for the past to catch up with me.

I'm kicking myself for not taking my car.

For trying to prove a point.

All I've done is freak the fuck out of myself.

I quicken my pace, gripping the straps of my backpack tighter, as if that'll somehow anchor me. The glow from campus begins to fade as I enter the residential area where I live. Greek row is right around the corner. Tons of parties take place here every weekend. But tonight is Tuesday, and it's quiet. There's not a soul on the street.

I peek over my shoulder again.

There's no one.

But that doesn't stop the odd sensation of being watched—*followed*—from invading my brain.

As I reach the next block, I realize that Hayes's house isn't far. It's closer than my apartment.

I'll stop there.

Even if he's not home, I can collect my scattered thoughts and rein in the terror flooding my bloodstream.

If I'm lucky, one of the girls will be there, and I can cajole them into driving me back to my apartment.

This exercise in trying to take a little control back from Nathan has totally backfired.

It's also made me realize just how paranoid I've become.

As loath as I am to bring him up to my parents, maybe it's time to tell them what's going on. For my own personal well-being and mental health, I can't live like this.

I walk faster, my breathing ragged from the cold air and the adrenaline spiking through my veins. As soon as the two-story blue Victorian comes into view, relief crashes over me.

Thank fuck.

I race across the front lawn before taking the rickety porch stairs two at a time. By now, I'm huffing and puffing. With my heart hammering in my chest, I press the doorbell and glance around. Other than the sound of passing traffic from a street over and the lone cry of a cat, there's nothing. But still, I can't shake the odd sensation that someone is stalking me from the shadows.

My Spidey senses are on high alert.

Is it nothing more than a trick of my imagination?

That's the problem.

I don't know.

And I'm unwilling to take a chance and find out.

Fear threatens to swallow me whole as I shift from one foot to the other. When there's no response, I rap the beveled glass with my knuckles. The lights are on, and music and laughter can be heard from inside the house.

Just as I raise my hand for a second time, the front door swings open, and Bridger Sanderson stares back at me from the other side of the threshold.

A chin lift accompanies his greeting. "Hey."

I glance past him, hoping to spot Hayes inside. "Hi."

With a tilt of his head, he narrows his eyes. "Aren't you Coach's daughter?"

I blink, thrown off by the question. "Um, yeah. Ava."

"Right." He doesn't move from where he's planted in front of the door. "So... what brings you to the hockey house, *Ava*?" Extra emphasis is placed on my name.

I shift my weight, feeling the uncomfortable heat of embarrassment creep into my cheeks. "Is Hayes here?" As casual as I'm trying to sound, a thin waver threads its way through my voice.

Bridger crosses his arms over his chest as his brows shoot up. "You're here to see Hayes?"

It would be impossible to miss the surprise in his voice.

"Yeah. Is he here or not?" For the first time, it makes me question the impulsive decision to stop by unannounced.

He gives me a long, considering look before stepping aside. "He's hanging out in his room. Go on up. Second door on the left."

It's on the tip of my tongue to ask if he's alone, but I can't force the words past my lips. Once the idea pops into my brain, it's impossible to shake loose.

I jerk my head in a tight nod before slipping past him, grateful he doesn't ask any further questions, but his parting words stop me in my tracks.

"Coach wouldn't like you hanging out here."

My spine stiffens before I turn back to meet his brooding gaze.

"Then you should probably do us both a favor and keep that info to yourself."

He presses his lips into a tight line and glares before turning toward the living room without another word.

With my heart lodged in my throat, I hurry up the stairs. Each step has more doubt creeping in at the edges. After the closeness we've shared, finding him with another girl would be devastating. By the time I reach the second-floor landing, I'm positive that's exactly what will happen.

What the hell had I been thinking getting involved with Hayes Van Doren?

Maybe he's turned out to have more depth than I expected, but does that really matter when he's a known player?

As I swing a left at the top of the stairs, my gaze lands on his door as it looms in front of me. My hand hovers in the air, but I can't bring myself to knock and discover the truth.

That I've been played.

I lean in, pressing my ear against the thick wood.

Not a sound can be heard from inside.

No voices.

No laughter.

Just silence.

I chew my lower lip before wrapping my fingers around the knob and turning it. The door creaks as I cautiously push it open. It's entirely possible that my heart is lodged somewhere in the middle of my throat.

The sight that greets me has my eyes widening and air stalling in my lungs.

Hayes is alone, lying naked on the bed.

The terror and concern from seconds ago melt away as my greedy gaze rakes over the length of him.

The man really does have a spectacular body.

His eyes are closed, and earbuds are shoved in his ears. Even if I'd knocked, he probably wouldn't have heard me. One of his brawny arms is tucked behind his head while his other hand grips his erection. His palm slides along the thick shaft. It takes a handful of seconds to realize that a laptop is on the chair near his bed and angled toward his torso.

Wait a minute...

Is he jerking off on camera?

My hand rises to my mouth as my eyes stay locked on the scene playing out in front of me.

I couldn't yank them away even if I tried.

Footsteps on the staircase catch my attention, and I slip farther inside the room before quietly closing the door. My spine hits the wall as I stand perfectly still, afraid to move a muscle.

When he arches, I realize how close to coming he is, and arousal explodes deep inside me.

His grip tightens, and a groan falls from his lips as the first spurts of cum erupt from the tip of his cock and land on his lower belly. My core shudders as my panties flood with heat. My mind tumbles back to the other morning when I'd taken him in my mouth. Memories of what he'd tasted like whip through me, and the urge to lick up all the pearly white fluid prods me into movement.

Before I can act on my impulse, his muscles loosen, and his eyelids flutter open. My heartbeat stalls as his heavy-lidded gaze slices to mine.

He freezes, and the energy in the room turns charged.

TENINCHESOF
COCKY

WILDCATS

I blink.

It's tempting to rub my eyes until the image of Ava dissolves, because there's no damn way she's standing in my room, staring at me in shock.

After I jacked off.

Online.

Fuck.

That thought spurs me into action as I roll to the edge of the mattress before ending the live feed and slamming the laptop shut.

Unsure what to say, I blurt, "What are you doing here?"

"I... needed to see you."

Before I can come up with anything else to say, she swallows up the distance between us and reaches out to run her finger through the jizz on my stomach.

My breath catches as she brings the digit to her mouth and sucks it.

Holy crap.

Her eyelids drift closed. "You taste just as good as I remember."

That throaty comment is all it takes for my cock to stir back to life.

She drops her backpack to the floor before unzipping her jacket and sliding the thick material from her shoulders. Then she toes off her shoes before climbing onto the mattress and crawling up my body until she's hovering over my groin. With her gaze pinned to mine, she laps up the sticky fluid. The velvety softness of her tongue slides over my lower abdomen until she's cleaned up the mess I made.

Holy shit. I don't think I've ever been more turned on in my life.

Until she kisses the tip of my dick and draws the hardening length between her pouty lips.

My eyes roll to the back of my head, and a groan rumbles up from deep within my chest.

Fuck, her mouth is heaven.

She slides down my cock before returning to the tip. I almost grieve when she allows the head to pop free. Until her tongue dances down the length to my balls. She circles one and then the other before drawing it into her mouth.

A garbled sound escapes from me. She releases one with a soft pop before giving the same attention to the other.

It's official.

Bury me now.

I've died and gone to heaven.

She licks around my clean-shaven sac before returning to the crown of my cock and drawing it back into the warm haven of her mouth.

If I could live in this moment for the rest of my life, I would.

It's that fucking amazing.

Unable to stand another second of this torment, I force myself to sit up before wrapping my hands around her ribcage. Once she releases my dick, I drag her up my body until she's stretched out on top of me.

Her gaze stays fastened to mine. "You didn't like that?"

"I think we both know I liked it a little too much. When I come again, it's going to be inside your sweet little cunt."

My dirty words have her pupils dilating.

And I love that as well.

This girl is so damn perfect.

I don't think I'll ever get enough of her.

That thought should have alarm bells ringing in my head.

What does it mean that they're not?

Instead, calmness falls over me as that knowledge settles deep inside my being.

I shove it from my head as I stare into her blue eyes, unwilling to inspect it any closer.

It's always been my family and hockey, without room for anything else. And it was enough. No one ever came close to touching that.

But that's no longer the case.

"I think you might be wearing too much clothing."

"Hmmm. That sounds like a problem. One you should do something about."

I smirk. "There's that sassy mouth again."

"Wouldn't you agree that a sassy mouth is much better at sucking cock?"

Yup... she's perfect.

In one smooth movement, I flip our positions. She gasps as I hover over her and take control of the situation. My mouth crashes onto hers. One sweep of my tongue against her lips and she opens so I can plunge inside. All I want to do is devour this girl in one tasty gulp.

But first things first. I need to strip off the clothing that keeps her gorgeous body from me.

My lips trail from her mouth to her chin before I scrape my teeth along the curve of her jaw. As I sink lower, she bares the delicate hollow of her throat. I press a kiss against the pulse that flutters madly like the wings of a hummingbird beneath. When I reach her collarbone, I'm met with the soft fabric of her sweater. I rise to my knees as my fingers grip the hem and drag it up her body and over her head.

It's a pleasant surprise to find she's not wearing anything beneath.

I flick a glance upward. "Where's your bra?"

"I don't always wear one." She glances at her breasts. "I don't exactly have a lot going on there."

My attention returns to her chest before my hands settle on the rounded softness, tweaking her nipples until they stiffen right up.

"They're perfect."

She arches into my palms as I toy with them.

"You like that, baby girl?"

"I do. They're sensitive, and I love having them played with."

I used to think my type was top heavy, like a dime. Turns out that's not the case. I love that Ava is toned and athletic. She might be petite and delicate looking, but it's misleading.

Both her mind and body are strong.

And there's nothing sexier than that.

I tease the tiny buds until she's writhing beneath me. Only then do I suck one stiff peak between my lips before giving the same attention to the other. As tempting as it is to continue tormenting her, I'm hungry for more. It's been way too long since I've had the taste of this girl on my tongue.

And I'm fucking famished.

I crawl down the length of her body, kissing and licking as I go, until I reach the waistband of her jeans. My gaze settles on hers as I flick open the button and lower the zipper. After tugging the denim down her hips and thighs, I raise one leg and then the other until the thick material is stripped away.

The only thing that bars her from my sight is a flimsy scrap of silky material.

For just a second, I sit back and allow my gaze to rove over her.

She's gorgeous with her golden hair spread out around her and the tips of her breasts in pouty little points. Her eyelids are lowered to half-mast, and her lips are already swollen from my kisses.

My cock throbs a painful beat as my gaze drops to the pale-pink material. I'm impatient to be inside her. I slip my fingers beneath the fabric before lowering them over the gentle flair of her hips and thighs. I want to stretch this moment out for as long as possible.

The sweet anticipation of it.

As soon as her mound comes into view, I place a chaste kiss against the bared flesh. She shifts, her breath catching in a soft whimper.

My guess is that it's not enough.

For either of us.

I lower the fabric a little more and repeat the caress. This time, I slip my tongue between her silky lips. Already they're drenched. I want nothing more than to lick up all that delicious cream.

Every fucking drop.

And then I want to make her sob all over again.

Unable to resist, I tongue the tiny silver hoop.

I wasn't kidding that night at her apartment when I said her nipples would look good pierced.

I'd have her in a fucking matching set.

And nothing more.

"Hayes, please…" Her voice trails off on a moan.

I glance up and meet her gaze.

There's nothing I love more than unraveling this girl.

"Please what, baby? What do you need from me? You know I'm happy to give you anything you want."

I've never meant anything more.

Her cheeks are flushed a pretty pink color, and her pupils look as if they've been blown out. I fucking love that I'm the one who can put that expression on her face.

"Remove the panties. Please."

"Well, since you asked so nicely." I straighten before dragging the scrap of material down her legs and tossing it to the floor so she's completely bared to my greedy sight.

My guess is that she's just as needy as I am.

Before I can ask, she spreads her legs wide until her knees hit the mattress, putting her gorgeous pussy on full display. I can't resist running my thumb over the silky folds that glisten with arousal. It's enough to make my mouth water.

Have I mentioned how flexible she is?

Fuck me.

I use both thumbs to pull her delicate lips farther apart so I can peek inside. It wasn't all that long ago that I jerked off. And now I'm ready to go off like a shot again.

It wouldn't take much.

A pump.

Maybe two.

Especially with that gorgeous view burned into my brain for all eternity.

I haven't even really touched her clit yet, and it's already swollen. The silver piece of jewelry glints from where it's nestled. I can't help but swipe my thumb over it before rubbing it in soft circles. Her hips jerk, and her spine arches until she's pressing herself into my touch.

"So fucking greedy, aren't you?"

"Yes." A fine tremble weaves its way through her voice.

"Tell me, will just any man's cock do?"

When she groans, I give her clit a tap. I know exactly how sensitive she is. Especially with the piercing. All I want to do is tease out her pleasure. By the expression on her face, that's exactly what I've done. I fucking love how responsive she is to my touch.

I stroke her clit. "I'm still waiting for an answer."

"Just yours."

"Good girl." When I swat the top of her slit for a second time, another whimper escapes from her. "You like that, don't you?"

Her teeth scrape across her lower lip as I stroke her sensitive flesh.

She's even creamier than before.

"You don't have to be embarrassed about the things you crave in bed. I want to give you all of it—everything you like. I'm going to take such good care of that little pussy. She'll cry every time you think about me."

Ava squeezes her eyes shut.

And that won't do.

I slap the top of her slit for a third time. "When I'm playing with your body, I want your eyes pinned to me so you can see the man between your thighs, giving you all this pleasure. When we're in bed together, there's nothing to be embarrassed about. Someone stole your power, and now you're going to reclaim it. Understand?"

Her eyelids fly open as intensity brews in her blue eyes, and she jerks her head in a tight nod. "Yes."

"Good."

I press a finger deep inside her drenched entrance. "Does your pussy need to be eaten?"

"Yes. That's exactly what it needs."

I give her a few slow pumps with my finger before withdrawing and lowering my face to her core. By now she's dripping.

With my gaze fastened to hers, I run the flat of my tongue from the bottom of her slit to her clit, licking up all the cream before circling the piercing with my tongue.

"You've made a real mess. All this sticky honey everywhere."

"It's your fault. You turn me on and make me that way."

"Mmm. I like the sound of that." A growl rumbles up from somewhere deep inside me as I lap her shuddering softness.

When she squirms, I wrap my hands around her inner thighs to hold her in place. This is exactly how I like her. The only thing better would be if she were pinned to the mattress with my cock.

"Please, Hayes... I need more."

I circle her swollen clit with the tip of my tongue. When her muscles tighten, I realize how close she is to finding her release. And I love that too. How easy it is to bring her to the precipice. Instead of allowing her to come, I pull back and leave her hanging.

A garbled protest catches in her throat.

Before she can ask any questions, I flip her over and drag her to the edge of the bed. "On your knees, baby girl."

She lies there, breathing hard. I slap one firm ass cheek and then the other. The resounding cracks shatter the silence of the room. With a squeak, she scrambles to do my bidding.

I rise to my feet and take up my position behind her. I massage her ass cheeks, tugging and stretching the rounded flesh. My palm settles between her shoulder blades as I press her chest to the mattress until it becomes necessary for her to turn her head so the side of her face rests against the navy comforter.

My gaze flicks to her backside.

"Spread your legs wider. I want to see both of those pretty holes."

Even though her breath catches, she does exactly as I ask.

She's so damn beautiful.

And mine.

Whether she understands it or not, this girl now belongs to me.

And I'll do whatever it takes to keep her.

The tips of my fingers caress her pussy. Even though I lapped up all her cream minutes ago, she's already soaked again. I continue stroking her flesh, gathering up her arousal before sliding my hand upward until one finger can settle over her tight little rosebud. Her body stills and her breath hitches. I watch her closely while massaging the puckered ring of muscle.

"Do you want me to touch you here?"

"Yes."

"If there's something you don't like, it's important that you tell me. All right? I don't want to do anything you're not comfortable with."

Her teeth scrape across her plump lower lip.

I press my face against her pussy and tongue it until her legs are shaking.

My warm breath whispers across her drenched flesh. "There's no judgment here. I want to give you everything you crave. Everything you need. I can't do that unless you're honest with me."

"I like what you're doing. It's been a really long time since anyone played with my body like this, and I miss it. But there's a part of me that feels bad for enjoying it. Like maybe Nathan saw something depraved in me."

"He couldn't possibly have known that. Your sexual preferences are what you enjoy, and it's nothing to be ashamed of. You need to let go of your guilt and simply embrace what turns your body on."

My teeth scrape across the curve of her ass cheek before I press my finger deeper inside her body. Her breathing picks up tempo as I advance and then withdraw, gradually falling into a steady rhythm. It doesn't take long before her muscles relax around the foreign intrusion.

"Does that feel good, baby girl?"

"It feels amazing," she says on a breathless sigh.

I fucking hate her coach for what he did to her. The ideas he drilled into her head. The way he made her feel guilty for enjoying the things he introduced her to. It's so damn twisted.

This girl should be worshipped.

More than that, she deserves every bit of pleasure she craves.

And from now on, I'll be the one who showers her with it. And I'll never make her feel bad or guilty for enjoying it.

When I remove my finger, a whimper trembles on her lips. I pull her cheeks apart to inspect her perfect rosebud. She has such a tiny gape.

"You really are gorgeous."

I massage both cheeks as I lean forward and lick her pretty little back hole.

When the tip of my tongue slips inside, she releases a soft moan, but she doesn't try to escape the intimacy. Instead, she strains closer.

When her cries turn to sobs, I give her one final lap before rising to my feet. My cock feels more like stone than flesh.

Thank fuck she's so close to coming because I have no idea how long I'm going to last.

I grab a condom from a drawer in the nightstand and tear the wrapper before sliding it over my hard length. Then I take up position behind her. She hasn't moved a single muscle. I swat one ass cheek and then the other before fisting my cock and lining it up with her drenched entrance. My finger slips back inside her rosebud as I surge forward and bury myself balls deep. I withdraw and repeat the movement.

I've never felt anything better than her tight heat strangling my dick. It's like coming home to a place I didn't realize I was missing.

Fuck.

Fuck.

Fuck.

Both my finger and cock fall into the same steady rhythm. It doesn't take long before her inner muscles contract around my hard length, squeezing the very life out of me. That's when I lose it, following her over the edge and into the abyss. The way she screams out my name only intensifies my pleasure. Stars dance behind my eyelids, and it's entirely possible the tip of my cock just blew off.

If that turns out to be the case, this experience will have been entirely worth it.

Zero regrets.

On the last thrust, my muscles loosen, and I collapse along the curve of her body. Our harsh breaths mingle together, becoming one, as I stay wrapped up in her sweet heat.

No matter how amazing the sex I've had in the past has been, nothing compares to this.

The kind of intimacy we've shared isn't possible with a one-night stand.

Maybe I wasn't ready for it before.

But I am now.

With Ava.

As I crash back to earth, my gaze settles on her face, needing to know I'm not the only one who had an out-of-body experience. Instead of the blissed-out expression I was hoping to find, she stares sightlessly at the far wall. I have no idea what thoughts are tumbling through her head.

And that's scary.

"Are you okay?" My chest constricts as my muscles tighten, bracing for her response. "Did I hurt you?" My voice dips as uncertainty gnaws at me. "Or do something you didn't want?"

With a blink, she turns her head just enough to meet my gaze.

And then does the last thing I expect.

She bursts into tears.

AVA

29

I have no idea where all the pent-up emotions come from. One minute, I'm enjoying the afterglow of the best sex I've ever experienced, and the next, I'm bawling.

Hayes's reaction is almost comical.

His eyes widen to the point of looking like they might fall out of his head before he pulls out of my body, then wraps the condom in tissue and throws it in the trash can near his desk.

Only then does he haul me into his arms.

"Tell me what I did, and I swear I'll never do it again." He rains soft kisses against the crown of my head. "Jeez, Ava. Tell me. Your tears are fucking killing me."

Even though I'm overflowing with emotion, I'm not sure how to put any of it into words. At least not ones that will make sense.

It continues to come out in a torrent of sobs.

"I-I'm sorry," I say when I'm finally able to speak.

"Baby, you don't have anything to be sorry about. I just want you to tell me what I did to cause this kind of reaction."

"You didn't do anything." I pause and rethink that statement. "Actually, you did everything."

"Fuck," he groans. "I knew it."

I chuckle weakly. "That's not what I meant."

Most guys would be jumping out of bed and gathering up their clothing to escape the awkwardness of this situation—especially being the first time we slept together. It would be the last time I saw them before they ghosted me.

What they wouldn't do is attempt to get to the bottom of what's going on.

At every turn, Hayes manages to surprise me.

"Ava, please. Would you just spit it out? I'm dying over here."

I draw in an unsteady breath, holding it captive in my lungs before gradually releasing it back into the atmosphere. It's important to take the time to gather my thoughts in order to explain them properly.

This man, above everyone, deserves the truth.

"Nathan was my first relationship—"

"It wasn't a relationship," he interrupts with a frown. "It was an abuse of power."

Everything inside me wilts. "I know."

It's taken a long time for me to come to terms with that knowledge. For whatever reason, it was easier to accept that I was eighteen years old and made the choice to get involved with my coach as a mature adult. I didn't want to believe that someone I loved and trusted took advantage of and manipulated me into doing something I didn't want.

It's a bitter pill to swallow.

"Whatever you want to call it, he was the only one I'd been with long term. There were a few guys after..." My voice trails off as I jerk my shoulders. "They made me feel bad for wanting certain things. And I began to wonder if I was normal. Especially when I couldn't get off from just regular sex."

His mouth drifts across my forehead. "You know that's not true. No one should have made you feel that way because you're more adventurous in the bedroom. I fucking love it."

My lips lift into a slight smile as I meet his earnest gaze. "I get that now."

He tugs me closer, wrapping me up in his arms. They have the rare ability to make me feel protected and safe. "I like every damn thing about you."

That admittance is all it takes for the tension swirling through my body to dissipate, leaving behind something I've spent the last year searching for.

Contentment.

We fall into a comfortable silence as my fingertips drift across his chest before I still. "So... are you going to tell me about what I walked in on earlier?"

When he releases a deep breath, I wonder if he'll bother with a response.

It would be a major disappointment considering I just experienced the best sex of my life and spilled my guts to this guy.

Honestly, if that happens, then I need to seriously rethink—

"Remember when you asked me about my job, and I said it was something online?"

My eyes widen as I jerk upright before swiveling to face him. "You get paid to jerk off online?"

Humor simmers in his green eyes. "If you want to bottom line it like that, then sure, I get paid to jerk off online. Although, I prefer to think about it as empowering people to live out their sexual fantasies."

My head spins with this revelation.

Some of the humor falls away from his expression as he searches my eyes. "Does it change what you think of me?"

My brows shoot up before I slowly shake my head. "Of course not. Why would it?"

He shrugs. "I don't know. It's not exactly something to be proud of."

"The fact that you're a full-time college student and a Division I athlete who's doing everything he can to take care of his family is admirable." I can't help but flash a grin as I tuck a stray lock of hair behind my ear. "Now that I've seen the goods up close and personal, I'm sure women are throwing a ton of money your way."

"Not to brag, but there are a few men as well."

A gurgle of laughter bursts from me. "That doesn't surprise me." There's a pause. "Does your mom know?"

His eyes widen as horror flashes across his face. "Hell no! She wouldn't accept a single dime if she even suspected where the money came from. She'd go out and get a second job just to make ends meet. Then the kids would never see her, and they'd have to raise themselves. That's the last thing my dad would have wanted." He shakes his head. "Next year, all of this will be a distant memory. I'll sign my contract with Nashville, and my family will have everything they need. More than what they need. Mom won't have to work her fingers to the bone, and everything will finally be good again."

My heart constricts at the earnestness in his voice.

That's all it takes for the last of the walls I've built around myself to tumble. It's also the moment I realize how hard I've fallen for him.

My fingers drift across his cheek before tracing his soft lips. His gaze stays locked on mine as he kisses them.

"You're a good man, Hayes Van Doren."

"Shhh. Don't tell anyone."

The corners of my lips hitch as I snort. "Don't worry. No one would believe me even if I did."

VAN DOREN
19

HAYES

I bring the steaming cup of coffee to my mouth and watch Ava as she glides effortlessly across the ice, her movements smooth and graceful. The way she skates is mesmerizing—almost as if she was born to do this, her ability innate. She executes a perfect spin, the same one from the photo I saw at her apartment. She's poetry in motion, a force to be reckoned with.

I could stand here for hours and watch her.

It's wild how much I've grown to care about this girl in such a short period of time. She's everything I didn't know I was looking for. Hell, I didn't even think I was looking for anything.

But Ava is different.

The connection between us is impossible to ignore.

She's burrowed beneath my skin, and I can no longer imagine my life without her in it.

Does she feel the same?

I really fucking hope so.

Each time we're together, I find myself revealing little pieces of who I am. The ones I don't allow anyone else to see. Not my teammates or my family. I've never felt so in tune with another person.

It's like she was made for me. Ava might have doubts when it comes to her sexual preferences, but I don't have any. When we're in bed together, I try to show her exactly how perfectly suited we are to one another.

She doesn't judge me for my past or for being here on a scholarship. I have plenty of teammates who were given money to play hockey at Western, but most don't need it to attend. It's more like the sweet cherry on top of a sundae.

The difference is that I wouldn't be here without it.

And she doesn't look down on me for the way I choose to support my family.

The fact that she accepts me for who I am means more than I ever imagined possible.

For the first time in my life, I've found someone I can be myself with. I don't have to pretend everything is a cakewalk or that nothing bothers me.

My heart catches when she leaps into the air, spinning before landing on one blade like it's nothing. I shake my head, awed by her talent. There's no doubt in my mind that Ava should be competing on a national level.

I understand the reasons why she stepped away from the figure skating world. After the scandal broke, the unwanted attention and scrutiny put her life under the microscope. What I hate is that she's allowed the past to dictate her future and steal her passion and joy. I can't imagine what it would be like to walk away from hockey.

It's in my blood.

A part of me.

Isn't competing the same for her?

Just as I'm about to take another sip of coffee, I catch movement from the corner of my eye, and it draws my attention. For the first time, I notice we're not alone. There's a guy standing near the edge of the rink, too far away for me to get a good look at his face. There's a ball cap pulled low over his brow, and something about him doesn't sit right with me. He's definitely not one of the usual staff or custodians who work this early.

My gut twists with unease as I watch him pull out his phone and lift it toward the ice.

What the hell?

Is he taking pictures of her?

I jump to my feet, the coffee forgotten as I move toward the guy.

As soon as he notices me, he tucks his phone back into his hoodie and walks away. The way he moves is too fast to be casual.

"Hey!" I shout, but he doesn't look back.

Without thinking, I break into a jog, determined to catch up with him. My heart pounds, not from exertion but from the realization that this could be her former coach.

As I push through the exit and into the hallway, I scan the empty space.

I grind my teeth, frustration bubbling up inside me as I take off down the corridor.

A faint whistling catches my ear, and I whip around the corner just as Tony walks by with his broom.

"Whoa!" His hands land on my arms as we nearly collide. "Where are you off to in such a hurry?"

"Sorry," I mutter, glancing past him. "Any chance you saw a guy walk by?"

With a frown, he shakes his head. "Nope. I clocked in about fifteen minutes ago, and you're the first person I've run into. Is there a problem?"

I clench my jaw, unsure what to say. "I don't know. I saw someone who didn't look familiar. It just seemed weird this early in the morning. He took off before I could talk to him."

Tony scratches his chin as his frown deepens. "You think someone was here messing around? I'll keep an eye out."

"I'd appreciate that." I force a smile, trying to shake off the thick tension that has gathered in my muscles. "Thanks, man."

He pats my shoulder. "It's not a problem. Maybe you should let Coach know. Can't be too careful these days."

I nod, though the last thing I want to do is bring this up to Coach. Not yet, anyway. "I'll be sure to do that."

My mind spins as I walk back to the rink. When I'm halfway there, it occurs to me that maybe I shouldn't have left Ava alone. What if that was Nathan and he drew me away in order to isolate her?

And I fell for it hook, line, and sinker.

The thought makes my stomach churn, and it's enough to have

me picking up my pace. By the time I burst through the door into the arena, my heart is pounding against my ribcage. Relief floods me when I catch sight of Ava gliding across the ice, seemingly unaware of what happened. Once she spots me, she skates over. Her cheeks are flushed from exertion as a small smile tugs at her lips.

"Where'd you disappear to?" she asks, planting her hands on her hips.

"Had to use the john," I lie, trying to keep my tone casual. "Are you ready to head out?"

The arena has always been a safe space for me, but that's not how it feels at the moment. I just want to get her out of here.

"Yup."

"Good. Let's get moving."

She raises a brow. "Hmmm... Who's the bossy one now?"

Despite my lingering unease, her teasing tone melts the tension coiled tight inside me. I can't help the smirk that tugs at my lips. "You haven't seen anything yet."

"Promise?"

"Yeah, Tink," I murmur, stepping closer. "It's definitely a promise."

Her laughter echoes through the empty arena as she reaches out and tugs on my hoodie, pulling me toward the bench where she's left her skate guards and duffel. The easy banter between us feels natural, like we've known each other far longer than just a few weeks.

The sense of protectiveness I feel toward her settles deep in my chest as she packs up her bag. I debate whether to tell her what I saw before nixing the idea and deciding to keep what happened to myself. At least for the time being. For all I know, it was nothing. A weird coincidence. She's got enough on her plate without worrying about some random creep.

But I'll be more vigilant from here on out.

I'm not about to let anything happen to my girl.

Once we're out of the arena and walking toward the parking lot, Ava glances at me, her expression softening.

"Thanks for coming with me."

"Anytime." I slide my hand into hers and give it a gentle squeeze. "I enjoy watching you skate. You're so damn talented."

Her eyes sparkle in the early morning light. "I think you might be biased."

"Nope. Not at all."

As we reach my truck, I realize that I don't just *like* being around Ava.

I need it.

I need *her*.

AVA

I tap on the frosted glass of Dad's office door before pushing it open. The familiar sound of game film plays in the background. Dad sits in his chair, eyes glued to the screen as he studies the plays. The moment he sees me, he clicks off the video and turns with a smile.

"Hey, sweetheart," he says, glancing at his watch. "I didn't think you'd be here for another twenty minutes."

"The professor let us out early." I drop my backpack to the floor and settle on the seat across from him. "So I came straight over."

"Good to know I'm getting my money's worth for your education."

I smirk. "Thanks to your position at Western, I'm getting a free ride, so you really can't complain."

"Hmm. Guess you're right. Speaking of classes, how are they going this semester?"

"They're fine," I say with a noncommittal shrug, avoiding his probing gaze. His desk is cluttered with papers, the remnants of what looks like an intense game analysis. His laptop is open next to his desktop, and I can see a familiar spreadsheet on the screen with stats and player rankings.

The disarray makes me itch to straighten it out, but I resist the urge. I learned enough in therapy to understand that controlling my surroundings is one way I cope when everything feels like it's falling apart.

"Any closer to figuring out a major?" Dad presses. "You're almost through your first year. It's about time to decide, don't you think?"

I shift on the chair. "No, I haven't made any decisions."

Even though I'm twenty-one years old, I only started college last fall, which makes me a freshman. Most of my classes are general education. Biology, English, math, psychology, and a graphic arts class.

The concern lurking in his eyes has guilt mushrooming up inside me for not having an answer. For not having my life figured out. For still being a mess.

"You could always visit the career counseling center and speak to someone."

I shake my head, brushing off the suggestion. "I'm not interested in talking to anyone else." I force myself to add, "At least not right now."

Just as he's about to push the subject, the door swings open and Mom breezes in, a large paper bag in her hands and a bright smile on her face.

"Hi!" she chirps, setting the bag down on Dad's desk. "I didn't think you'd beat me here! I thought you had class."

"He let us out early," I repeat, my tone softening as I watch her move around the room. There's a certain warmth to my mom that makes everything seem a little less overwhelming.

"Perfect timing!" She plants a quick kiss on Dad's cheek.

They've always been so in love. Always holding hands or sitting next to one another. There were times when I'd walk into the kitchen and find them hugging or kissing. When I was younger, their affectionate displays embarrassed me. I remember grumbling under my breath that they needed to keep their hands to themselves. Now, I think it's sweet that after twenty-five years, they're still so in love.

Mom turns to me, brushing a few loose strands of hair away from my face before kissing my forehead. The gesture is so familiar and comforting, that some of the tension drains from my body.

She unpacks the subs, placing them on the desk next to the drinks. Turkey and swiss for Dad, tuna for her, and an Italian for me.

The smell makes my stomach rumble, and we settle into a familiar rhythm of conversation while eating.

Dad doesn't bring up my lack of major again, and for that, I'm grateful. The pressure to figure out my path forward weighs heavily on me. It feels like my entire life has been about skating, and now that it's gone, I have no idea what to fill the void with.

The thought leaves me feeling empty.

Adrift.

It doesn't take Dad long to demolish his sandwich, and soon he's finishing off half of Mom's as well. The casual banter shifts to hockey, with Dad detailing the upcoming schedule, and Mom talking about her new job. For a while, I let the conversation flow around me, attempting to ignore the nagging unease at the back of my mind.

The restlessness that's been there for weeks.

Ever since Nathan resurfaced.

I still haven't mentioned the messages to them.

The last thing I want is for Dad to fly off the handle or Mom to blame herself again. The concern that was a constant presence in her eyes has finally faded. I'm loath to do anything that will disrupt it.

I've stopped responding to the texts. My hope is that he'll get bored and leave me alone. I ignore the little voice that nags at the back of my brain, reminding me it has yet to occur.

After a quick glance at my phone, I push to my feet. "I should probably head out. Thanks for lunch, Mom. We should do this more often."

Her gaze flicks to my dad. A second or two of silent communication passes between them. I've seen it before. Especially after they found out about my relationship with Nathan.

A pit of unease blooms at the bottom of my belly. My gaze shifts from one to the other before narrowing. "What's going on?"

When Dad remains silent, Mom gives him a nod of encouragement. "Tell her."

It's carefully that I lower myself back to my seat as my tone escalates. "Tell me what?"

Dad clears his throat before balling up his sandwich wrapper and tossing it into the trash. The way his attention stays pinned to me sends a wave of anxiety rippling through me. "Nadia Petrovic reached out to me the other day."

My heart stutters in my chest. "Nadia Petrovic?" I echo, my voice barely above a whisper. The name alone is enough to send a shiver racing down my spine.

The woman is a legend in the figure skating world. Olympic gold medalist, world champion, and coach to some of the greatest skaters in history. I idolized her when I was younger, back when I still believed that dream could be mine.

Why would she reach out?

Especially now, after all this time?

Dad hesitates, and when he speaks, his voice is gentle. "She's interested in training you."

"What?" I shake my head, unable to process what he's saying. "I don't understand. Why would she want to do that? I haven't skated competitively since—" I stop, the words catching in my throat.

Since everything fell apart.

Dad doesn't flinch or look away. "I might have sent her a video of you skating recently," he admits quietly. "And told her you were ready to make a comeback."

My heart races as a potent concoction of anger and disbelief rushes through me. "You did what?"

Before Dad can respond, Mom steps in, her tone soft and pleading. "Honey, we didn't want to tell you until we knew it was a real possibility. You've been so lost this past year, and we just hate seeing you like this. We thought... maybe this could help."

I swallow hard, the weight of their expectations looming over me. "You should have talked to me first."

Mom's eyes fill with sadness, but she doesn't back down. "We were afraid you'd say no before giving it a chance. We just want you to be happy."

Her words hit me hard, right in the gut. I've been telling myself that I'm fine and don't need skating anymore. Deep down, though, I can't help but wonder if she's right.

The thought of returning to that world is terrifying.

Dad's voice drags me from the whirl of my thoughts. "Will you at least meet with Nadia and hear what she has to say?"

"I'm not in competition shape," I whisper, my hands trembling. "I just skate for fun now. I'm not... I can't—"

"She knows how talented you are and what you're capable of, Ava," Dad says, leaning forward. "She's watched you for years. She believes in you."

Tears burn the backs of my eyes, and I stand, desperate to escape before they fall. "I need time to think."

After more than a year away from the competitive circuit, I can't envision what it would be like to train full time again. Nor can I imagine how people would react if I just showed up at a competition.

The knowing smirks.

The hushed whispers.

The gossip would be rampant.

Am I willing to subject myself to that all over again?

The thought is enough to have me shrinking in on myself.

"Take all the time you need," Mom says gently. "But don't let fear hold you back."

With a nod, I grab my bag and head for the door. As I step into the hallway, her final words echo through my mind.

As much as I don't want to admit it, that's exactly what I've spent the last year doing.

AVA

32

Seven hours later and Nadia Petrovic's name continues to repeat in my head. My thoughts are a swirling mess of disbelief and confusion.

One of the greatest figure skating coaches in the world is interested in me.

It doesn't feel real.

As I step out of the library and into the cool evening air, I pull my jacket tighter around me. My mind is still stuck on everything Dad said at lunch, and my body continues to buzz with all the possibilities. Nadia had always been kind whenever our paths crossed at competitions, throwing a few compliments my way, but this isn't something I ever expected.

She can work with her pick of athletes. Skaters who are still competing, still relevant. Why would she bother with someone like me, a girl who hasn't been on the competitive circuit in over a year?

It doesn't make sense.

Lost in my thoughts, I cut a path through the parking lot toward my car.

I'd be lying if I didn't admit that part of me wants to at least speak with the Russian coach and hear what she has to say.

But there's a larger part that's grown comfortable with my life at Western. I may not have everything figured out yet, but I've found friends—real friends like Britt—and for once, I don't feel the constant pressure weighing on me like I did when skating was my entire world.

And then there's Hayes.

Thoughts of him send a warm tingle through my chest. I haven't known him for long, but something about what we're slowly building feels different. Solid. Real. It's more than just sex. Although, the sex is incredible. He makes me feel safe, understood in a way no one else ever has. We've shared pieces of ourselves, parts of our past we don't let anyone else see. With him, I don't have to pretend.

I can just... be.

"Ava! Wait up!"

I halt in my tracks and glance around to find Hayes jogging toward me from the direction of the arena. A smile tugs at my lips before I can stop it.

Seeing him has that effect on me.

As he gets closer, his smile mirrors mine, and his presence puts me at ease. His blond hair is slightly damp from practice, curling a little at the ends, and even in the dim parking lot lights, I can see the energy buzzing through him.

"I didn't know you'd still be on campus this late," he says as he reaches me, his breath visible in the cool air.

"I had a lot of homework to get through, and I've got a test coming up, so I camped out at the library for most of the afternoon."

He tilts his head toward the arena where a few guys are still making their way to their cars. "We just wrapped up practice."

"What are you up to now?" I ask, shifting closer. "Any interest in coming over?"

I could use the distraction. Something to take my mind off the whirlwind of thoughts surrounding Nadia, and the unexpected decision that now looms over me.

My heart stutters.

It would mean leaving Hayes.

Why didn't that occur to me before?

His gaze drops to the phone in his hand. "I've got something to take care of first. How about I come over around nine?"

A mixture of arousal and excitement dances in the pit of my belly. "What needs to be taken care of?"

Humor sparks in his green eyes as he reaches out to tuck a stray lock of hair behind my ear. It's a simple but intimate gesture. His touch lingers on my cheek, his thumb brushing against my skin.

"You know exactly what needs to be done."

My pulse quickens at the intensity in his gaze, and for a moment, I forget about everything else.

Nadia.

Skating.

My parents.

Nathan.

Right now, it's just Hayes and me, standing in the middle of an empty parking lot.

He leans in, his mouth sweeping against mine in a kiss that's gentle but full of promise. I tip my head, deepening it, savoring the feel of him. Every time his lips brush against mine, it's like the world falls away and nothing else matters.

When we finally pull apart, there's a warmth in his eyes that makes my heart flutter.

My tongue darts out to moisten my lips as my palms settle on the broad expanse of his chest. "Can I watch?"

There's a moment of silence as his brows rise. "You want to watch me jerk off on camera?"

My mouth turns cottony at the vivid image his words paint in my head. "More than anything."

An answering heat ignites in his eyes. "Yeah, all right." He presses a kiss against my lips. "Meet back at my house?"

I nod as he takes a step in retreat, his hand trailing down my arm before falling away. I can't help but stare after him as he turns and heads toward his truck. My body hums with excitement.

It takes effort to pull myself from my thoughts and slide into my car. Just as I start the engine, my phone buzzes with a text.

TENINCHESOFCOCKY:

See you soon, Tink.

I smile at his contact name, which also happens to be his screen name, biting my lip as I pull out of the parking lot.

I might not know exactly what this is between us or where it's going, but one thing is for certain—I'm not ready to let it go.

Anticipation hums through my veins as I follow him back to the old, blue Victorian. By the time I exit the vehicle, he's standing at the driver's side door. His arm slips around my waist as he leads me up the front porch stairs and into the house.

Now that everyone is home from practice, the place is bustling with activity and noise. A few of his teammates call out for us to join them. He shakes his head and waves them away with a smile.

By the time we reach the second floor, I'm unable to think about anything other than the image of Hayes stroking his hard cock, bringing himself to orgasm.

I have no idea why that turns me on so much, but it does.

Once he twists the lock on the door and drops his athletic bag on the carpet, he flicks a glance my way. Doubt fills his eyes. "Are you sure you want to stay and watch? You could always chill out downstairs for a while."

Wild horses couldn't drag me away.

"I'm sure."

"Okay." With that, he grips the hem of his sweatshirt and yanks it over his head before letting it drop. The black Western Wildcats T-shirt is the next to get stripped away before it meets the same fate. Once his gray joggers are shoved down thick thighs, he stands before me in nothing more than white socks and black boxer briefs.

I point to his feet. "Are you keeping them on?"

He cocks his head and arches a brow. "What's wrong? Not sexy?"

Laughter falls from my lips. "Not in the least."

"How do you know? Maybe the fans will love it."

I shake my head. "Take them off."

"Fine." He lifts one foot and removes a sock and then the other.

"Trust me, your fans will thank me."

"Guess we'll never know."

My gaze drops to his briefs. "Aren't you forgetting something?"

He slides his thumb beneath the elastic band and snaps it against his trim waist. "Nah. I was thinking tonight could be more of a let-your-imagination-run-wild kind of show."

"How about you take them off and show me the goods?"

He lifts his chin. "You want them off so badly, why don't you do it yourself?"

I shed my jacket before tossing it over the chair tucked neatly beneath his desk. It only takes a half a dozen steps to eat up the distance between us. My gaze stays pinned to his as I reach out and stroke his cock through the thin cotton material.

"That feels good, baby girl. But the fans like to watch me get hard on camera. It's part of the fun."

"Oh well." I slip my hand into his underwear and wrap my fingers around his thick length. It feels more like steel. When the urge to take him into my mouth pounds through me, I drop to my knees. Not once do I release his gaze as I guide the head of his erection to my lips. My tongue darts out to lick the slit. Already, it's beaded with moisture.

He loosens the band holding my hair in a ponytail. As soon as the blonde strands tumble around my shoulders, his fingers tunnel through them, tightening around my scalp to hold me in place. "Fuck, baby. That feels amazing."

Unable to resist, I suck him deep inside until he nudges the back of my throat. "Have I told you how much I love your mouth? Especially when it's wrapped around my big dick?"

His dirty words have more arousal gathering in my core. We've barely done anything and already my panties are soaked.

Just thinking about Hayes turns me on.

And I love it.

Love how easy everything feels with him.

A low groan vibrates through him as he gently pushes me away.

When I give him a questioning look, he growls, "If you keep that up, I'll come, and that's definitely not part of the regularly scheduled programming."

My tongue flicks over his swollen tip. It wouldn't take much for him to lose it, and there's a part of me that wants to push him over the edge.

With another growl, he drags me to my feet. Before I can say anything, his mouth crashes onto mine. "You want to fuck with me, baby? Just remember, turnabout is fair play."

A shiver of excitement dances down my spine as my pulse picks up tempo.

He smirks. "Somehow, I don't think that's the punishment I meant it to be. Maybe it would be best if you headed out." He brushes another kiss against my mouth. "You're too much of a distraction."

I force my lower lip out in a pout. "Fine. I'll be good. Promise."

He glances at the clock on his nightstand. "I've got three minutes to lose the boner."

Without thinking, I reach out to stroke his cock.

He shakes his head as his hand tightens around my wrist, and he brings my fingers to his lips before pressing a kiss against them. "As much as I love your touch, that'll only make matters worse."

After releasing my hand, he swings toward the desk to grab his computer. He clicks a few buttons before dragging the chair next to the bed and positioning it. Then he snags a pair of earbuds and settles on the mattress. The boxers are the last to get stripped away, leaving him completely naked.

My gaze licks over every inch of him. He's so gorgeous. Staring at him is enough to get me all heated up. I drop down on an armchair in the corner of the room that's out of view from the camera. He shoves the buds into his ears and reclines against the pillows before closing his eyes. His chest rises and falls with every deep breath he draws into his lungs.

Once his boner has wilted, he rolls toward the camera and hits a button or two before resettling.

I can't help but watch in fascination as he strokes both hands over his chest. His muscles ripple beneath his fingertips. Arousal gathers in my core like wisps of smoke, and I shift on the cushion, trying to alleviate the growing ache.

He tweaks both nipples until they're hard points before tugging at them.

It's like there's an invisible thread connecting his body to my core.

Who would have thought watching him stroke his chest would be such a turn on?

His hands continue their slow descent to his groin. It's only when he reaches his destination that I notice his cock has stiffened back up again and is standing at attention.

Another wave of desire crashes over me, and I shift on the chair as my pussy throbs a harsh beat that vibrates throughout my entire body. I'm not sure if I've ever felt so turned on in my life. It doesn't take long before my fingers are twitching with the urge to touch myself.

When he swirls his fingertip around the tiny slit, spreading clear fluid on the blunt head of his dick, I just about come undone. Before I realize it, my fingers grip the hem of my sweater and I'm lifting it up my torso and over my head. His gaze snaps to mine, and heat sparks in his eyes when I unsnap my bra and drop it to the floor.

Unwilling to overthink my actions, I rise to my feet and remove my jeans and panties until I'm just as naked as he is. Only then do I resettle on the chair. I press my spine against the cushion before spreading my legs wide enough for each one to dangle over the armrests so I'm completely exposed.

He turns his head toward me as his fingers tighten around his cock, and he slowly strokes the hard length.

As I watch him pleasure himself, I can't help but feel the rush of excitement build deep down inside of me. I pinch and tweak my nipples until they stiffen, mimicking the actions of his hands on his own body. Anticipation heightens with each second that ticks by.

The intensity in his gaze is palpable as green fire snaps from his eyes, and he picks up speed. My own hand drifts downward, to the part of me that pulses with a life all its own. That first brush of my fingertips against my sensitive lips is enough to have a groan rising from my chest. I force it back, not allowing it to escape.

He growls as his fingers loosen from around his erection and slide lower before cupping and squeezing each ball.

Holy fuck.

Heat floods my core as my fingers circle my drenched entrance before finally dipping inside.

He releases another garbled sound as I spread the wetness around before circling my clit with lazy strokes and flicking the little piece of jewelry. It's so tempting to close my eyes and enjoy the sensations that ripple outward to the very tips of my fingers and toes. This is the first time I've touched myself and actually felt like I was about to come.

My gaze stays locked on Hayes. I couldn't look away even if I wanted to. The sight of him playing with himself is so damn hot. I can understand why women pay good money to watch him.

When a scream builds within me, my teeth sink into my lower lip to keep it trapped inside.

I'm so damn close to shattering into a million broken pieces.

With a tilt of my hips, I spread my legs wider. Even from here it would be impossible not to notice the way his pupils dilate, the black swallowing up the green, as they smolder with heat.

When I can't stand another second, my eyelids flutter shut as I tweak my nipple with my fingers while the other hand plays with my pussy, pushing me closer to the edge and into oblivion.

It's almost a shock when a deep growl erupts from him. My eyelids fly open just in time to see him roll toward the computer and slam the lid shut before jumping to his feet and swallowing up the distance between us with three long-legged strides.

I gasp when he drops to his knees between my parted legs, his eyes focused and intense. His strong fingers grip my inner thighs as he spreads the lips of my pussy apart, exposing my delicate flesh. Without hesitation, he leans in and kisses my center, his tongue lapping up the wetness. He teases my clit with quick flicks of his tongue, sending bursts of pleasure through my body. I arch, wanting more, as he moves his tongue around my piercing. Just when my inner muscles begin to tighten, he pulls away and the cool air hits me, making me shudder. Before I can protest the loss, he gently slaps my clit with his fingertips, creating a delicious mix of pain and pleasure that only pushes me closer to release.

"You distracted me." He swats me again.

Only this time, I anticipate it and press closer, craving the sting before pleasure rushes in to drown it out.

"You love it, don't you?" he asks, a tortured groan following the question.

"I do," I admit as the familiar ache between my legs intensifies. "I love it all."

"You're so fucking perfect."

His lips fasten on me again as he sucks the tiny ring into his mouth. With his thumb, he gathers up some of the wetness before pressing it against my rosebud and penetrating the tight ring of muscle.

It doesn't take more than that for me to splinter apart. And then I'm lost in an intense sea of pleasure. A scream tears from my throat before I can think of tamping it down.

At this point, I don't give a damn who hears me cry out my orgasm. I only care about the spasms that rack my body.

As soon as the last tremor fades, Hayes rises to his feet until his hard cock bobs inches from my face. His fingers tangle through the thick strands of my hair to hold me in place.

"How about you finish what you started earlier?"

My lips quirk as he pulls me closer. When the bulbous head of his cock brushes my lips, I open wide, but he only gives me the tip.

When my lids drift shut, he snaps, "Eyes on me, baby girl. Pretty sure we already had a conversation about this. I want your gaze pinned to me the entire time you suck my dick."

He continues to tease me, inching farther inside.

With a moan, my eyes plead with his.

"Need more?"

With one smooth thrust, he nudges the back of my throat.

The stretch of it feels amazing.

So does the lack of oxygen.

The way tears prick my eyes.

Maybe it shouldn't.

Maybe it should be painful, and I should hate it.

But I don't.

"Damn, that feels so good. Can you take more, baby?"

With his thick erection down my throat and his hands in my hair, it's impossible to nod my head. I moan around his girth, hoping he understands he has my consent.

In the short time we've known each other, I've come to trust that this man will take care to walk that fine line and push my limits without stepping over any boundaries. That knowledge has the shackles falling away so I can free my mind and allow my body to soar.

I want to give him the same gift.

My attention stays locked on him as he presses so deep down my throat that my face is flush against his groin. I focus on drawing air in through my nostrils as he holds me in place.

"From the first moment I saw you, I knew you'd look beautiful with your mouth stuffed full of my cock."

Even though I just came, heat floods my core. The possessive light that fills his eyes is my undoing, and I moan around him.

He withdraws, allowing me to suck in a shuddering breath.

"Ready, baby? Ready to take me back inside?"

"Yes."

When I raise my hand to wipe away the spittle, he shakes his head. "Leave it. I like the way you look when you're all mussed-up." His thumb swipes across my swollen lips, gathering up the wetness before pressing it to my mouth. "Open."

I draw his finger inside before sucking it.

It's only after his lids turn heavy that he slips it free before wrapping his hand around his erection and bringing it to my lips again. "Beg for it, baby. Beg to suck my cock."

"Please. I want to taste you in my mouth."

He lifts a brow. "That really the best you can do?"

I shake my head as desperation floods through me. "Please, Hayes. Please let me suck your big dick. I need it." There's so much truth in the plea. I do need it. I need *him*. "I love the way my lips stretch around it and the way it feels to take you deep into my throat. I want to feel you come so I can drink down every last drop."

"Fuck. You're such a good girl. Know that, baby? Now, open wide. I'm going to give you exactly what you begged so prettily for."

I do as instructed as his fingers tangle in my hair, and he slides between my lips. I never thought I'd enjoy the feel of it, but I do.

With one continuous movement, he glides all the way down my throat until my nose is buried in his groin and breathing becomes impossible.

"A few more strokes and I'm going to give you exactly what you crave. What you need."

I moan as he retreats. This time there's no reprieve or chance to catch my breath. He uses my mouth for his own pleasure, and I revel in every single second of it.

On the last thrust, his hips stay flexed as he draws me closer. He groans as thick jets of cum erupt from the tip of his cock and hit the back of my throat. I greedily swallow down every drop just like I promised.

His release seems to last forever as my gaze stays pinned to him.

With his head thrown back, I'm only able to see the bob of his throat and the rigidly held muscles.

Tears stream down my face as he huffs out a breath and carefully slips free. His hands loosen from around my scalp as he crouches in front of me. That's when I realize my legs are still thrown over the armrests of the chair. His gaze drops to my splayed pussy before he presses a kiss against the wet flesh. The velvety softness of his tongue slides between my lips and a whimper breaks loose from me.

No matter how much I have of this man, I'm still hungry for more.

Just when I think he'll make me orgasm for a second time, he rises until we're eye level with each other before searching my gaze carefully, as if looking for signs of remorse.

He won't find any.

"Open."

My lips part enough for him to peer inside.

"I love seeing your throat painted with my cum."

One hand snakes around the nape of my neck before he pulls me forward, and his mouth presses to mine. He licks deep strokes until it feels as if he'll devour me in one tasty bite. A tangy flavor fills my mouth, and I realize it's the taste of my pussy on his lips.

He pulls away just enough to press his forehead against mine as we look at each other. "There's nothing better than the taste of our combined arousal on my tongue."

My belly swoops as my core tightens.

That's the moment I realize just how deep I'm in with this guy.

TENINCHESOF
COCKY

WILDCATS

33

With my back facing the hot spray, I allow the water to pound my shoulders, easing the tension from two grueling hours spent on the ice.

Physically, I'm wiped.

But mentally?

My brain refuses to shut off.

I'm struggling with a dilemma. Part of me realizes I need to tell Coach what's going on with his daughter. He should know in order to keep her safe. But another part realizes that Ava will be pissed when she discovers I took matters into my own hands.

I know that creepy fucker is still bombarding her with messages. I sneak peeks at her phone when she walks out of the room.

Is that an invasion of privacy?

Probably.

But I'm concerned that she's downplaying the situation.

I have no idea if the guy at the rink taking pictures was Nathan. I couldn't get a good look at him, but I've got a bad feeling about the way it all unfolded. It's too much of a coincidence.

If some dude was messing with Kia, I'd want to know about it.

So I could bury him six feet under.

Every morning, I drive Ava to the rink and then stick around to watch her practice. I've also been picking her up after her night classes. There's no way in hell I'm going to let her walk home alone.

Whenever I bring up the subject of her former coach, she brushes it off like it's nothing, even though we both know that's not the case.

By the time I twist the shower knob so the spray becomes more of a trickle, I've arrived at a decision.

No more procrastinating.

I need to tell Coach.

Ava might hate me for it, but I'd rather beg her forgiveness than have this guy take his obsession to the next level.

With a towel in hand, I make quick work of drying myself off before wrapping the damp material around my waist and heading back to my locker.

"Hey, Van Doren," Colby calls out from a few lockers down. "Are we grabbing something to eat after this? I'm fucking famished. I'll call the girls. They can all meet us at Taco Loco."

"Nah, I'm good."

He waggles his brows. "I'm sure Britt will invite Ava."

I give him the finger. "I'll call her myself."

Bridger, who's changing nearby, smirks as he pulls on a pair of boxers. "Seems like shit's getting serious around here."

"It is."

He cocks his head and studies me. "Aren't you getting bored?" He throws a quick look at Coach's office before dropping his voice. "Or does this have more to do with the thrill of sneaking around behind the guy's back?"

His words hit an unexpected nerve, and I glare at him. "This has nothing to do with sneaking around, man. I *like* her." The word is too small for what I feel for Ava, but I say it anyway.

Bridger arches a brow, clearly not buying it. "Really? You sure about that?"

"Yeah, I am," I say, more forcefully than intended. The last few weeks have changed everything.

Ava isn't just some girl.

She's *the* girl.

He shrugs. "I'm just saying, Coach isn't gonna be thrilled when he finds out. You've got a reputation, and it's not exactly squeaky clean. If he catches wind that you're with his daughter, he'll probably bench your ass."

He's right.

Coach would flip if he knew.

Which is one reason to keep silent. But I just can't do it. This situation has become dangerous, and I'll do whatever it takes to keep Ava safe. Even if that means taking the brunt of Coach's ire.

Ford pops his head around the corner. "You sure you don't want to come with us? Tacos sound pretty good right now."

I shake my head, knowing exactly what I need to do. "Maybe later."

Ford takes off, and soon, the rest of the guys trickle out of the locker room, leaving me alone. I pull on my clothes and mentally prepare myself for what needs to happen.

With one last look at my reflection in the mirror, I suck in a deep breath and make my way to Coach's office. Each step feels heavier than the last.

As I knock on the office door, the sound of game film drifts through the frosted glass before he calls out, "Come in."

My heart pounds as I push the door open and step inside. "Coach?"

There's no turning back now.

He glances at me, surprise flickering in his eyes. "Hayes? What are you still doing here? I thought everyone cleared out."

I stuff my hands into the pockets of my joggers, unsure where to start. "Yeah, they did. I just... needed to talk to you."

He clicks off the computer screen and swivels in his chair to give me his full attention. "Take a seat. What's going on?"

My mouth turns cottony as I drop down on the chair opposite him. "It's about Ava."

"My daughter?" His brow furrows, and I can feel the weight of his scrutiny. "What about her?"

Fuck.

This is more difficult than I anticipated. I hate that I'm betraying her trust. Especially when it wasn't easily given.

I drag a hand through my damp hair, trying to figure out the right way to say this. My gaze bounces around the room before settling on a photo of Ava with him and her mother. They're all smiling, looking as if they're on top of the world.

"Hayes?" he prompts, drawing my attention back to him.

"Her former coach has been texting her," I blurt, needing to get it out. "It's been going on for a while now, and he won't leave her alone."

There's a long silence, the kind that stretches and twists in the air between us. Coach's face goes stone-cold, his expression unreadable. "How do you know about this?" he asks, his voice tight.

"Ava told me," I admit, knowing this conversation is about to take a turn.

"Why would she do that?" His gaze sharpens, like he's piecing something together.

"Because..." I take a deep breath, preparing myself for the fallout. "Because we've been seeing each other."

"Let me get this straight." His jaw tightens. "You've been seeing my daughter?"

"Yes, sir," I say, my voice steady. "I'm sorry you had to find out this way, but I'm concerned. He's sending harassing messages every day."

He leans back in his chair, rubbing a hand over his face. "Why didn't she come to me herself?"

"She didn't want to worry you," I say quietly. "But it's bad. The other day, at the rink... I saw a guy taking pictures of her. When I went to talk with him, he took off."

Coach's hand falls from his face, his eyes narrowing. "Taking pictures of her?"

"I can't be sure who it was, but it looked suspicious."

He swears under his breath, pulling off his ballcap and dragging a hand through his hair. "Does Ava know you're here?"

"No."

Even though his shoulders relax just a bit, thick tension continues to vibrate off him in heavy waves. "I appreciate you making me aware of the situation."

"Keeping her safe is my number one priority."

Coach studies me in silence. "It sounds like you really care about my daughter."

I meet his gaze with an unwavering one. "I do. And I don't want to see anything happen to her."

He nods, his eyes softening. "I believe you."

I stand, ready to leave, but Coach's voice halts me in my tracks. "Did Ava mention that a very prestigious skating coach is interested in training her?"

I blink, thrown off by the shift in conversation. "No, she didn't."

Coach leans back in his chair, his expression turning thoughtful. "This is a once-in-a-lifetime chance for her. More importantly, she'll be in Colorado, and there'll be security. Ava will be safe there. With everything going on, I think that's the best option for her. Don't you?"

The words hit me like a kick to the nuts.

Colorado.

That's far away from here.

From *me*.

"Nadia will be with her night and day, helping her get back into competitive shape. There won't be time for anything else," Coach adds, his meaning clear.

Translation: there won't be time for me.

I open my mouth to argue, but the words stay trapped inside, refusing to budge.

When I remain silent, at a loss, he continues, "Skating has always been Ava's life. You have no idea how much it broke her to walk away. Not only is this her chance to reclaim it but to be safe." There's a pause as his tone gentles. "If you really want what's best for Ava, you'll let her go."

The heavy weight of his words presses down on me, crushing the air from my lungs. As much as it kills me, I think he might be right.

I have to let her go.

AVA

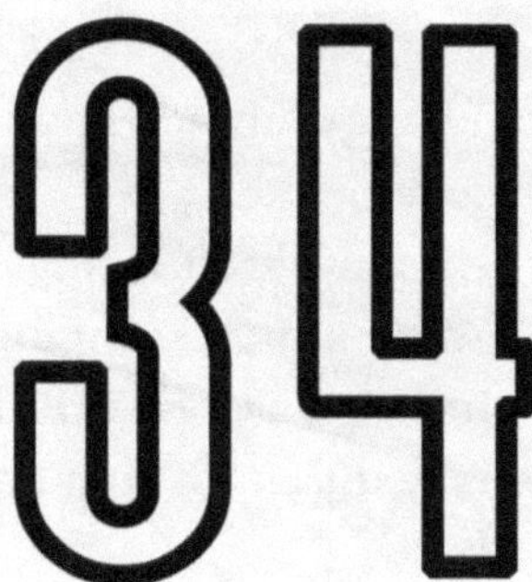

I stare at my phone, the latest text from Nathan flashing on the screen like a ticking bomb.

UNKNOWN NUMBER:

Answer me! I won't be ignored any longer!
What we had was special.

My hands shake as I read the message for a second time.
He's changed his number.
Again.
The next message makes my stomach twist into a series of painful knots.

UNKNOWN NUMBER:

I'm the one who made you what you are
today!

I clench my jaw, forcing back the bile rising in my throat. Before I can close the app, another message pops up.
This one feels like a knife to the gut.

UNKNOWN NUMBER:

There's no way that kid can give you what
you crave. I know how you like to be
touched. I'm the one who created the need.
And I'm the only one who can feed the
monster that lives deep inside you.

I stop dead in my tracks, the chill of the air no match for the icy fear that floods my system.

The only way he could know about Hayes is if he's here at Western, watching my every move.

That thought sends a violent shiver racing down my spine.

I glance around the quiet campus, scanning the shadows, as paranoia tightens its grip on me. I can't resist throwing cautious glances over my shoulder. I'm terrified that I'll spin around and find Nathan standing there.

I pick up my pace, nearly breaking into a jog, as I make my way toward Hayes's house. I texted him half an hour ago, and normally he's quick to reply.

But there's been nothing.

I have no idea when it happened, but he's become my safe space.

My pulse hammers in my ears as I cross the street toward the hockey house, my thoughts swirling. I can't ignore this anymore. I'll tell Hayes about everything. The relentless texts and the creeping fear that Nathan might be closer than I suspected.

That he's here.

On campus.

For a second or two, I consider texting Hayes and telling him what's going on. But I'm so close to his house. Only a few more blocks. I'd rather tell him in person. I know he's going to be pissed.

I suck in a deep breath as I arrive at another decision.

And then we'll talk to my parents in person. We can tell them about what's happening with Nathan and that we've been seeing each other.

I'm fed up with all the secrets and lies.

By the time I reach Hayes's house, my heart is pounding for an entirely different reason. The blue Victorian looms in front of me like a sanctuary. If I can just get to Hayes, everything will be okay.

I hurry up the steps and knock on the beveled glass, my pulse still racing.

A moment later, the door swings open and disappointment rushes through me. Instead of Hayes, I find Bridger Sanderson.

This feels like déjà vu.

His piercing gray eyes remind me of the embarrassing messages that have been broadcast to the university at large. If there's someone stalking my every move, I imagine he must feel the same way.

Strange that we would have that in common.

"Hey, Ava," he says, leaning casually against the doorframe. "What's up?"

Loud music and voices spill from inside the house, and I catch a glimpse of people laughing, the sounds of a party in full swing. Bridger blocks most of the view, standing in front of me like a bouncer.

"Is Hayes here?" I ask, shifting from foot to foot. I want to get inside, out of sight, but something in Bridger's expression makes my anxiety spike.

He hesitates, guilt flickering in his eyes before it's quickly masked by indifference. "Yeah, but he's kind of got his hands full at the moment."

Hands full?

My stomach plummets.

What does that mean?

"He's too busy to talk?" My voice wavers as I try to peek past him into the house. It's difficult to keep my cool when every instinct inside me is screaming that something isn't right.

Bridger's muscles tense, his jaw tightening. "Yeah. Should I let him know you stopped by?"

I bite down on my lip, trying to keep it together.

Hayes hasn't responded to my texts, and now he's too busy to see me?

With everything going on, he's supposed to be the one person I can count on.

"Just tell him to call me as soon as he can." I hesitate before adding, "It's important."

His muscles loosen. I'm sure he was expecting more of a fight. "Will do."

I make a move to turn as if I'll go back down the stairs to the sidewalk. Instead, I bolt toward the door, pushing him aside and slipping past.

"What the fuck!" Bridger barks, reaching for me, but I'm already halfway across the entryway. I make it five steps, just enough to see into the spacious living room before Bridger's fingers lock around my upper arm, halting me in my tracks.

When his hand tightens, I give him a death glare before jerking free.

My heart spasms painfully beneath my breast when I find Hayes sprawled on the couch, two girls curled up against him, their hands trailing over his chest. I recognize them immediately—the brunettes from The Roasted Bean. The ones who couldn't take a hint. One of them leans in, whispering something in his ear, and he smirks, his eyes heavy-lidded with lazy amusement.

Tears sting the backs of my eyes as I watch them, my body frozen in place.

Bridger steps up behind me, his voice low and mocking. "Have you seen enough, or do you want to stick around and see what happens next? Spoiler alert—you're not going to like it." He gives me a considering look. "Unless you're cool with sharing?" There's a beat of silence. "Some chicks are." He shrugs. "Hayes's motto has always been 'the more the merrier.'"

I whirl around and glare at him, trying to hold back the tears. "Screw you."

Betrayal and humiliation crash over me. I don't know how I'm still standing. How I haven't collapsed under the crushing weight of the emotion.

How could I have been so stupid?

How didn't I see him for the player he truly is?

Was he sleeping with other people the entire time we were together?

The acidic taste of bile rises in my throat.

I need to get out of here before I throw up.

That would be the icing on the cake.

I stumble toward the door, grateful Hayes hasn't caught sight of me. Every step feels like I'm walking through quicksand. I thought Nathan's texts were the worst thing that could happen today.

I was wrong.

"Still want me to tell him you stopped by?"

I blink back the tears before refocusing my attention on Bridger. If I didn't know better, I'd think there was a mixture of sorrow and remorse filling his eyes. But how can that be?

"That won't be necessary."

"Probably for the best."

"Yeah." It takes effort to hold the sob inside as I keep moving. Even though I'm frightened about what waits for me out there, there's no way I can stay here for another second.

Just as I open the door, someone steps in front of me, blocking my path.

"Ava?" Concern laces Britt's voice. She takes one look at my face and her own expression hardens. "What's wrong? Did something happen?"

I try to swallow the lump in my throat, but it's no use. Tears spill over, and before I know it, Britt's arms are slipping around me and holding me tight.

"Oh my God," she whispers. "What did Hayes do?"

"That's not really fair. How do you know Hayes did anything?" Colby mumbles from behind her.

She shoots him a sharp look before turning back to me.

"Sorry. Stupid question," he says grudgingly. "What did the jackass do?"

"Can you please drive me back to my apartment?" My voice cracks as I try to speak. "I need to get out of here."

Britt doesn't release her grip on me. "Of course. We'll grab something to eat, and you can tell me everything. Okay?"

With a nod, I let her lead me out the door.

Even though it feels like my heart has been ripped out of my chest, I know one thing for sure.

I was a fool for ever trusting Hayes Van Doren.

TENINCHESOF
COCKY

WILDCATS

TenInchesofCocky
VAN DOREN
19
19
81
HAYES

"It's done, dude."

Bridger's words hit me like a sledgehammer to the chest. The weight of them sinks in, adding to the mixture of sorrow and grief swirling inside me. I've done a lot of hard things in my life—balancing school and hockey, supporting my family—but this...

Hurting Ava like this?

It's on a completely different level.

It feels like I've ripped out my own heart.

Unaware of my inner turmoil, Cassidy's and Kendall's hands continue drifting over my chest. Their touch makes me sick to my stomach. I fucking hate that Ava saw them doing it, and that she believes I'm just another player who used her for a good time.

Without a word, I shove up from the couch, needing to get away from them, from everything. All I want to do is take a hot shower and scrub away the shame that clings to me like sweat.

"Come on, Hayes." Cassidy pouts, reaching for my arm, but I jerk it away before she can touch me again. "What's your deal?"

My deal?

My deal is that I just destroyed the best thing that ever happened to me. And now all I want is to forget this entire night ever happened.

When I arrived at the house earlier, Cassidy and Kendall were all over one of the younger guys. He'd looked like he'd died and gone to heaven.

Ever since my conversation with Coach, I'd been bouncing back and forth all day, trying to figure out what to do.

"Pretty sure you just broke her fucking heart, man."

He's right.

I did.

I just didn't think it would break mine in the process.

Making Ava think she was just another girl I'd hooked up with seemed like the only way to create a clean break. I figured it would be easier for her, that she'd hate me and move on. From the corner of my eye, I saw her face crumble and the pain in her eyes. That's all it took for doubt to creep in at the edges.

"I still don't understand why you had to hurt her like that." Bridger's voice is low but pointed. "You should've seen the fucking look on her face."

I wince as a fresh wave of guilt slams into me.

The last thing I want to do is picture Ava's expression again, but Bridger's right. It's impossible not to see it. The way her eyes filled with tears, the disbelief, the betrayal. If I let myself dwell on it for too long, I'll be in my truck, speeding over to her apartment to beg her forgiveness and spill the truth about everything.

But then I think about what Coach said—that the only way to keep Ava safe is to let her go. To let her leave for Colorado, where Nathan can't get to her.

Fuck.

My mind races as I rake a hand through my hair and pace the length of the living room.

I know what I did was for her safety and for her future.

She deserves this shot with Nadia Petrovic, and she needs to focus on skating.

Ava has too much talent, too much potential, to let Nathan ruin it all.

She needs to be far away from him... and me.

If only knowing all of that made it easier to stomach.

It certainly doesn't stop the ache that gnaws at my chest or the urge to go to her, tell her everything, and promise that I'll protect her.

The sad truth is, I don't know what to do anymore.

I've never been so conflicted in my life.

"I had to make sure she'd leave," I mutter, more to myself than to my teammate. "She needs to be safe. And she won't be if she stays here."

In order to get his help, I had to let Bridger in on what's been going on with Nathan.

He releases a long breath and crosses his arms over his chest. "Yeah, I get that. But did you have to be so brutal about it? Now she thinks you don't give a shit. That you never gave a shit."

"I do care." My tone is harsher than I intend. "I care about her more than anything, which is why I had to do it. If something happens to her because of that asshole…"

"So what now? You're just going to let her think you're the world's biggest dickhead and hope she's better off without you?"

I grind my teeth and stare at the floor. "If it keeps her safe, then yeah. Do you have a better idea?"

With a shake of his head, he remains silent. He might not like how everything went down, but we both know this was the only way. Ava needs to get out of here, away from Nathan's obsessive bullshit, and the only way to make sure she goes is if she thinks there's nothing left for her here.

But God, the thought of her leaving, of never seeing her again… It feels like my insides are being ripped apart.

"I'm gonna head out," I say abruptly, beelining for the front door. "I need to clear my head."

"Maybe what you really need to do is figure out a way to fix this mess before it's too late," Bridger mutters, his tone sharp.

I don't bother with a response.

I don't know if there is a way to fix it, or if I even should.

Maybe the best thing for Ava is for me to stay out of her life, no matter how much it fucking kills me.

AVA

I wipe another tear from my face. My reflection in the window tells me everything I need to know. My eyes are red and my cheeks blotchy.

For the second time in eighteen months, my world feels like it's crumbling around me. The pain and betrayal are all too familiar, and I hate it.

Hate that I let myself trust someone again.

Hayes said all the right things, and I fell for it.

I should've known better.

Britt rubs soft circles on my back. "Aw, babe, I can't stand to see you like this."

I nod, choking back another sob, though it feels pointless at this stage. "I'm sorry for being such a mess," I mutter, embarrassed by how much I've cried tonight. I've been like this for over an hour, and yet the tears keep coming.

Who knew a person could cry so much?

"There's no need to apologize," she says softly, but the words do nothing to stop the ache gnawing at me.

Across the room, Colby cracks his knuckles, his expression serious. "Want me to take him out?"

I blink, momentarily distracted from my grief. "No."

"Are you sure?" he presses, raising a brow. "Hayes is one of my best friends, but I'd still do it."

Despite the hollowness in my chest, a tiny smile tugs at the corners of my mouth. "I don't think that's necessary."

Colby shrugs. "Just saying. It's an option if you change your mind."

"Thanks, I appreciate the offer." I try to sound lighter than I feel, but it comes out flat.

Britt nibbles on her lower lip as she stares at me in concern. "Don't you think you should talk to him? Maybe there's more to what you saw."

The memory of Hayes, surrounded by those girls, laughing with them, as if nothing else in the world mattered, flashes in my head.

In that moment, I felt invisible. Something I've never felt in his presence. He has the rare ability to make me feel like I'm all he sees.

All that matters.

My heart constricts.

"I don't know if I want to hear whatever excuses he has. I saw enough to know I don't mean anything to him."

As detached as I try to sound, like I'm already past it, the truth is, it's ripping me apart.

How could he so easily dismiss everything we found together?

The intimacy we shared felt so real.

At least it did to me.

But now... I don't know what to believe.

Maybe none of it was real.

"You meant something to him," Britt says quietly. "I know you did. I could see it."

Even though her words are meant to offer comfort, they only make me ache more.

If I meant something to him, why did he let me think I didn't?

Why did he let me walk away without a fight?

I swallow hard, pushing back more tears. "I'm going to head over to the rink and clear my head." I glance around my apartment. Everywhere I look is a reminder of Hayes.

His smile, his laugh, the way he made me feel like I mattered.

I need to escape.

Britt's worried gaze stays pinned to me. "Are you sure? Do you want us to come with you?"

With a shake of my head, I rise from the couch. "No, it's okay. I just need some space." I feel like I'm suffocating. I can't even go in the bedroom without being slammed with memories.

Maybe I'll sleep at my parents' house tonight.

Or for the next week.

Thoughts of Nadia Petrovic flood my brain.

In light of my current situation, I don't have anything to lose by talking with her and hearing what she has to say.

As I step into the cool night air, the silence surrounds me. The weight of everything that just happened presses down on me. It takes effort to put one foot in front of the other and keep moving forward.

I need the ice.

Even when my world is falling apart, it's the one place that still makes sense.

I part ways with Colby and Britt outside my apartment building.

My friend pulls me in for one last hug before squeezing me tight. I can't help but sink into the warmth of her embrace. I feel bad for not telling her about what's going on with Nadia. But what's the point when it might not turn out to be anything?

"Call me if you need to talk, okay?" She pulls back just enough to search my face. "I mean it."

I offer a weak smile. "I will. Promise."

She nods as Colby slips his arm around her waist. Those two are so perfect for each other. They mesh so well.

And here I'd hoped—

As soon as the sly thought tries to sneak inside my brain, I cut it off.

Nope. I refuse to go there.

With one final wave, I slide behind the wheel of my car and start the engine. I hadn't realized how late it was until we'd walked outside.

During the short drive to the rink, the sight of Hayes with those girls plays on a constant loop in my brain. It's enough to make me sick. Even though it's only nine o'clock, there's not much traffic on the street, and when I pull into the arena lot, three cars are parked there.

It's a relief that Dad's SUV is one of them.

I grab my bag from the trunk and rush toward the entrance. Unease prickles at the bottom of my belly. I can't help but glance over my shoulder and search the shadows for anything that looks out of place.

The rink feels different at night.

Almost eerie.

It's the kind of silence that wraps around you and makes your skin crawl. The lights overhead buzz softly, casting a dim glow that barely reaches the edges of the rink. The ice glistens, untouched and perfect. I've skated here a hundred times, but tonight, with no one around, it feels like the arena is holding its breath, waiting for something to happen. And that only ratchets up my own nerves.

The familiar routine does nothing to soothe my paranoia. I came here tonight to clear my head, not to let my imagination run wild. The hum of the refrigeration system is the only sound that fills the space. It's a low, constant drone that vibrates through the floor and into my bones.

My fingers tremble as I slip off my shoes and lace up my skates. That's when footsteps catch my attention. My head jerks up, gaze locking on a solitary figure as my movements stall.

"Hey, sweetheart. I wasn't expecting to run into you this late. Weren't you here this morning?"

Dad.

It takes a moment for my heartbeat to settle.

I shake my head. "No, I was up late studying, so I thought I'd get a quick skate in."

He glances at his watch. "Don't stay too long. They'll be locking the place up soon."

"I won't."

He searches my eyes. "Have you given anymore thought to meeting with Nadia?"

I draw in a deep breath and hold it captive. It's only when my lungs begin to burn that I release it back into the atmosphere. There's a good possibility that my life will change if I agree to this meeting.

When I remain silent, his gaze softens. There's an intensity to his voice when he finally speaks. "Ava, this could be your chance. You've got so much talent, and I know you've been through hell, but Nadia could help you get back to where you've always belonged—on the ice, competing again. At the very least, hear her out."

Competing.

It's what I've wanted for so long, but everything is so uncertain now. And I'm not sure if I'm ready to open that door again and step back into that world.

"Meet with her," he urges gently.

His words circle through my brain. It's almost a shock when I blurt, "Okay. I'll listen to what she has to say with an open mind."

"That's all I'm asking. Just give it a chance."

It's only when his lips lift into a smile and relief floods his eyes, easing the heavy lines of tension, that I realize how stressed he appears.

My brow furrows as I search his face. "Is everything all right?"

"Oh, you know... just heading into the playoffs with a new team."

I nod, accepting the response. There's no reason for him to lie. Plus, I know how much he enjoys his position at Western. If the team doesn't do well, there's the possibility his contract might not get renewed.

And then he would be on the hunt for a new coaching position, which means more upheaval in our lives.

As tempting as it is to tell him about Nathan, now doesn't seem like the right time.

"You guys are going to crush it." I force a smile. "You'll probably end up winning the championship."

"From your lips to God's ears." He glances at the watch wrapped around his left wrist. "Do you want me to hang around until you're done? I don't like the idea of you being here alone."

"No, I'll be fine." I shake my head, knowing he probably has a ton more work to do before he goes to bed tonight. "I won't stay long."

Indecision flashes across his face before he gives me another tight smile and heads toward his office in the locker room.

When he's about a dozen or so feet away, he swings around. "Text me when you get back to your apartment, all right? I won't sleep well unless I know you're safe."

My rigidly held muscles loosen. "I will."

"Love you, sweetheart."

"Love you too."

Once he disappears, I turn my attention to the ice. The familiar chill of the air settles around me, soothing the tension in my body. This is exactly what I need. An escape from everything gnawing away at the back of my brain.

As soon as my blades cut through the smooth surface, a sense of calm washes over me. The rink has always been my sanctuary. Even after everything that happened with Nathan, it still feels like home.

It's the one constant in my life.

But it's still not able to fully erase the pain of a broken heart.

Not tonight.

As I glide across the ice, my mind drifts back to the conversation with Dad. As much as the thought of skating under Nadia excites me, the idea of leaving everything I've built here at Western —the friends I've made, the life I'm trying to piece together—is terrifying.

No matter if I return to skating or not, I can't shake the feeling that something just as important has slipped through my fingers.

Hayes.

As I push off and glide forward, a chill runs down my spine. It's colder than usual. Or maybe it's just me. I pick up speed and try to shake off the strange feelings by losing myself in the rhythm of my skates as they cut through the ice.

Breathe in.

Breathe out.

The movements come easily at first, the familiarity of my routine taking over. A spin, a turn, a jump that I land perfectly. The sound of my blades hitting the ice echoes in the empty rink.

No matter how fast I go or how many times I push my body to its limits, the disturbing sensation that I'm not alone continues to linger.

I remind myself that there's no one else here.

As much as I don't want to admit it, the shadows at the edges of the rink seem darker tonight.

Deeper.

Almost as if something is hiding just out of sight, watching me.

I spin again, harder this time, hoping that if I go fast enough, I can blur out everything around me.

But the sound of my skates isn't enough to drown out the silence. I keep expecting to hear something.

A footstep.

A creak.

Anything.

But there's nothing.

Just the empty arena and the weight of my thoughts pressing in on me.

I attempt a triple lutz. It's a jump I've done a thousand times before. As I rise in the air, there's a split second where it feels like the ice pulls away from me. My landing is solid, but my heart is pounding in my chest, louder than the scrape of my blades.

I force myself to keep moving, to focus on the steps, the jumps, the spins. But it's hard. My mind keeps wandering back to everything I've been trying to forget.

What I walked in on at the hockey house.

Nathan's refusal to leave me alone.

And Nadia.

What if she decides that my best years are already behind me? Even though I'm not sure if I want the chance, I want to be the one who makes that decision.

Another jump that flows into a spin. I'm desperate to quiet my mind. It seems like the harder I push, the more the rink pushes back at me. The ice feels too smooth, too slick. Almost as if it's playing tricks on me, waiting for me to crash and burn.

My breath comes in sharp bursts as I slow down, finally coasting to a stop near the center of the rink. The hum of the lights seems louder now, like they're buzzing right in my ears. I glance around, half-expecting to see someone standing at the edge of the rink, watching me.

But there's no one.

Just the shadows.

I exhale sharply, trying to laugh it off, but it comes out shaky. I'm being ridiculous.

I've been skating alone for years.

Why does it feel so different now?

I take one last deep breath and close my eyes, trying to force everything from my mind.

The cold.

The shadows.

The fear that Nathan is actually stalking me.

Not from across the country but from here at Western.

I focus on the sound of my breath, the feel of the ice beneath my feet, the familiar tension in my legs.

I push off one last time, gliding across the rink in a long, sweeping arc. The cold air rushes past my face, and for a moment, I lose myself in the motion. It's just me and the ice, nothing else.

But when I stop, the silence presses in again. It's heavier now, more oppressive. I stand alone in the middle of the rink, my breath misting in the air. And I realize that no matter how fast I skate, no matter how hard I try, I won't be able to outrun the feelings eating at me.

My breath is ragged, chest heaving, as I stare out across the rink. The shadows at the far end seem darker, like they're closing in.

I blink.

It's just my mind playing tricks on me.

My heart skips a painful beat when I spot him. For a second, I want to believe I'm imagining things.

It can't be him.

Not here.

Not now.

But it is.

My old coach stands half-hidden in the shadows, just outside the reach of the dim light. His silhouette is unmistakable—the tall, broad-shouldered frame. The way he stands with his hands shoved in his pockets, as if he's waiting for me to acknowledge his silent presence.

"You still look good, Ava." His voice is low, almost conversational, but it sends a shock of fear through me. "It's a shame you quit."

The terror that slides through me is icy and sharp. My mouth turns cottony, making it almost impossible to force out the question. "What are you doing here?"

With a shrug, he takes a step forward, his shoes crunching against the ice. "You refused to talk to me. What was I supposed to do?"

I swallow hard as he moves closer, his steps deliberate. The thin barrier of space between us feels like nothing. My skates wobble beneath me, making it impossible to escape.

My heart flutters in panic as the frigid air around us turns suffocating.

"You're not really going to work with that woman, are you?" he asks, his voice smooth as the whiskey he was always partial to, as he takes yet another step in my direction. "You have to realize we were meant to be together, right? We were so perfect. And we could be again."

"No." I shake my head, stepping back instinctively, my blades scraping against the ice. "You crossed so many lines... and you don't even realize it."

Nathan's lips lift. It's a patient, infuriating smile that makes my skin crawl. "It sounds like your parents filled your head with lies," he says softly. "I was able to unlock something in you because of our emotional connection. Every move you made was like watching art come to life. It was effortless, fluid, beautiful."

"What you did was wrong," I snap, my voice trembling but firm.

His smile never falters. "Did it feel wrong when we were together?" His tone is calm, almost condescending. "I molded you into the perfect skater. No one will ever understand you the way I do. Only I know how to tease out a flawless routine. Deep down inside, you know it's the truth. You're nothing without me."

My breath escapes in shallow bursts as I try to hold my ground. "You manipulated me."

"No," he says quietly, shaking his head. The unwavering smile on his face feels like a taunt, the kind of patience that makes me want to scream. "I brought out the best in you. We could be on top again."

"Stop." My tone turns desperate. "You're a predator. You belong locked up behind bars."

His smile breaks, but only for a second, as his eyes darken, and he takes another calculated step. "You don't really believe that," he says, voice hardening. "You've been brainwashed."

I force myself to retreat, but the ice feels unforgiving. The cold, hard surface beneath my trembling legs makes it impossible to feel grounded.

He pulls his hand from his pocket and a glint of metal snags my attention. I'm so transfixed by the small object that I barely notice when he takes another step forward.

My breath hitches and my blood turns to ice as I stare at the gun, unable to tear my eyes away from it.

"Nathan..." My voice comes out sounding as if I'm being strangled from the inside out. "What are you doing?"

"It's simple. If I can't have you, no one will."

His chilling response hangs heavy in the air as it echoes through the arena. Or maybe it just reverberates hollowly in my head. Icy tendrils of fear and panic wrap around my heart, constricting it until movement becomes impossible. Even as he approaches, my brain screams at me to flee. But my feet are slow, the ice beneath me too slick, and my stilted movements are clumsy compared to his steady approach.

"Nathan, please." My voice cracks as it turns pleading, and my hands shake. I lift them, trying to make him see reason. "Don't do this."

He doesn't respond as his eyes stay locked on me.

Only now do I realize how empty and emotionless they are. He takes another step and raises the gun, pointing it directly at me.

My knees turn to jelly as my body quakes.

As much as I want to glance around and get my bearings, I can't take my eyes off him. I'm afraid of what he'll do if I look away for even a second. I'm running out of space and options. A cry escapes from me when my back hits the boards at the edge of the rink, and I realize there's nowhere left to go.

The cold metal of the barrier presses against my spine, but it's nothing compared to the icy terror that spreads through my veins.

"Nathan," I gasp. "Don't do this."

"I made you." His voice remains low.

Eerily calm.

As if what he's saying makes perfect sense.

"No one will ever push you to be the best the way I did. You need me, Ava."

My teeth chatter as my heart jackhammers against my chest.

There's nowhere for me to run. He has me trapped.

The only thing I can focus on is the gun in his steady hand.

My tongue darts out to lick dry lips. "Nathan, please—"

His finger hovers over the trigger, and time slows.

My chest constricts until breathing becomes impossible.

Until thought becomes impossible.

Until there's nothing left for me to do but pray.

TENINCHESOF
COCKY

WILDCATS

y foot is heavy on the gas pedal as I speed through the quiet streets, gripping the wheel so tightly my knuckles ache.

I fumble with the phone, redialing her number, trying to get a hold of her.

Just like the previous times, it goes straight to voicemail.

As I pull into the parking lot of her building, I look for her apartment on the fourth floor. The place is shrouded in darkness. Only then do I glance around for her silver Jetta and realize it's not here.

Fuck.

I shouldn't have pushed her away. I told myself the right thing to do was to let her go so she could follow her dreams. Just like Coach said. But right now, all I can think about is how I screwed everything up. And now I can't shake the feeling that something is wrong.

Where would she go at this time of night?

I rack my brain, trying to think, as my heart hammers in my chest.

Then it hits me.

The rink.

I rev the engine and squeal out of the lot, taking the turn sharply and flying toward the arena. Skating is her refuge, the one thing that has the power to calm her. But as I pull into the parking lot, something feels... off.

Ava's car is here, parked in its usual spot, along with a few others.

My gaze settles on a vehicle I don't recognize with out-of-state plates, and a cold wave of unease rolls over me.

I cut the engine and rush inside the arena. As soon as the glass door slams shut behind me, the familiar chill hits me, but it does nothing to calm the rising panic in my chest.

The rink, the place that's always felt safe, now feels too quiet.

Unnaturally still.

My footsteps echo off the walls as I move through the building.

The need to find her pounds through me like a steady drumbeat. Each step only intensifies the feeling.

As I come to the second set of doors, I catch sight of her.

Ava's at the far end of the ice, backed up against the boards. She's pale, and even from here, the stark terror written across her expression is palpable.

And she's not alone.

Nathan is on the ice, standing too damn close, with a gun pointed at her.

My heart stutters before beating into overdrive.

"No one will ever push you to be the best the way I did. You need me, Ava."

The chilling calmness of his voice has my blood freezing in my veins.

"Nathan, please—" she whispers.

My body moves before my brain can catch up, slipping toward the benches. I need to find a way to get him to stop pointing the gun at her. I crouch lower, keeping behind the boards, moving quickly but quietly. Ava shifts, turning slightly, and Nathan follows her movement. His back is to me, the gun remaining trained on her.

This is my chance.

It might be the only one I get.

I leap over the boards and hit the ice hard. It doesn't take long for me to regain my balance. Nathan is too focused on Ava to notice me just yet. Even though he continues to talk, I barely hear him over the rush of blood that pounds in my ears.

"I didn't want it to be like this," he says, his voice cracking as it rises. "But you let them twist everything. Do you have any idea how much I loved you?"

I'm closer now.

His grip tightens on the gun, and I see the barrel shift, moving away from Ava. My heart seizes when I realize where it's now pointing.

He's turned it on himself.

"Nathan!" I shout, but it's too late. He squeezes the trigger just as I crash into him, my body slamming into his with every ounce of my strength.

The gun goes off, the sound splitting the air.

We hit the ice hard before sliding across the smooth surface. The gun flies out of his hand and spins away. My ears ring as my breath comes out in short, sharp gasps.

Ava screams my name, but it's distant, muffled. Almost as if I'm underwater.

"Get your phone!" I yell, my voice hoarse as I push myself up. My hands shake as adrenaline rushes through me. "And call the police!"

Ava's frozen for a second, her face leeched of all color, but then she snaps into action, rushing toward her bag at the edge of the rink.

I refocus my attention on Nathan. He's lying on his back, staring up at the ceiling as blood pools beneath him from a wound in his shoulder. His chest heaves with ragged breaths, and his eyes are wide, unfocused.

"You..." Nathan's voice is barely audible now, broken and full of pain. "You'll never love her the way I do."

My hands shake as I press down on the wound and try to stem the bleeding. I glance over my shoulder to see Ava is talking on the phone. It would be impossible not to notice the way her body trembles. From the corner of my eye, I see Coach rush from the locker room and onto the ice. It doesn't take long before he has her wrapped up in his arms. Our gazes lock for one moment as he turns her away, shielding her from the view.

Nathan's breath rattles, his eyes still fixed on the ceiling. "I loved her," he whispers, voice fading. "I made her what she is."

I don't bother with a response.

There's nothing left to say.

Police and EMTs burst through the doors with a flurry of activity as I press harder on his wound, trying to keep him alive. I have no idea if he'll make it. After everything this man has done, I honestly don't know if he deserves to.

But one thing is clear—he'll never hurt Ava again.

Not ever.

AVA

The harsh fluorescent lights of the police station make everything feel surreal, like I'm watching my own life unfold from the outside. It's a peculiar sensation. I sit in the small, stiff chair, with my parents on either side of me. Their hands clasp mine, offering silent support. My body still hums with nervous energy, but my mind feels distant.

Numb.

I still can't believe this happened.

That Nathan would—

The officer sitting across from us closes his notebook, his expression remaining neutral.

"We'll be in contact if we have any further questions," he says. "Nathan is at the hospital. The guy is lucky to be alive."

"What happens now?" my dad asks, his voice low and steady, but I can hear the tension fighting to break through.

"A psych evaluation, for starters," the officer replies. "And then, depending on the results, he'll be charged. Stalking, assault, illegal possession of a firearm. He's not walking away from this."

His words should have relief flooding through me that it's finally over, but instead, all I feel is exhaustion, a bone-deep tiredness that makes it hard to think, hard to breathe. I just want to go home and pretend this nightmare never happened.

It's almost difficult to believe there was ever a time when I thanked my lucky stars that Nathan Covington found me, saw something in me that I didn't realize was there, plucking me from obscurity.

Now the opposite is true.

"Thank you, Officer," my mom says softly, squeezing my hand. I nod, my eyes fixed on the door, only wanting to get the hell out of here. I want to fall face-first into bed and sleep for days. Long enough to forget about the terror pumping through my veins when he'd pointed that gun at me. I never believed it when people said their lives flashed before their eyes, but that's exactly what happened.

We stand to leave, and I follow my parents out of the room. I appreciate their comforting presence now more than ever. As we walk into the lobby, my heart stutters in my chest when I catch sight of Hayes. I wasn't sure if he would take off after the police were done talking to him.

He jumps to his feet the moment he sees us, his face a mix of relief and something else.

Guilt, maybe?

My pulse quickens, and it takes everything I have inside not to run to him. To throw myself into his arms and forget about everything that happened.

But I don't.

I can't.

We're not together.

Maybe we were never really together.

That thought cuts as deep as a knife.

Hayes shoves his hands into the pockets of his jeans as his gaze searches mine. "Do you have a moment to talk?"

Dad steps forward, his protective instincts kicking in. "I think it would be best if you and Ava spoke another time," he says. "She's pretty shaken up."

"I'm so sorry I didn't get there sooner," Hayes whispers, his voice low and thick with regret. He looks at me again, and the weight of his words presses on my chest.

What if he'd gotten there ten minutes later?

Or not at all?

A shiver scurries down my spine, not wanting to imagine either of those scenarios playing out.

"It's not your fault." I glance at my parents as guilt threatens to swallow me whole. "I should have told them about the texts. Or that I thought I saw him following me." I shrug, wishing it were possible to go back in time and make different decisions. Better ones. "I thought I was just being paranoid."

When a heavy silence falls over our group, Dad's hand settles gently against my back, attempting to steer me toward the exit.

It's a surprise when Hayes steps in front of us, desperation flooding his green eyes. "Please, Coach? It's important."

Dad hesitates before shooting a glance at me. "Is that what you want?"

I nod, unable to trust my voice, as my mom brushes a kiss against my forehead.

"All right. We'll wait in the car." Dad squeezes my hand before wrapping an arm around my mother. She leans her head against his broad shoulder. Barely do I hear the soft sob that escapes her as they walk out, leaving me alone with Hayes.

The moment the door swings shut behind them, I feel the weight of Hayes's gaze pinning me in place.

He looks wrecked.

His eyes are full of an apology that doesn't need words.

"I'm so sorry, Ava. For everything," he says, his voice hoarse. "I thought I was making the best decision for both of us, but it turned out to be the wrong one."

I frown as confusion mixes with the swirl of emotions I'm still trying to manage. "I don't understand. What are you talking about?"

"Your dad told me about the coach who wants to work with you." Remorse clouds his face as he looks away. "I thought if I ended things, you'd move to Colorado to focus on skating, and that you'd be safe there."

"He did?" With that, understanding dawns. I exhale as the pieces finally click into place. "Is that why you were with those girls? Why you pretended we were nothing more than a hookup?"

He drags a hand through his mussed hair, and I get the feeling I'm not the only one trying to keep it together. "Yeah. You're too damn talented not to compete. I didn't want to be the reason you didn't reach your full potential."

I shake my head as frustration bubbles up inside me. "That wasn't your decision to make."

"You're right," he says, his voice rough. "It wasn't. And I'm sorry. It was never my intention to hurt you. I just..." He pauses, his jaw clenched. "I only wanted what was best for you."

Silence stretches between us as the tension turns oppressive. I search his eyes, desperate to see the truth behind his words.

"Did you ever consider that you're what's best for me?"

As soon as the question is out of my mouth, Hayes steps forward, bridging the distance between us. My breath catches when his hand rises to cup my cheek, and his thumb brushes against my skin.

"If that's true," he admits, seriousness shining brightly from his eyes, "then I would consider myself the luckiest bastard in the world."

Unable to hold back for another second, I lean in so my lips can drift over his. The kiss starts off soft, almost tentative, as if we're both testing the waters. It doesn't take long for the floodgates to open, and everything I've been holding back—the fear, the pain, the longing— pours out into that one caress.

Hayes tugs me closer before wrapping his arms around me, as if he'll never let go, and for the first time since this nightmare began, I finally feel safe.

Really, truly safe.

And I know with every fiber of my being that this is exactly where I'm supposed to be.

TenInchesofCocky
WILDCATS
VAN DOREN
19
19
81

TENINCHESOF
COCKY

HAYES

WILDCATS

39

The roar of the crowd fills my ears as I line up at center ice, my heart already thudding with the adrenaline that surges before the puck drops. Playoff games are always tense and electric.

But tonight is different.

I look up into the stands and scan the crowd until I find her.

Not only is Ava sitting with all the other girlfriends—Juliette, Carina, Fallyn, Viola, Stella, Britt, and Willow—but she's wearing my jersey. Seeing her there has something tightening in my chest. I never expected to find someone who made me feel complete. It's crazy. She crashed into my life when I least expected it, and now I can't imagine being without her.

Nor would I want to.

Even Willow's roommate, Holland, is here tonight.

I stifle a grin.

That girl scares the hell out of me. She's all sharp edges and attitude, the kind of person who won't hesitate to cut you down with a single look.

I don't know what it is, but she gives off this vibe, like you never really know what's going on in her head.

Bridger glances at the stands, and his gaze narrows when it locks on Holland. There's something between those two, but for the life of me, I can't figure out what it is. He's been dealing with a lot lately—

the BS with the messages and his father—and it's been weighing on him. You can see it in the way he moves and his sullen demeanor.

Bridger's a good friend. I wish there were more I could do to help, but there isn't. The only thing I can do is be there for him if he needs me.

I shove those thoughts from my head and refocus my attention. I've got a game to win and a girl to impress.

My mom, Ollie, Theo, and Kia are also here, cheering me on. I want my siblings to see that anything is possible with enough hard work and a shit load of determination.

As soon as the puck drops, everything around me fades to the background.

I play hard. Every shift, every pass, every check feels like it's propelling me toward my future. And knowing that Ava's in the stands, wearing my number, cheering for me, makes me push myself past my limits.

I want to win, not just for the team but for her.

It doesn't take long before I'm locked into the rhythm of the game. The feel of the puck on my stick, the way my legs burn as I skate up and down the ice. It's when I catch a clean pass and break away from the defense that everything slows. The goalie shifts, trying to anticipate my shot.

I see my opening and fire the puck.

A second ticks by.

Then another.

When it hits the back of the net with a satisfying thud, the arena erupts. The roar is deafening, and I can barely hear my own thoughts over the sound of the crowd. I skate toward the glass and point at Ava. She's on her feet, grinning from ear to ear. The sight of her has something clicking inside me.

Even though the fans are going crazy, shouting my name, she's the only one I'm cognizant of.

I've never been in love before. Never even thought about the possibility. But seeing her there, wearing my name, my number, cheering like I'm the only guy on the ice...

It's like the world finally makes sense.

This has to be what love feels like.

The undeniable pull toward someone who makes everything brighter and better. The feeling manages to ground me while lifting me up at the same time.

As the game continues, I glance up at her whenever I can. It's like she's my anchor, the one thing that keeps me steady in all this chaos.

I have no idea how I got lucky enough to find her, but I do know one thing—there's no way in hell I'm letting her go.

Not now.

Not ever.

TENINCHESOF
COCKY

WILDCATS

TenInchesofCocky
VAN DOREN
19
HAYES

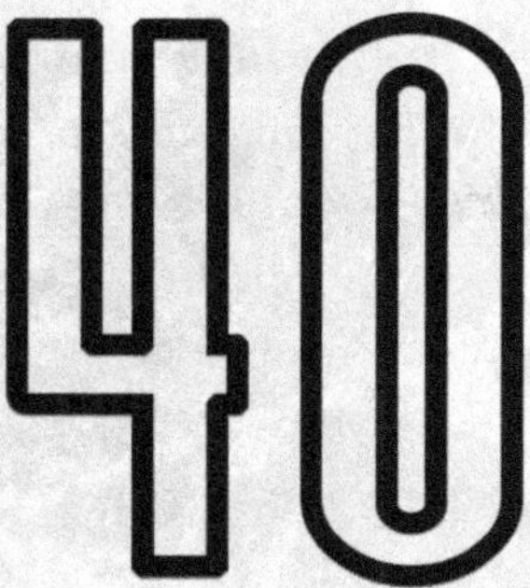

By the time the team arrives at Slap Shotz, the place is packed to the gills. Everyone is still riding high from winning our first playoff game.

It's tradition—after a win, this is where we go to celebrate.

Fans are sporting jerseys and buzzing from the game, as if they were the ones on the ice tonight. There's a frenetic energy that charges the air and is impossible to ignore.

I should be soaking it all in, enjoying the glory of the win and the attention. Hell, there are a few groupies hitting on me right now, tossing out flirty comments and batting their eyelashes, hoping I'll give them a bit of attention or a word of encouragement.

But there's no way in hell that's going to happen.

I can't take my eyes off Ava.

And if I'm being truthful with myself, that's the way it's been from the very beginning.

She's across the room, talking with Fallyn and Juliette, laughing, her smile bright enough to light up the whole damn bar. In a short period of time, she's become my everything. I never expected to feel this pull toward her. Now that I do, I can't imagine a single day without her. She's still wearing my jersey, and every time she glances at me, my heart skips a beat.

As soon as our gazes collide, she rises to her feet and cuts a direct path to me. The moment she's within striking distance, I nab her fingers and pull her close enough to wrap up in my arms.

It's exactly where she belongs.

It's the best feeling in the world to be here with my girl and my teammates, celebrating our first playoff win. Ryder was just on stage with Juliette, singing some ridiculous duet that makes the whole place swoon and cheer. Wolf jumped up there after them, crooning a love song to Fallyn. I flick a glance at his wife to see she's eating it up.

Even Bridger's here, which is a surprise. There's a black Western Wildcats ballcap pulled low over his eyes, and he's sitting off to the side, nursing a beer and looking like he'd rather be anywhere else.

The poor bastard can't seem to catch a break.

"Last song of the evening," Sully, the bar owner, announces.

A slow grin spreads across my face as Ava's eyes widen, and she shakes her head.

"No way. You've heard me sing. It's not good. We'll get booed off the stage for sure"

"We have to, Tink." I glance around at my teammates. "Apparently, it's another tradition. Are you really going to be the one who breaks it?"

She huffs out a breath before muttering, "I guess not. But consider yourself warned if things go south quickly."

The second I pull Ava onto the stage, the noise of the bar fades away, leaving only the thud of my heartbeat to fill my ears.

Her gaze darts nervously at the crowd as I give the song selection to Sully, and he cues it up.

When John Legend's "All of Me" starts, her expression softens, and something shifts in the air. It's like the world narrows down to just the two of us as the soft melody fills the space. I hold the microphone close, and when I start to sing, it's not just to the crowd—it's to her. As soon as she joins in, her voice intertwines with mine, and the room seems to disappear.

Her lips curve slightly as she sings. I can't help but lay it all out there for everyone to see. There's no hiding how much this girl means to me, especially when I came so close to losing her.

Each glance, each note shared between us, is a promise, something deeper than we've dared to voice out loud. My throat tightens, not from the lyrics but from the weight of what's passing between us.

The world could burn down, and I wouldn't notice. It's just me and Ava, the connection between us tangible, like a thread we're holding on to in the quiet pauses of the song.

By the time the final notes ring through the air, I realize the bar has gone silent.

Emotion rushes through my veins as I tug her into my arms, and my lips brush across hers. Ford leaps to his feet and whistles, and the crowd bursts into catcalls and applause.

Ava shakes her head as our gazes hold.

"I think you're it for me, Tink."

She cups my cheeks with her palms. "I can't begin to imagine my life without you in it."

"Guess it's a good thing that you'll never have to."

Just as the night hits its peak with everyone laughing, singing, and soaking in the irrepressible energy from our win, there's a sudden buzz.

When my pocket vibrates, I pull out my cell. That's when I realize the same mass text has hit everyone's phones at the same time.

It's a picture of Bridger at the bar, and there's a girl standing close to him with her hand on his chest. The caption beneath says

Make sure someone sends the hockey ho penicillin in the morning. We all know she's gonna need at least one dose. Maybe two.

"Shit," I mutter.

The mood shifts as everyone stares at their phones.

I glance at Bridger and see his expression has darkened. He swears under his breath as his narrowed eyes scan the bar, like he's trying to figure out who the culprit is. He clenches his hands as tension vibrates off him in suffocating waves.

This is the last thing he needs.

I see the exact moment his gaze lands on Holland, who's parked at a table next to Willow. Whatever she's thinking is hidden behind a mask of indifference. You would have to be blind not to see the sparks that fly between them the second their gazes collide. Bridger's jaw tightens, looking as if it's in imminent danger of shattering, as Holland flips him the bird and goes back to her drink like nothing happened.

Ava catches the exchange, her brow furrowing as she glances between them. "Any idea what their deal is?" she asks, tone curious but laced with concern.

Now that Willow is dating Maverick McKinnon, her roommate and bestie, Holland, has been hanging out with the girls. She and Ava have become fast friends.

"Not sure," I say with a shrug, watching as Bridger's eyes narrow at Holland as she continues to ignore him. I'm almost afraid to voice the thoughts that have crept into my head. "I really hope she's not the one behind all the messages. Bridger will make her life hell if that turns out to be the case."

Ava frowns, biting her lip like she's trying to figure out a puzzle. The last thing I want is to get drawn into whatever drama's brewing between them. That's his mess to handle. All I care about is the girl standing next to me, looking up at me with those wide, blue eyes that are capable of making me forget my own name.

I drop a kiss on the top of her blonde head. The floral scent of her hair teases my senses and turns me on like nothing else. "You ready to get out of here, baby girl?"

She looks up at me, the corners of her mouth lifting in a soft smile, and nods. "Yeah, let's go."

My grip tightens around her hand as I lead her through the crowd, away from the chaos of the bar, and into the night. The only thing I have on my mind is getting Ava alone and showing her exactly how much she means to me.

And I'll do it with my mouth.

My hands.

And my cock.

Exactly the way she likes it.

AVA

EPILOGUE

It's hard to believe almost a year has passed since I started working with Nadia Petrovic. To say that it's been grueling would be an understatement. She demands perfection every second I'm on the ice. What can't be denied is that I've become a better skater with her coaching. The long hours, the sweat, the exhaustion—it's all been worth it. I didn't realize how much I missed the thrill of competition until I was back in it. Every jump, every spin, every glide across the ice feels like I've found a part of myself that I'd long forgotten.

The hardest part is being separated from Hayes.

He's playing for Nashville now, and the NHL season runs for nearly eight months, sometimes longer if the team makes it to the playoffs. If I'd been secretly worried that a long-distance relationship might be the end of us, the opposite has turned out to be true. When we're able to arrange our schedules and fly to the same city, it's always explosive between us. We can't keep our hands off each other and end up spending most of our time in bed. There's no other place I'd rather be than wrapped up in his arms. Our connection has only flourished, deepening over the past year.

When we're together, nothing else in the world exists.

I'll see him again in two weeks at a competition, but right now, I miss him so much, it hurts.

I grab my laptop and open it, settling on the queen-sized bed in my apartment. Anticipation hums through my veins as I stare at the dark computer screen, waiting for him to start a private show just for me.

It's become our thing, a way to bridge the distance when we can't be in the same city. One of my favorite things is to watch him get off on camera. I love the way he runs his hands down his chiseled chest and over his defined abs, each movement causing his muscles to flex and ripple. I can't stop from touching myself, imagining his hands are the ones bringing me pleasure as I watch him fist his thick erection with precision and control. What we've found together is raw and intimate, a part of our relationship that we've grown into, where we can explore our needs without judgment.

Hayes indulges me in ways I never thought possible, turning all my fantasies into reality.

With him, I feel free.

And safe.

I grow impatient as the screen remains blank. With a frown, I scoop up my phone and call him. He answers on the second ring.

"Hey, what's going on?" I click a few more keys, only wanting to see his gorgeous face.

"Hold on, babe." His voice crackles through the line. "I'm having some technical difficulties on my end. Just give me a second or two to work through the kinks."

A few more minutes slip by, and still nothing. I sigh as disappointment creeps in at the edges. Today was rough. Nadia had me practicing one part of my new routine over and over until it was perfect.

My legs ache, and my body feels like it's been through a war. The thought of seeing Hayes tonight, even if it's just through a screen, was what got me through it all.

But now...

It doesn't look like that's going to happen.

My head snaps up when there's a knock on the apartment door. "Someone's here," I mutter with a frown.

"Expecting company?"

"Not that I know of."

"I'll wait while you go check who it is," he says as I slide off the bed and pad barefoot to the door.

With a twist of the handle, I pull it open. A gasp catches in my throat, and my heart stutters before beating into overdrive. Standing on the other side of the threshold is Hayes. A smile lights up his face.

My eyes widen, and before I can even think, I launch myself at him with a small squeal of happiness. He catches me easily, his strong arms banding around me as I bury my face against his neck and inhale his masculine scent.

God, I've missed it so much.

I've missed *him* so much.

A heavy wave of emotion crashes over me.

I can't believe he's standing at my door.

After spending weeks apart and trying to coordinate our schedules, I didn't think it was possible.

"What are you doing here?" I ask, my voice muffled against his shoulder before I pull back just enough to search his handsome face. "We talked about it. You said you wouldn't be able to make it this weekend!"

His grin widens as his eyes twinkle with amusement. "I wanted it to be a surprise. Are you surprised, baby?"

Tears well in my eyes as I pull him closer. "You have no idea." I've missed him so much, and now that he's here, everything feels right again. Like I can breathe again.

He's changed so much since college. He's more muscular, his body harder and thicker, and I love it. I can't stop my hands from roaming over the firm planes of his chest and arms, feeling the strength that lies tightly harnessed beneath his skin. As soon as I wrap my legs around his waist, he palms my ass cheeks.

"I've missed you," I whisper, kissing him again, this time slower, savoring the taste of him.

He chuckles against my lips, carrying me toward the bedroom without breaking our connection. "I've missed you too, babe. I couldn't go another day without seeing you. Holding you. Kissing you."

Once we're in the bedroom, he lowers me onto the mattress, his body hovering over mine. The warmth of his presence seeps into me and chases away the exhaustion of the day.

Now that he's here, everything else fades to the background.

Nothing else matters but this man.

He's become my everything.

The reason I draw air into my lungs.

And I can't imagine that ever changing.

He presses a kiss against my lips before pulling away and staring deep into my eyes. "You know how much I love you, right?"

I nod. He shows and tells me every single day.

Not once have I ever doubted it.

Even when I watch his games on TV, and I see all the women sporting his jersey and cheering for him. One even held up a sign that said she blew him in college.

I really hope she enjoyed it because that's not something that will ever happen again.

I'm the only one who gets to blow my husband now.

Oh, did I forget to mention that we're married?

We tied the knot three months ago.

It was during a weekend trip to Vegas to watch him play. A bunch of his college teammates flew out to the game. Afterward, we went out to celebrate and had a few too many drinks. One thing led to another, and an Elvis impersonator presided over the nuptials.

We haven't told anyone else.

For the time being, it's our little secret.

The only time I wear the wedding band he bought for me is when I'm alone in the apartment. I can't wait until next July when we have a formal ceremony, and I can wear his ring all the time.

In his eyes I see every drop of love he feels for me.

It's always shining brightly from his green depths.

"I do. And I love you just as much. Thank you for planning this. You have no idea how much I needed to see your face in person." My fingers trail over the light stubble on his cheek.

"I know, babe. It won't always be like this. Hopefully, if the trade happens, we'll be living in the same city."

I squeeze my eyes closed and pray with every fiber of my being that his agent can work a little magic. Hayes Van Doren is a hot commodity in the league. We won't know for another month or so if they were able to hammer out the finer details of the contract, though.

His gaze trails down my body. "I think you might be wearing a bit too much clothing."

Before I can say a word, he grips the hem of my shirt and drags it up my torso before dropping it to the floor beside the bed. His attention stays fastened to my chest as he palms the soft flesh.

"I love when you don't wear a bra. Easy access."

With a whimper, I arch into his touch. It's been so long since his hands have been on me, branding me as his own.

And I've missed it.

Missed *him*.

He tweaks my nipples until the little peaks stiffen before tugging them in tandem. It's enough to drag another moan from me. His face lowers until he can suck one pert tip between his lips, drawing it deep inside the warmth of his mouth. My fingers tunnel through his thick blond hair to hold him close. He releases my nipple with a soft pop before giving the same attention to the other one.

"Hayes, please..." My voice trails off as pleasure floods every cell in my body.

He lifts his head until his gaze can capture mine. "Please what, baby girl? Tell me what you want. You know I'll give you exactly what you need. All you have to do is ask."

It's not an empty promise.

He means every damn word.

He proves it to me every time we make love. And that's exactly what it is.

Love.

"I want you to flip me over and take me hard."

"Fuck, baby. That's sweet music to my ears." With a growl, he yanks my leggings down my hips and thighs before they meet the same fate as the shirt.

He spreads my legs wide and stares at my naked core. "No panties, huh?"

I shake my head.

His thumb glides over my slit. A deep rumble of approval comes from his chest. "Already wet for me."

"I was so excited to see you that I would've fucked you in the hallway."

"Mmmm. Don't care if you would've given all your neighbors a show, huh?"

The idea is thrilling and only sends my arousal spiking. "Let them watch. All the ladies would be drooling over your big cock, wishing they had something half the size."

He smirks. "You're the only one I want drooling anywhere near my cock. Preferably all over my dick while you're choking on it."

More wetness gathers in my core. "I think that can be arranged."

"Oh, I'm counting on it, Tink." He smears my arousal around, rubbing soft circles against my clit before flicking the little piece of jewelry. I can't help but arch my back and widen my legs, needing more.

Needing everything.

"Always so fucking greedy."

"For you."

"Better only be for me."

When he slides one finger deep inside my body, my inner muscles clench around him. With his other hand, he toys with my nipple while leisurely pumping inside my pussy until my eyelids are fluttering shut as waves of pleasure pummel my senses.

It wouldn't take much to make me come.

A second finger joins the first, filling me even more. Stretching me for his girth. My eyelids crack open when he pauses. I find his gaze locked on my spread pussy. Only his fingertips remain inside me.

"Such a gorgeous cunt. I'm going to enjoy fucking and eating it this weekend. I've missed the taste of you on my tongue. I hope

Nadia gave you the day off tomorrow, otherwise you'll be calling in sick."

"She did," I say with a gasp.

The thought of him doing all those delicious things to me only gets me wetter. I'm probably drenched right now.

He smirks. "You love the dirty talk, don't you, baby girl?"

"You know I do."

A slow grin spreads across his face. "Yup, I do. I just love hearing you admit it."

We couldn't be more perfectly suited. His appetites match my own, as if we were made for each other.

"How much does this pussy need to be fucked?"

I spread my legs impossibly wide as he caresses my lips. "Please, I need you."

"Trust that I know exactly what you need."

"I do, Hayes. I trust you to always take care of me."

His eyes soften before he leans down and licks my slit from the bottom to my clit before sucking the silver ring into his mouth. I can't help but shift, silently begging for him to push me over the edge and into oblivion.

It certainly won't be the last time tonight.

And I can't wait.

I gasp when he pulls back and slaps my clit with the tips of his fingers. Pleasure explodes in my core before reverberating throughout the rest of my body.

His hands settle on my hips before tightening. It doesn't take much for him to flip me over and drag me to the edge of the bed. He swats one ass cheek before doing the same to the other side. It's not hard. Just enough to have pain blooming into pleasure.

"Ass in the air, baby girl. You know how I like to see both your pretty little holes."

My belly dips at his dirty words.

I press the side of my face into the sheets. My back arches, raising my ass in the air, as I spread my legs nice and wide.

Just the way he likes it.

The way I like it too.

I wouldn't do anything I didn't enjoy.

And Hayes wouldn't ask it of me either.

"So damn beautiful," he whispers as his hand drifts across the curve of my ass before his fingers separate the flesh even more so he can stare at the most secret part of me.

He pumps one finger in my pussy before sliding it over my rosebud, massaging the tight ring before gradually pressing inside. My breath catches and my eyelids feather shut at the delicious intrusion. He strokes in and out of me until every muscle loosens, and my body turns pliant.

"You have the most perfect heart-shaped ass. I miss it so damn much when we can't be together."

"I miss the way you play with me too."

I suck in a breath as he pushes in deeper. He crouches down until his warm breath can ghost across my delicate flesh as he presses a kiss against me.

"I wish I could wait longer, but I can't. I'll take my time with you later."

"Well, I did ask you to take me hard."

With a strained chuckle, he rises to his feet. In one swift movement, his cock slides deep inside my body, filling me to the brim.

Another groan falls from his lips. "Right here, baby. Pure bliss."

It doesn't take long for our bodies to fall into a natural rhythm. And then we're both falling over the edge.

Together.

The way it was always meant to be.

TENINCHESOF
COCKY

WILDCATS

TenInchesofCocky
VAN DOREN
19
HAYES

EPILOGUE

The arena buzzes with both excitement and energy as I take my seat among the crowd. I've never been more nervous in my life. Not even during my own championship games. I bite my nails as my gaze stays glued to the ice. If I know Ava, she's cool, calm, and collected.

My wife has nerves of steel.

That, in and of itself, is a fucking turn on.

A few minutes later, the crowd applauds as she steps onto the ice and takes her position in the center of it. My in-laws are seated on one side of me, and my mom and siblings are on the other. They're all munching on popcorn.

"She looks so pretty," Kia says with a sigh. "All those sparkles."

I grin at her. "Maybe figure skating isn't so bad after all, huh?"

She presses her lips together, as if giving the question serious consideration. "I still like hockey. I get to knock the boys on their butts."

"She's savage. Some of the boys are actually afraid of her," Ollie mutters.

Kia grins as a wicked light dances in her eyes.

I slide my arm around her slender shoulders and pull her close before pressing a kiss against the top of her blonde head. "That's my girl. Keep giving them hell."

When music fills the cavernous space, we all fall silent. More like the entire arena quiets as Ava glides effortlessly through her technical program, throwing in more jumps and tricks than I can count, each one more difficult than the previous. She's a vision out there, the way she moves with such grace, like she was born to do this.

My mind tumbles back to the first time I saw her on the ice, all those years ago at Western. She looked so beautiful, so strong and poised, like every movement she made was an extension of her soul.

I knew then that she was special, but seeing her here at the Olympics, it's like I'm watching her in a whole new light. She's one of the best women's figure skaters in the world, and I couldn't be prouder.

Nadia, her coach, has taken her to an entirely new level. Every jump, every spin, every combination is perfectly executed. It's not just her technical skills that make her stand out. It's the way she lights up the ice and captivates the crowd. Skating has always been her passion, and you can see it in every polished movement, every flick of her wrist. This is her world, and she commands it with a kind of quiet power that's impossible to look away from.

I can barely breathe as she nails her final jump, landing it so flawlessly it brings the entire arena to their feet. The crowd roars, and my heart swells with pride. Ava beams, grinning as she skates to the center of the ice, picking up the teddy bears and flowers fans throw in celebration.

She's worked so hard for this moment, and now it's hers. She glances up at the stands, right at me, and blows a kiss.

All I can say is that I'm the luckiest bastard alive.

As she and Nadia head over to the kiss and cry, a place where skaters and coaches wait for the scores to come in, I push my way through the crowd, clutching the bouquet of flowers I picked out earlier. My heart is still pounding, but this time, it's not from nerves.

It's from love.

Pure, overwhelming love for the woman who just took everyone's breath away. A few years ago, I could never have imagined feeling these kinds of emotions.

Fast forward two years, and I can't imagine *not* feeling them.

When I reach the televised area, Ava's sitting next to Nadia, still catching her breath, her cheeks flushed with excitement. I step forward and offer her the flowers, grinning like an idiot. "You were amazing, Tink. Pure magic."

Her face lights up when she sees me, and she stands on her skates, throwing her arms around me. I can feel her joy, her excitement radiating off her in heavy waves.

"Thank you. They're gorgeous," she says with a laugh, her voice muffled against my chest before she pulls away just enough to meet my gaze.

A spark fills her eyes. It's the one that always makes me feel like I'm exactly where I belong.

Where I want to be.

With her.

"Hayes!" a reporter calls out, trying to shove the microphone in my face. "Any word on if you'll be traded at the end of the season?"

"Actually, if you don't mind, I'd much rather focus on my wife's performance. She really smashed it out there, didn't she?"

"She sure did!" he says, turning his attention back to her.

Over the last two years, we've become America's sweethearts. The hockey player and the ice-skating queen. It still feels surreal sometimes, like it's all a dream I'm afraid to wake up from.

But right now, at this moment, none of that matters.

As the scores come in, I hold her close, kissing her temple. "I've never seen you skate better. No matter what the judges say, your performance was perfect."

She looks up at me, her eyes shimmering with emotion. "I couldn't have done it without you. You've always been by my side. My biggest champion and supporter. I love you. More than anything."

With a smile, I lean down to press my forehead against hers. "I love you too, baby girl. And I plan on proving it to you every day for the rest of our lives."

Hours later, after celebrating her silver medal with our families and friends, I run a bath, knowing she'll need to soak her exhausted muscles. She's been training so hard for this moment.

Both physically and mentally.

And it paid off.

Pride fills me with everything my wife has accomplished. She's become a force to be reckoned with in the competitive skating world.

When the tub is almost filled, and steam is rising from it, I turn off the taps and return to the bedroom where she's waiting.

A smile curves my lips when I see she hasn't moved a muscle.

"Such a good girl," I say, offering my hand for her to take.

Her pupils dilate at the endearment as she places her fingers in mine, and I help her to her feet.

I press a kiss against her lips before turning her so her back is to me. After her performance, she cleaned off all the makeup and washed her hair. It hangs in loose waves around her shoulders. It's carefully that I gather up the golden-blonde strands.

"Hold this up?"

Her arms rise to do as I've asked. I make quick work of the zipper, tugging it down the long line of her back. Once the material gapes open, she releases her hair so I can shove the material from one shoulder and then the other. The silky fabric puddles around her bare feet until she's standing before me in nothing more than a black thong. After the tiny scrap of underwear gets stripped away, I sweep her hair aside and press a kiss against the delicate curve of her neck before reaching around and cupping the warm weight of her breasts. I can't resist tugging at the little bars that pierce her nipples.

Fuck, but they're sexy.

Her head falls back to rest on my chest as a soft sigh drifts from her lips. "That feels amazing."

"Yes, it certainly does." I continue stroking them because I know just how much she loves having her breasts played with.

Especially with the piercings.

Those were a surprise for our one-year anniversary.

I sweep her up into my arms and carry her into the bathroom before gently setting her on the marble counter. The room is steamy and warm from the bath. Unable to help myself, I take a step back to admire the pretty picture she makes sitting naked in front of the mirror with both sets of piercings on full display.

That's all it takes for my cock to stiffen up.

I lean forward and kiss one breast before nipping at the hardened tip, sucking the little piercing into my mouth. Then I give the same treatment to the other one. A whimper falls from her lips as she arches into my touch.

I lick a hot trail down the middle of her ribcage to her bellybutton before sinking lower. My hands slide to her inner thighs, spreading them wide until my mouth can settle on her pussy.

When I swipe my tongue over her opening, circling the silver hoop, Ava groans and arches further. My hands slide from her thighs back up to her breasts to toy with the little bars.

When she's dancing on the edge, I pull back, not wanting her to spiral out of control.

At least, not yet.

"Hayes, please don't leave me hanging like this," she says on a whimper.

A strained chuckle escapes from me as I press one last kiss against her pouty lower lips and tweak her nipples before rising to my feet. I might be tormenting her, but I'm doing the same damn thing to myself in the process.

"Be patient, Tink. I promise I'll take care of you."

She grumbles in response.

Before scooping her into my arms, I take another step back and admire just how gorgeous my wife is.

Both inside and out.

Her arms tangle around my neck as I sweep her up and carry her to the bath before gently lowering her into the warm water until she's settled against the sloped porcelain. A sigh of contentment slips free as her body sinks into the steaming water. When she's fully submerged, she widens her legs until she's completely exposed. My gaze dips to her spread thighs before skimming up her body to settle on her face.

"Need more warm water added?"

"No." With a shake of her head, her eyelids slide closed. "It's perfect."

My gaze roams over her naked body as I strip off my button-down and T-shirt. Her eyes crack open to watch me. I can practically feel the heat of her gaze licking over my chest. My fingers flick open the button of my khakis before lowering the zipper and shoving the material down my legs until I'm left in nothing but my boxers.

And then those get peeled away as well.

Her attention drops to my erection before she licks her lips and slants her gaze upward to meet mine. My guess is that the heat in her eyes is echoed tenfold within my own.

"Have I mentioned how hot my husband is?"

I smirk. "Nope, not lately."

"Then I've been remiss."

I fist my hard dick before stroking it. Her pupils dilate, and the black swallows up the blue. "I know the perfect way you can make it up to me."

Her shoulders shake with laughter. "I'm sure you do."

"Just saying."

"Oh, I know exactly what you're saying, and I'm happy to oblige."

"Scoot up, baby."

She scoots forward so I can step behind her before settling in the water and stretching out my legs on either side of her. My hands wrap around her ribcage before drawing her backside against me. When she's positioned perfectly between my thighs, I press a kiss against her cheek. She turns her head until our lips can brush.

"I love you, baby. So fucking much it takes my breath away."

The expression on her face softens. "I love you too. I can't imagine my life without you in it."

I squeeze her against me. "You'll never have to."

She twists in my arms until we're facing one another. Only then does she rise and straddle my thighs. The piercing glints from between her spread lips as her fingers wrap around my cock before stroking the hard length. I can't help but strain against her, loving the feel of her touch.

With her fingers still wrapped around my thick erection, she guides me to her entrance before slowly sliding down the length.

We both let out quiet sighs. Once she's fully seated, her hands settle on my shoulders as she rocks against me until we fall into a steady rhythm. When her pussy spasms, it sets off my own orgasm. Our gazes stay locked as she takes me over the edge.

No matter what I experience in my life, nothing will ever feel as amazing as sliding inside her tight heat because it feels very much like coming home.

And that's exactly what Ava will always be.

My home.

The End

Thank you so much for reading Ava's and Hayes's story! I hope you enjoyed it as much as I loved writing it! Ready for the next couple in the Western Wildcats series?

Check out Never Your Girl!

Can you really blame me for loving the scandalous texts exposing Bridger Sanderson for the jerk he is? As far as I'm concerned, it's sweet karma for ghosting me after we hooked up two years ago. Cocky, infuriating, and way too gorgeous for his own good, Bridger thinks he's untouchable.

The best part?

He's convinced *I'm* behind the messages.

I wish.

Unfortunately, my life takes a turn for the worst when Bridger uncovers my secret side hustle. Now he's blackmailing me, forcing me to stick close—we're talking 24/7—until he figures out who's airing his dirty laundry on campus.

I should hate him for dragging me into his mess.

And I do...

Mostly.

Except... the more time we spend together, the harder it becomes to ignore how he looks at me. It's almost like he can see straight through the walls I've built to protect myself. Or how his own guard slips, revealing cracks in his armor when he thinks I'm not paying attention.

The only person who's ever gotten this close is *ColdAsIce17*, my anonymous confidant on the school chat app. With him, I can totally be myself.

But what happens when the lines blur between the guy I hate and the one I can't stop thinking about?

What happens when I realize they... might be the same person?

One-click Never Your Girl now!

If you haven't read Hate You Always, the first book in the Western Wildcats Hockey series, turn the page for an excerpt...

HATE YOU ALWAYS

JULIETTE

"I had a really good time tonight," Aaron says, gaze pinned to mine with an intensity that has me wanting to take a quick step in retreat.

Instead, I force a smile. "Yeah. Me, too."

It's not a total lie. I did have a good time. But that's all it was—*good*. Kind of like when we study together at the library or grab coffee at the Roasted Bean before class.

He glances away and shoves both hands into the pockets of his perfectly pressed khakis. "I hope we can do this again." There's a pause before he tacks on, "Soon."

I'm treated to a long, soulful stare that leaves me feeling borderline uncomfortable.

Yeah...I'm pretty sure that's not in the cards for us.

Aaron is nice.

Really nice.

Super-duper nice.

There's just no spark between us.

I'm searching for that elusive little tingle you get at the bottom of your tummy whenever you're near that person or even catch a glimpse of them from across a crowded room. It's the kind of irrepressible energy that sizzles in the air, charging it until drawing a full breath into your lungs feels impossible.

No matter how much I might wish otherwise, Aaron and I just don't generate that kind of chemistry.

There's only one person—

No.

I take a deep breath, slamming the door closed on those thoughts.

What I feel for that guy isn't attraction.

It's irritation.

Annoyance.

Aggravation.

Trust me, if you gave me enough time, I could come up with a laundry list of descriptive words that start with a vowel.

I blink back to awareness, only to realize that Aaron is patiently awaiting a response.

Oh, right. He wants to do this again.

As I open my mouth to let him down gently, the words stick in my throat. The last thing I want to do is lead him on, but at the same time, I don't want to hurt him either. What I need to do is strike the perfect balance. We have several pre-med classes together this semester. If I'm sick and can't attend class, Aaron is the one who catches me up to speed and makes sure I have all the notes.

They're usually color coded and placed in order of importance.

If there's been one lesson learned this evening, it's that I should avoid dating guys I see on a daily basis.

As Carina, my roommate, would say—don't shit where you eat.

She's right about that.

He inches closer. "If you're in agreement, I'd like to move this relationship forward. I like you, Juliette." He glances away briefly before his muddy-colored eyes refocus on me with a mixture of heat and intensity. "I'm probably getting a little ahead of myself here, but I think we could be a real power couple. We share similar aspirations —both of us have set our sights on furthering our studies in medicine and becoming physicians. I've never found someone who fits so perfectly into my five- and ten-year plan. It's almost like we were made for one another."

My eyes widen as a garbled sound escapes from me.

A little ahead of himself?

Five- and ten-year plan?

We've been out precisely three times, and the chances of there being a fourth have dwindled to the single digits.

I need to tell him that this—whatever he thinks *this* is—isn't going to happen. "Aaron..."

He perks up and sways closer. "Yeah?"

There's so much hope and expectation packed into that one word.

Argh.

Why does this have to be so difficult?

The problem is that he really *is* a nice guy. And what he said is absolutely true, we *do* have a lot in common. It's the reason I talked myself into giving him another chance.

And then a third.

There are a lot of douchey guys at this school who are only interested in sleeping with a chick before moving onto the next warm body. Sometimes within the span of the same evening. They don't have five- or ten-year plans that involve one specific girl. They don't even have twenty-four-hour plans that involve the same female.

So, when you happen to find a guy who has the opposite mindset, you need to take the time to delve deep and really get to know him before tossing him back into the wild for someone else to snap up.

"I had a nice time, too," I say carefully.

"Good." The tension filling his narrow shoulders drains as he beams in relief.

Aaron has a wiry build. His limbs are long and lean, much like a runner. Unlike some of the football or hockey players that strut around campus with their muscles on display as if they're god's gift to the female species.

Ugh. They seem to be everywhere.

As I stare into his earnest eyes, I make a last ditch effort to convince myself that he's exactly the type of guy I'm attracted to.

Deep down, in a place I'm loath to acknowledge, I know it's a lie.

Carina, damn her, would also tell me that the worst lies are the ones we tell ourselves.

That girl really needs to stay out of my head.

His hands reemerge from the depths of his pockets before rising to my face. It would be difficult not to notice their slight tremble. I force myself to stand perfectly still and not evade his touch at the last moment. And if that doesn't tell you everything you need to know about this situation, I'm not sure what will.

His eyelids droop to half-mast. "I'm going to kiss you now, Juliette," he mutters thickly. "I hope that's all right."

And with that, the mood has officially been killed.

Not that there was much of one to begin with, but still...

Unlike him, my eyes stay wide open as he moves toward me in slow motion. I steel myself for impact instead of flinching away.

Maybe I'm wrong.

Maybe Aaron will surprise the hell out of me and will end up being a phenomenal kisser. I'll magically lose myself in the caress as time and space cease to exist.

It's tentatively that his lips settle over mine. They're dry and papery to the touch. It's kind of like being pecked by a distant aunt or uncle.

Everything inside me deflates with the knowledge that this isn't going to end any other way than me carefully letting him down, because there's no way in hell I can do this again.

In fact, I'd pay good money to never do *this* again.

I press my palms against Aaron's chest to push him away when someone clears their throat. Aaron jumps back as if he just stuck his finger in an electrical outlet.

My gaze slices to the tall, muscular blond guy who has ground to a halt beside us.

Ryder McAdams.

My belly does a strange little flip before I swiftly stomp out the sensation.

Dark blue eyes pin me in place for a drawn-out heartbeat, making it impossible to breathe before shifting to Aaron. It's only when I'm released from his penetrating stare that the air trapped in my lungs rushes from me and I realize there are five more oversized hockey players crowded in the hallway outside my apartment door.

Ford Hamilton, Wolf Westerville, Colby McNichols, Riggs Stranton, and Hayes Van Doren are seniors on the Western Wildcats hockey team. Wherever they go, fangirls are sure to follow. I glance around only to realize they're all by themselves. It's weird not to see their entourage trailing after them.

Is it possible that hell has officially frozen over?

Colby flashes an easy-going grin as he snags my gaze. "Hey, McKinnon. Looks like someone has a hot date tonight." Like Ryder, he's blond and entirely too handsome for his own good.

His dimples are lethal to any female with a beating pulse in the vicinity.

Present company excluded.

Heat scalds my cheeks until it feels like they've caught on fire. The last thing I need is for the pretty hockey player to open his big yap to my brother.

Like I need the fifth degree from him.

Hard pass, thank you very much.

I might be the older sibling by fifteen months, but that, apparently, doesn't matter. Maverick takes his protective brother duties seriously. Dad drilled that into his head when he arrived at Western the year after I did.

Before I can snap out a response, they jostle and joke their way down the hall to the apartment next door. Ford lives there with Wolf and Madden while Ryder and five other teammates have a place located a couple blocks off campus known around school as the hockey house. For the last three decades, the residence has been exclusively occupied by Western hockey players. The current group of guys who rent the property will select the teammates who live there the following year.

It's a whole thing.

Eyeroll.

Thankfully, my brother lives off campus at the house. He's the only junior who was invited to do so and that has everything to do with Ryder. They've been tight since elementary school. I seriously don't think I could handle having him in the same building. He's all up in my business enough the way it is.

My skin prickles with awareness when I realize that Ryder hasn't followed his friends down the hallway. His gaze is still locked on Aaron, who looks seconds away from pissing himself.

And I get it.

Ryder McAdams can be intimidating.

Especially when he glares.

Which is exactly what he's doing at the moment.

Poor Aaron. In comparison, he looks like a scrawny, underdeveloped high schooler.

Awkwardness descends.

My date clears his throat before mumbling, "I, ah, should probably go."

There's a pause before he hesitantly sways toward me again. He only gets a few inches before Ryder crosses his thickly corded arms over his brawny chest. Aaron's movements stall as his face turns ashen.

"Umm..." He releases a high-pitched laugh that's strained around the edges. "How about a hug instead?"

When Ryder's eyes narrow, Aaron gulps, his throat muscles convulsing with the movement. In the silence of the hallway, the sound is deafening.

He finally reaches out, wrapping his sweaty palm around my hand before giving it three hearty pumps and promptly releasing it. I don't even get a chance to say goodbye as he swings around and races to the elevator like the hounds of hell are nipping at his heels.

He stabs the button a bunch of times and glances over his shoulder at us warily. When the bell chimes, announcing the car's arrival, he shoves his way inside before the doors have a chance to fully open, disappearing from sight.

Once the metal contraption closes, I scowl at Ryder. "Why'd you do that?"

One thick brow slinks upward. It's enough to have me gritting my teeth.

"Do what? I never said a word."

True enough. But still...

I'm aggravated with him for messing with my date. There was absolutely no reason for it.

"You purposefully stood there and made him feel uncomfortable."

Why am I picking a fight?

It's not like I wanted to kiss Aaron. If anything, I should be thanking Ryder for his timely interruption.

I almost snort, because there's no way in hell *that's* going to happen.

"How'd I do that? By standing here and patiently waiting for an introduction?" His gaze stays locked on mine as he tilts his head and scratches his shadowed jaw. "Seems kind of odd."

I bare my teeth before swinging away to dig through my purse for the apartment key. As soon as my fingers wrap around cool metal, I yank it out and jamb it in the lock with more force than necessary. The door reverberates on its hinges as I step inside and swivel to face Ryder once more before promptly closing it with a loud bang.

One-click Hate You Always now!

CAMPUS PLAYER

DEMI

"**M**orning, Demi!" Gary, one of the stadium custodians, calls out with an easy smile and wave as he saunters toward me. "Up and at 'em bright and early this morning, I see."

My heart jackhammers beneath my ribcage from the twenty-minute run as I flash him a grin. "Always!"

"You have a good one! I'll see you tomorrow!"

Since I've already moved past him, I holler over my shoulder, "Same place, same time!"

Even with *The Killers* pumping through my earbuds, I almost hear the deep chuckle that slides from his lips. Our morning greetings are a ritual three years in the making. I've been running through the wide corridor that leads to the stadium football field since I stepped foot on campus freshman year. This will be something I miss when I graduate in the spring. Five days a week, I'm up at six, logging in a four-mile run before returning home, jumping in the shower, and heading off to class.

At this time of the day, the stadium is still relatively quiet, with only a few people wandering the hallways. There's something both serene and eerie about it. I've been here on game days when there are thirty thousand fans packed shoulder to shoulder, rooting on the Western Wildcats football team. Three-fourths of the stadium filled with black and orange is an amazing sight to behold. Football is a religion at Western. Unfortunately, the same can't be said for the women's soccer team. We're lucky if there are a couple of hundred spectators in the stands.

I've come to terms with it.

Sort of.

I keep my gaze trained on the light at the end of the tunnel and push myself faster. As soon as I burst out of the darkness, bright sunlight pours down on me, stroking over the bare skin of my arms and shoulders. It's late August, and summer is still in full swing. A whistle cuts through the silence of the stadium, and my gaze slices to the field. Nick Richards has been head coach of the Wildcats for the last decade. He also happens to be my father.

Two days a week, the guys are up at six in the morning for yoga. Dad is a big believer in flexibility. Even though I'm winded, a smirk lifts the corners of my lips. Watching two-hundred-and-eighty-pound linebackers contort their bodies into Downward-Facing Dog, the Warrior II Pose, and the Cobra is enough to bring a chuckle to my lips. Some of the guys actually like it, but most grumble when they think Dad isn't paying attention. Little do they know that he sees and hears everything.

My father catches sight of me and flashes a quick smile along with a wave in my direction. He has a black ball cap pulled low and aviators covering his eyes. There's a clipboard in one hand as he paces behind the instructor.

When I point to the field, he shakes his head. He might make the guys do yoga, but he refuses to participate. Something about old dogs and new tricks. Every once in a while, I'll tell him that he needs to get out there and set a good example for the team. He usually shoots me a glare in return.

Every Wednesday night, Dad and I get together. Our weekly dinners became a thing when I moved out of the house and into the dorms freshman year. He's busy coaching football, and my schedule is packed tight with school and soccer. Getting together once a week is the best way for us to stay connected. It doesn't matter if we're in the middle of our seasons; we always make time for each other. Especially since Mom lives in sunny California. After eighteen years of marriage, she got fed up with being a distant second to the Western University football program. She packed up her bags and walked out. I hate to say it, but Dad didn't notice her absence for a couple of days. Which only proved her point. Now she's remarried, learning to surf, and is a vegan. I visit for a couple of weeks during the summer before soccer training camp starts up at the end of June.

Even though it's only the two of us, our weekly dinners are set for three people.

I tell myself to stare straight ahead and not glance in his direction.

Don't do it!

Don't you dare do it!

Damn.

My gaze reluctantly zeros in on him like a heat-seeking missile. Long blond hair, bright blue eyes, sun-kissed skin, and muscles for miles. And he's tall, somewhere around six foot three.

I'm describing none other than Rowan Michaels.

Otherwise known as the bane of my existence.

My dad discovered the talented quarterback the summer before we entered high school and took him under his wing. Which has been...aggravating. In the seven years since, Rowan has become an irritatingly permanent fixture in my life. He's the brother I never wanted or asked for. He's the gift I wish I could give back. He's the son my father never had but secretly longed for.

On a campus with over thirty thousand students, one would think that avoidance would be easy to accomplish. That hasn't turned out to be the case. Somehow, we ended up in the same major—Exercise Science. I get stuck in at least one class with the guy each semester. This time it's statistics, which is a requirement. Three times a week, I'm forced to see him. And then there are the weekly dinners at Dad's house.

Every Wednesday, Rowan shows up without fail.

It's so annoying.

No, *he's* annoying!

Our gazes collide, and electricity sizzles through my veins before I immediately snuff it out and pretend it never happened.

I am not attracted to Rowan Michaels.

I am not attracted to Rowan Michaels.

I am not attracted to Rowan Michaels.

Maybe if I repeat the mantra enough times, it'll be true. That's the hope I cling to. I've made it through the last seven years trying to convince myself of this. I only have to get through our final year together, and then we'll go our separate ways—me to graduate school or maybe to the Women's National Soccer League, and Rowan to the NFL. He's one of the most talented quarterbacks in the conference. Hell, probably the country. There is little doubt in my mind that he'll be a first-round draft pick come next spring.

Trust me when I say that Rowan Michaels fever is alive and well at Western University. His fanbase is legendary. The guy is a major player.

Both on and off the field.

Girls fall all over themselves to be with him. They fill the stands at football practice, show up at parties he's rumored to be at, and basically stalk him around campus.

It's a little nauseating. Don't these girls have any self-respect when it comes to a hot guy?

I wince at that unchecked thought.

Fine...I'll begrudgingly admit it; he's good-looking.

I shake my head as if that will banish the insidious thoughts currently invading my brain. Enough about Rowan. It's time to focus on the reason I'm at the stadium at this ungodly hour. I rip my gaze from him as I hit the cement staircase. After half a flight, all thoughts of the blond quarterback vanish from my mind. How could they not when my quads, glutes, and calves are on fire, screaming for mercy as I force myself to the nosebleed section. By the time I finish, my legs are Jell-O, and I still have a two-mile run back to the apartment I share with my best friend off-campus.

I give Dad a half-hearted wave before leaving. It's the most I can muster. His lips quirk at the corners as he shakes his head. He thinks I'm crazy. At the moment, I can't argue with his assessment of the situation. Although, it's the extra training I put in that helps me run circles around the other team in the second half of the game.

The jog home feels like it will last forever. By the time I unlock the apartment door, I'm ready to collapse. I beeline for the shower and jump in before it's fully warm. My skin prickles with goose flesh, but it feels so damn good. Twenty minutes later, I'm dressed and ready to take on the day. My hair has been thrown up in a messy bun, and I'm making a protein smoothie that will fuel me for my morning classes.

Just before taking off, I poke my head into Sydney's room. I know exactly how I'll find her, and that's buried beneath a small mountain of blankets. She doesn't disappoint. We met the summer before freshman year in training camp and have been besties ever since. She's the yin to my yang. The peanut butter to my jelly. The Thelma to my Louise. Where I'm more introverted and cautious, she's loud and boisterous. She's been known to leap without necessarily looking at what she's jumping into. Every so often, it gets us into trouble. Sydney and I have lived together since sophomore year. I gave up trying to cajole her ass out of bed for a six o'clock run after the first week of us cohabitating when she nearly took my head off with an alarm clock.

"It's that time again," I sing-song obnoxiously, "rise and shine."

There's a grunt and then some shifting from under the blankets that tells me she's alive.

When I chant her name repeatedly, each time escalating in volume, she growls, "Get the fuck out!"

"Awww," I mock, "that's so sweet. I love you, too."

Sydney snorts before a hand snakes out from beneath the blankets to give me a one-fingered salute. Then she grabs a pillow and tosses it in my general vicinity. It falls about five feet short of its mark.

I stare at the dismal attempt. "If you're trying to cause bodily harm, you'll have to do better than that."

"Piss off."

"All right then." I shrug. "See you after class." With that, I close the door behind me.

My farewell is met with another indecipherable mouthful. If this weren't something we went through on the daily, I'd worry she was in the midst of a stroke. Sydney is definitely not a morning person. She's more of an early afternoon person. Another thing I've learned over the years? The action of waking up to a brand-new day is a gradual process. She's like a bear rousing prematurely from hibernation. It's not a pretty sight. She's lucky I don't take her insults personally.

I grab my backpack from the small table crammed into the breakfast nook area along with a coffee before heading out the door. The apartment I share with Sydney is located three blocks from campus, which is highly sought out real estate. We're fortunate Dad is friends with the guy who manages the building. It's probably one of the only perks of having a father who is a head coach of a college football team.

You'd think there would be more, but you'd be wrong. Honestly, being Nick Richard's daughter is more of a hindrance than anything else. People assume you receive special treatment on campus, from professors, or that you have an in with all the football players.

Or worse...

Much worse.

After a bunch of ugly—not to mention untrue—rumors circulated freshman year, I've done my best to distance myself from the Wildcats football team. They're a great bunch of guys, but I don't need all the ugly gossip and speculation that comes along with being friends with them.

As I reach Corbin Hall, the mathematics building for my stats class, my gaze is drawn to a clump of students standing around outside the three-story, red-brick building. In the center of that crowd is Rowan. I don't have to see him physically to know that he's close. The muscles in my belly contract with awareness. It's like a sixth sense. One I wish would go away. He's the last person I want to be cognizant of.

As I jog up the wide stone stairs to the entrance, my gaze fastens on him. A smirk twists the edges of his lips, and my eyes narrow before I drag them away and yank open the door to the building. Relief rushes through me as I step inside the air conditioning and disappear from sight.

"Hey, Demi, wait up!"

I turn at the sound of my name before slowing my step. The dark-haired guy jogging to catch up smiles before falling in line with me.

Justin Fischer.

He's a baseball player and teammates with Sydney's boyfriend, Ethan. We've been seeing each other for about a month. It's still casual at this point. With school and soccer, I don't have a ton of time to invest in a relationship. He seems to understand that and isn't pushing to be more serious.

When he leans in for a kiss, I angle my head. At the last moment, he tilts in the opposite direction, and we end up bumping teeth instead of locking lips. With a grunt, I pull away and chuckle. My fingers fly to my mouth to make sure I haven't chipped a tooth.

Maybe I've been reluctant to admit it to myself, but that kiss sums up our relationship perfectly.

Awkward and a step out of sync with each other.

"Sorry," he murmurs with a slight smile. I search his face and wait for any telltale sign of sexual chemistry to ping inside me. Unfortunately, my insides remain completely unfazed, which is disappointing but not altogether unexpected. I had a sneaking suspicion when we first got together that it might turn out this way.

"No problem," I say, hoisting my smile and brushing aside those thoughts.

"I haven't seen you for a couple of days," he remarks as we turn a corner and continue walking.

"It's been busy." Which isn't a lie. School might have recently started, but the academics at Western are rigorous. And being a Division I athlete is more like a job. If you're not ready to put in the work, don't bother showing up. There's no half-assing it around this place.

"When's your next game?" he asks.

"Tomorrow at six." My gaze flickers in his direction. Not that I expect him to come, but...

Fine, so maybe I do. If he wants to be my boyfriend, then he needs to show a little support.

His dark brows draw together. "That sucks. I've got a mandatory study hour I have to attend."

I shrug off the disappointment. It's another nail in the coffin of this relationship as far as I'm concerned. "That's cool. It's not a big deal."

"But I'll see you tonight?"

Oh. Right.

Tonight.

Well, damn. In a moment of weakness, I threw out an invitation to join our Wednesday evening dinner. It's one I now regret. If only there were a gracious way to rescind the offer.

"If you're busy, I totally understand—"

"Are you kidding? No way." With a grin, he shakes his head. "I wouldn't miss it for the world. I'm looking forward to meeting Coach Richards."

Great. So this is more about my father than me? Exactly what every girl wants to hear.

I force a brittle smile. "Awesome. He's excited, too."

That might be something of an overstatement.

Justin nods toward the end of the corridor. "I better get moving. Professor Andrews is a real stickler for punctuality."

"Yup. See you later."

This time, when he leans in, our lips align perfectly. The kiss is nothing more than a fleeting caress. There and gone before I can sink into it.

And I'm left feeling...absolutely nothing.

I bury the disappointment where I can't inspect it too closely before giving him a wave as he takes off. For a moment, I stand rooted in the hallway and watch as he disappears through the crowd. There's nothing to distinguish Justin from the thousands of guys who look exactly like him on campus. He's of average height and build with dark hair and espresso-colored eyes. He's nice enough. Although, if I'm completely honest, he's a little self-absorbed. He talks about baseball all the time. If Ethan hadn't introduced us, he's not someone I would have looked twice at. We don't have a ton in common.

As much as I hate to admit it, this relationship has probably reached its expiration date.

Now it's a matter of pulling the plug.

Ugh. I hate breakups. Although, it's doubtful this will end up destroying him. I'll have to make it through tonight and figure out the rest.

With a sigh of resignation, I head to the classroom and find a seat tucked away in the far corner of the small lecture hall. A lanky guy I recognize from a few of my other classes settles beside me. He flashes a dimpled smile as we empty our backpacks.

The tiny hair at the nape of my neck rises seconds before Rowan enters the room. It's like my body knows when he's within a thirty-foot radius. I glance at him from beneath the thick fringe of my lashes before shifting away. Air becomes wedged in my lungs as I wait for him to take a seat. And it won't be next to me because I'm—

"Hey man, would you mind moving?"

Surrounded on both sides.

Damnit. I'm hoping the cutie next to me will tell Rowan to go take a flying leap.

What? It could happen. Not everyone at this university is enamored of the football-playing god. Although I realize the odds aren't stacked in my favor. Rowan is the most recognized athlete on campus. People fall all over themselves to accommodate him.

It's a little sickening.

Okay, maybe more than a little.

"Sure, no problem, Michaels." The guy next to me hastily packs up his books before vacating the desk. Unable to ignore him any longer, I glare as Rowan slides onto the seat next to me.

"Did you really think you could evade me that easily?" Laughter brims in his deep voice. A voice, I might add, that does funny things to my insides.

"One can always hope, right?"

"Oh, answering a question with a question." He leans closer, eating up some of the much-needed distance between us. "I like it."

I roll my eyes as his lips stretch into a satisfied grin. Irritation bubbles up inside me when sexual tension blooms at the bottom of my belly. Or maybe that tension has settled a little lower.

It's definitely lower.

I'm tempted to swear like a sailor. How is it possible that I feel nothing for the guy I'm actually dating, and yet my pulse skitters out of control for someone I don't even like? It's so freaking ironic. It's been this way since we met, and nothing I do stomps it out. I can try to fool myself into believing it's not there, but that doesn't make it any less true.

It's a relief when Professor Peters takes his place at the podium and clears his throat. Once he's captured everyone's attention, he delves headfirst into the probability of dependent and independent events.

Grateful for the excuse to ignore Rowan for the next fifty minutes, I open my textbook and concentrate on the lesson. Just as the blond boy fades into the background, his bare knee bumps into mine. Electricity ricochets through my entire being. I glance at him to see if he's noticed the strange energy we always seem to generate and find his ocean-colored gaze fastened to mine.

My guess is that he does.

Damnation.

One-click Campus Player now!

MORE BOOKS BY JENNIFER SUCEVIC

<u>The Campus Series</u> (football)

Campus Player (Demi & Rowan)

Campus Heartthrob (Sydney & Brayden)

Campus Flirt (Sasha & Easton)

Campus Hottie (Elle & Carson)

Campus God (Brooke & Crosby)

Campus Legend (Lola & Asher)

<u>Western Wildcats Hockey</u>

Hate You Always (Juliette & Ryder)

Love You Never (Carina & Ford)

Always My Girl (Viola & Madden)

Dare You to Love Me (Stella & Riggs)

Never Mine to Hold (Fallyn & Wolf)

Never Say Never (Britt & Colby)

Mine to Take (Willow & Maverick)

Break my Heart (Ava & Hayes)

Never Your Girl (Holland & Bridger)

<u>The Barnett Bulldogs</u> (football)

King of Campus (Ivy & Roan)

Friend Zoned (Violet & Sam)

One Night Stand (Gia & Liam)

If You Were Mine (Claire & JT)

<u>The Claremont Cougars</u> (football)

Heartless Summer (Skye & Hunter)

Heartless (Skye & Hunter)

Shameless (Poppy & Mason)

<u>Hawthorne Prep Series</u> (bully/football)

King of Hawthorne Prep (Summer & Kingsley)

Queen of Hawthorne Prep (Summer & Kingsley)

Prince of Hawthorne Prep (Delilah & Austin)

Princess of Hawthorne Prep (Delilah & Austin)

<u>The Next Door Duet</u> (football)

The Girl Next Door (Mia & Beck)

The Boy Next Door (Alyssa & Colton)

<u>What's Mine Duet</u> (Suspense)

Protecting What's Mine (Grace & Matteo)

Claiming What's Mine (Sofia & Roman)

<u>Stay Duet</u> (hockey)

Stay (Cassidy & Cole)

Don't Leave (Cassidy & Cole)

<u>Stand-alone</u>

Hate to Love You (Hockey) (Natalie & Brody)

Just Friends (Hockey) (Emerson & Reed)

Love to Hate You (Football) (Daisy & Carter)

The Breakup Plan (Hockey) (Whitney & Gray)

<u>Collections</u>

Claremont Cougars

The Barnett Bulldogs

The Football Hotties Collection

The Hockey Hotties Collection

The Next Door Duet

ABOUT THE AUTHOR

Jennifer Sucevic is a USA Today bestselling author who has captivated readers worldwide with her sizzling new adult romances. With over thirty novels to her name, her stories of love, heartbreak, and swoon-worthy heroes have been translated into six languages, including German, Italian, and Portuguese, making her a truly global voice in the genre. Armed with a bachelor's degree in history and a master's in educational psychology from the University of Wisconsin-Milwaukee, Jen initially worked as a high school counselor before embracing her passion for writing full-time. Her background in psychology lends a depth to her characters that resonates with fans everywhere.

When she's not crafting irresistible love stories, Jen enjoys biking along scenic trails and soaking up the sun at the beach. She currently resides in Michigan with her family, where she continues to dream up heroes and heroines you'll want to fall in love with again and again.

If you would like to receive regular updates regarding new releases, please subscribe to her newsletter here-
Jennifer Sucevic Newsletter

Or contact Jen through email, at her website, or on Facebook.
sucevicjennifer@gmail.com

Want to join her reader group? Do it here -)
J Sucevic's Book Boyfriends | Facebook

Social media links-
https://www.tiktok.com/@jennifersucevicauthor
www.jennifersucevic.com
https://www.instagram.com/jennifersucevicauthor
https://www.facebook.com/jennifer.sucevic
Amazon.com: Jennifer Sucevic: Books, Biography, Blog, Audiobooks, Kindle
Jennifer Sucevic Books - BookBub

www.ingramcontent.com/pod-product-compliance
Lightning Source LLC
Chambersburg PA
CBHW061112310726
48974CB00002B/493